# A PARAMOUNT KILL

Also by Gaylord Larsen

*An Educated Death*
*The 180-Degree Murder*
*The Kilbourne Connection*

# GAYLORD LARSEN

A PARAMOUNT KILL

E. P. DUTTON  NEW YORK

Published in the United States by E. P. Dutton,
a division of NAL Penguin Inc.,
2 Park Avenue, New York, N.Y. 10016.
Published simultaneously in Canada by
Fitzhenry and Whiteside, Limited, Toronto.

Library of Congress Cataloging-in-Publication Data
Larsen, Gaylord, 1932–
A paramount kill.

I. Title.
PS3562.A734P3   1987      813'.54      87-19652
ISBN 0-525-24592-8

COBE

DESIGNED BY STEVEN N. STATHAKIS
1 3 5 7 9 10 8 6 4 2
First Edition

When you believe in an ideal, you don't own it.
It owns you.

—Raymond Chandler

# A PARAMOUNT KILL

 arling, time to get up."

There was no response so she sat on the bed and shook the calf of his left leg through the covers. "Ray. Ten-thirty story conference. Remember?"

"Oh Lord," he groaned and cast a dead eye toward his alarm clock. 9:35. He rolled onto his side and waited for his brain to make the same trip.

"I thought you might need this to get you going."

She held out a tumbler containing a familiar dark red concoction. He hadn't needed one in a long time, but he needed it this morning. But as he reached for it he marveled at how steady his arm was. Maybe he hadn't drunk as much as he thought he had.

He took two bitter sips and looked at his wife and tried to smile. Without his glasses on, she was as beautiful as ever. She had opened his bedroom blinds and the morning sun was playing on her light frizzy curls like a dazzling backlight in some distant silent movie. How appropriate. She would have been at her zenith back then. Her pink silk dressing gown was snug about

1

her thin waist and the light on the curve of her neck and throat brought back a flood of memories. Titillation and desire. Then the memory of youthful lust and passion for a mature woman. He didn't regret anything. Not for a minute.

She sat quietly at the foot of his bed while he planned his next move. She was too still, in fact, and he knew instinctively what it meant. They had long since reached the time when married couples find it difficult to keep secrets. Mornings were the worst part of the day for her now. He had planned on setting the alarm so they could eat a leisurely breakfast together, but the drinking bout had taken care of that idea. He got his feet on the floor and sighed.

"Is there a problem I should know about?" she asked.

"Cissy, I don't want you worrying about things."

"I worry more not knowing."

He sighed again and reached for his glasses. "It's this damn story conference. It has the aroma of deadly revisions about it."

She turned her head just enough to show a question, as if she were asking, "Is a heavy story conference enough to get the drinking started now?"

"Y. Frank Freeman is scheduled to attend, along with my old sparring partner, Billy Wilder, the Austrian dictator. They don't call up the heavy artillery unless there are serious problems. I don't have the fortitude for this story-by-committee business. Is there any coffee?"

She rose to head for the kitchen. "No. I didn't think you'd want any."

"Don't bother. I'll put it on before I shower."

He caught up with her at the door. Putting an arm about her waist he walked her slowly through the small dining room of their two-bedroom rental and into the kitchen. She rested against the sink counter while he got down the Chase and Sanborn.

"I don't think you have anything to worry about. Your story line is very good"—she waited for more air, then went on—"I think it's the best mystery plot you've ever done . . . and you're not exactly without credentials, you know."

She started a cough, but over time she had developed a coy

2

little technique of making it sound like she was only clearing her throat. He acted as though he didn't notice.

"Maybe I should bring you along to remind them of my 'credentials.' They have a gnawing habit over there of making writers feel about as welcome as . . . as a cold sore on a debutante."

"Very good," she smiled. "Let's save that one for future reference."

After a minor skirmish with the aging gas stove, he got the flame going under the pot, then he blew out the match and watched the smoke curl upward in the cool still air of the kitchen.

"They keep insisting on happy endings," he mused at the ceiling. "They don't admit as much, of course. They keep using words like denouement and fulfillment, but what they really mean is the boy gets the girl. I keep reminding them that any mystery worthy of the name is a bittersweet experience at best. If you're not sad about the murder victim you certainly are about the murderer when he is revealed and caught, assuming of course he or she's been drawn with a modicum of sympathy and three-dimensional logic in the first place. But they keep tacking on these love interests and turning up the violins. God save me from Hollywood's happy endings."

"Oh, I don't know. Happy endings sell a lot of tickets, you know."

"Oh, do they now? Well then, by all means, we must sell those tickets, mustn't we. And let the devil and the story values take the hindmost."

"Tragedy doesn't seem to play well in the movies."

He snorted a short laugh. "Believe me, our current epic is destined for a unique tragedy of its own design. They've cast Veronica Lake opposite our hero. Ending up with her at his side is tragedy enough for any man, Greek or otherwise."

"Raymond, I do hope you aren't going in there just to be sarcastic."

She watched his facial expressions and she didn't like what she saw. There was a smile on his lips but there was no humor in his eyes. His sharp glances darted about the room as they often did when he was deep in thought. Finally he spotted the incessantly ticking clock on the wall and his mood broke.

"Are you going to be all right today?" he asked.

"Yes. Some of my old cronies from Pasadena are coming over. If I feel up to it, they're taking me to lunch at the Tick-Tock."

"Good. And you'll call me if you need me." He said this half as a question and half as a statement on his way toward the bathroom.

"Ray, it's all right to let them win a few arguments," she called after him. "After all, it's their studio. You aren't your own boss, you know, like you are when you're writing a boo—"

She heard the shower start and gave up. She had delivered different versions of this last admonition often enough before. He didn't need to hear how it ended.

Cissy dropped two pieces of Helm's Olympic white bread into the toaster, then moved into the dining room and did some paper straightening at the dining room table, where her husband had set up his typewriter and "writing place." The small study where he normally worked had become unbearable with the onset of the warm weather. He did most of his script work at the studio, but he was trying to get a new short story of his own underway, and it wasn't going well. The last page looked the same as it had when she had read it last week, except now some pencil doodles had been added in the corner.

Cissy cut a fresh stack of half pages, eight-by-eleven sheets cut in two, which he liked to work with. He said it cut down on the retyping when revisions were needed. Then she slid the latest ledger notebook over to her side of the table, opened it at the tab marked "Similes" and wrote the entry in a light feminine hand: "At Paramount, writers are made to feel as welcome as a cold sore on a debutante."

Chandler swung his late-model grey-green open Packard up to the De Mille gate and waited. Clarence, the morning-duty guard looked out and smiled and waved a friendly greeting as he started the old wrought iron gate into action. Clarence was a real mystery buff. He had followed the exploits of Chandler's characters since the *Black Mask* mystery magazine days and went out of his way to give his favorite writer special treatment. It was Clarence, in fact, who had first allowed Chandler to park in a shady corner between buildings. It kept the sun off his leather seats and it was nice and close to the writers' building. The spot was supposed to be reserved for studio bicycles but exceptions and special treatment seemed to be part of studio life. Nearly everyone in the studio had some little favor to offer and this was Clarence's. Chandler had discovered that measuring your collection of perks was a good weather vane by which to judge your standing. All three of the films he had worked on had been successful—there had even been an Academy nomination for his work on *Double Indemnity*—so no one was about to tell him where to park. At least not yet.

Chandler gently herded his big touring car through the narrow studio streets. He was slightly short-waisted and in order to see over the dash he was forced to tip his head up, giving him the air of a British aristocrat. This morning Simone, the little receptionist from the writers' building, was standing at the bike rack, apparently waiting for him, for as soon as she saw his car she checked her watch and hurried to his door.

"Oh good, you're here. They're all over in Mr. Dozier's office waiting for you. The Navy's there, too."

"Good Lord, we're under invasion."

She gave him a short laugh. She couldn't live with a building full of writers without knowing a cue line when she heard one. "I'm supposed to get you over there as soon as you show up."

Chandler eased out of the driver's seat and bowed to Simone to lead the way, if she insisted. Always the gentleman where ladies were concerned, he bounced along at her side in a solicitous way, making sure he could always dart ahead in time to open doors or help fend off careless delivery boys on their hurried rounds.

Raymond Chandler and Hollywood did not mesh well in many ways, and that included physical appearance. Although Southern California was the suntan capital of the Anglo-Saxon world, Chandler managed to continue sporting a pale, almost transparent complexion. With his tweed jacket, his tight, four-in-hand, conservative tie, round horn-rimmed glasses, and his somewhat historical flannel slacks, Chandler looked more like an Oxford don who had gotten lost in a time warp on his way to a poetry class than he did the author of hard-boiled American detective novels. But his dialogue "crackled," and if there was one thing Hollywood needed it was crackling dialogue. And if there was one thing Chandler needed it was some of Hollywood's money.

The producers' office building, like most of the permanent buildings on the lot, was designed with a variety of period facings. The original intent, no doubt, was so that they could double as sets for small budget productions. The outside of Mr. Dozier's ground floor corner office sported Tudor timbering. The large casement windows were already swung open and men's voices could be heard.

Simone and Chandler stepped inside the entry under a shield that read, "Ye Olde Crowne and Thistle." Simone knocked on Dozier's private entrance and whispered "Good luck" to her charge.

Apparently she really had been under orders to hand deliver him. Not an unusual event in the life of a Paramount writer. Ever since the halcyon days when Ben Hecht and Charlie MacArthur put a match to the sprinkler system in the writers' building and soaked everyone just so they could have an afternoon at the races, the studio writers were looked on as a bunch of pranksters and not to be trusted. And there always seemed to be a few on staff who liked to maintain the reputation.

Behind William Dozier's desk sat a large animated man dressed in Navy whites. Three rows of decorations showed on his left breast and an honest-to-goodness whistle hung from the black braided rope that wound around his right epaulet. As Chandler entered, the officer was regaling the civilians in the room with an account of the Navy's heroics in capturing the heavily fortified island of Saipan from the Japanese. Dozier, the studio's story editor, was pacing the room between a box of Kleenex on his desk and the wastebasket in the corner, waiting for a courteous moment to interrupt the war story. When it came he introduced "the writer" to Commander Crane, U.S.N.—Special Services. The Commander granted Chandler a semi-salute, "Just grab a seat anywhere, partner."

The question was, where? The couch opposite the desk was already filled with the film's director, George Marshall, the producer, Joseph Sistrom, and his new associate, John Houseman.

6

They sat exchanging glances that seemed to indicate the problem of locating an additional chair was beyond their comprehension. The only other chair in the room was the lounging site of a smiling Billy Wilder, who wasn't about to relinquish his seat for the writer or help him look for one of his own. Finally, Dozier got his secretary to bring one in from the outer office.

With the furniture quandary settled, Dozier started to apologize for his summer cold. He would try to stay over by the windows with his Kleenex box and out of their way. While this was going on, Wilder tap-tapped on the desk with his little malacca cane to get the Navy officer's attention.

"Listen," he stage whispered in his confidential manner, "I want to hear more about this Saipan thing. There might be a movie in it. Later we talk, see."

The Commander agreed readily and they exchanged knowing nods.

"Our problem at hand," Dozier went on, a bit louder, "is our Ladd vehicle. Joe Sistrom and I have been over all this but I wanted this meeting so everyone knows how things st—"

Bill Dozier got a tissue to his nose just in time to catch a sneeze. "You'll have to excuse me. Mr. Freeman and I were at a sneak preview in San Francisco last night. We must have sat in a draft on the plane back. He's home in bed and that's where I should be, but I know how important time is to this project.

"Anyway, as you know, we let the different branches of the service read our scripts in the early stages, just so we don't inadvertently do anything to hurt the war effort. After all, we're all in this thing together and we want to do everything we can for our boys out there doing the fighting."

Chandler looked around at the other faces to see if he could tell where the war effort pep talk was leading. Sistrom had been friendly and supportive in the past; there was even a slight smile on his lips now, but was the smile for Chandler? Sistrom's eyes were virtually invisible behind his thick glasses. Houseman and Marshall were hanging on Dozier's every word. Wilder was busy sighting down the shaft of his pet cane while he twisted it about in his hand. No doubt he was entering a miniature billiards tournament as soon as the meeting was out of the way.

Dozier finally got to the point: "The Commander here has

put his finger on something that I think needs our attention. As *The Blue Dahlia* script now reads, the murderer turns out to be a sailor friend of our hero, Alan Ladd. He has just been released from a Navy hospital, but he seems to be a bit disoriented because of a combat head injury. And he ends up killing Ladd's estranged wife while in a mentally confused state. And then he forgets that he did it until the end, of course, when he is exposed.

"Now the Commander here has two problems with this—correct me if I'm wrong, Commander—number one, he doesn't think it's good to have a returning veteran shown as a murderer. The way the war is going now, we hope it won't be long before all our boys will be returning home and the public should be looking to them as conquering heros. Dwelling on mental problems and such is just going to put our audience in the wrong frame of mind. Make them start wondering about our boys . . . ."

The Commander was nodding his head—yes, this was exactly his point—then he shook it from side to side—no, we don't want this kind of image.

Dozier went on. "Secondly, it is obvious that William Bendix—that's who we've cast as our murderer—that Bendix should never have been released from the hospital in that condition. You see, this shows our Navy Medical Corps in a bad light. What's a guy like that doing out on the street?

"Does that about capsulize your feelings, Commander?"

The Commander gave a thumbs-up signal. "First-class job, Bill. A first-class job. I'm not here to tell you folks your business, but I think you can see my point."

Dozier looked at Chandler, then everyone else in the room did the same. The silence after all the chatter was noticeable.

"Well, Ray, what do you think? This cause any problems for you?" Dozier asked.

Chandler had been tamping a load into his old briar pipe and he continued with this procedure, perhaps ramming the tobacco down with a bit more gusto than usual. There was a slight smile on his thin lips but his eyes and his forehead muscles suggested something else. It wasn't until he brought his match up to the pipe that he looked across the desk at the naval officer. The dramatic effect of the long sucks on the stem and the billowy smoke and the steel-eyed stare through the smoke made Wilder

8

stop playing with his cane. The Commander cleared his throat and secured his hands on the arm rests of Dozier's chair, as if he were getting ready for high seas.

"And what, pray tell, would you say would be the solution to our problem?" Chandler asked.

The Commander shrugged, "Someone else will have to be the murderer."

"I see. Just like that, eh?"

"Well, of course it might take a bit of thinking. But then after all, that is your job, isn't it? To figure these things out?"

"Commander Crane," Chandler boomed in his top-drawer public school British, "I want you to know how delighted I am to make your acquaintance—"

"Why, thank you," Commander Crane interrupted, "I'm real pleased to know you too, sir—"

"You see, Commander, knowing you helps me to understand how the United States Navy could blunder into an unmitigated fiasco like Pearl Harbor."

Wilder was the quickest in the group; he stifled a laugh and suddenly found a burning need to retie his shoelaces. The three on the couch looked like they wanted to go out on the back lot and scout up more chairs. Dozier forgot his nose and started to explain that we all have our duties to perform and the Commander, however unpleasant, had his, too. The Commander turned all the colors of his ribbons and shook a threatening finger at Chandler until he found some words.

"Say, now just who do you think you're talking to? You, you Hollywood writer, you."

"Now before we say anything more," Dozier was counseling, "let's remember we're all here to do the same thing. To make the best films we know how. Right, Ray? Isn't that what we're here for?"

"Just what the hell do you think I've been doing, Mr. Dozier?"

"I know, Ray. I know. And I like your story line very much. But don't you think he's got a point?"

"I do not."

"Okay then, let's hear your side of it. But no more personal stuff. Okay?"

9

"You talk about generating sympathetic feelings within the American public for our servicemen. Okay, fine. Let's do that. But let's at least have the guts to do it honestly. Not this comic strip stuff the Navy's trying to pull here. It so happens I know a bit about how these men feel. I was there once myself. I know about being under fire and losing your company . . . about looking at your friend one minute and looking at a hollow shirt where his head used to . . ." The tough-guy act Chandler had been displaying now had to give way. He was getting too close to home. After fumbling with his pipe, he found it needed relighting, but he was afraid his hand would shake if he struck a match. Then he went on in a softer voice, "I know about coming home to a world that doesn't understand. About unbelievable loneliness in a town full of people. About living in strange bedrooms and in strange towns where jobs with any dignity or respect to them were not to be had. It gets at your guts and pretty soon you're hit with the conviction that you're helpless to do anything about anything. The fates or the powers in the world are all beyond your ability to control them. You're powerless to change anything.

"That's what I'm getting at in this story. Our central character loses his son while he is overseas and he is powerless to do anything about it. His wife wants out of their marriage and he is powerless to do anything about it. His buddy is injured and he comes home with him, hoping he can do something for him to help him snap out of his bad moods. But even that backfires on him and when he is accused of his wife's murder he ends up clearing his own name, but only at the expense of exposing his Navy buddy who has his own set of insurmountable problems.

"In the end our guy is searching for some way of life, some plot of ground where he can begin to carve out his own destiny, some place where his fortunes will be the result, at least partially, of his own wisdom or folly.

"The boys coming home don't want medals and pats on the back. They don't see themselves as heroes. What they're going to need is our understanding and support. This is the kind of story that'll lend itself to that understanding." He rested his case.

"That was beautifully expressed, Ray," Houseman said.

Dozier scratched the back of his neck and scowled. "I don't

know, Ray. That's an awfully complex concept. I sure didn't get all that from reading the script. I thought it was just a nice, tight little mystery."

"Exactly," the Navy concurred. "An idea like that will go right over their heads. Remember what P.T. Barnum once said: 'I never lost a nickel underestimating the intelligence of my audience.' " He laughed, pleased as punch with himself.

Dozier smiled and coughed. "Commander, I wonder if you would excuse us now."

"Of course, Bill. I have some more reading to do anyway."

"I'll be in touch with you before you go."

"How about lunch?"

"Sorry, not today. There's a producer's meeting this afternoon I have to get ready for."

Dozier ushered out the naval officer with more platitudes and assurances that everything could be worked out to everyone's satisfaction, then came back in and closed the door.

"Ray, we can't afford to antagonize the United States Navy."

Chandler's only response was two more heavy drags on his rejuvenated pipe. Dozier opened more windows and sat behind his desk.

"I'd like to hear what the rest of you feel about this."

"Well, I can go either way," Marshall said. "I feel about the same way you do, Bill. I thought of it as a corking good mystery. Who the murderer is doesn't affect me one way or the other."

Marshall was what was known in town as a house director. He knew the camera angles and how to keep the actors from bumping into one another. But he could never be accused of intellectualizing a story line. And he would never be arrested for setting off Roman candles in a darkened theatre.

Houseman supported Chandler's angle and said he felt the story could be brought off with taste and a good deal of understanding for the returning veterans. The success of the film would put the Commander's objections to rest.

"Anything further, Joe?" Dozier turned to Sistrom.

The producer pushed his glasses up and rubbed at the pink indentations on his nose. "We gotta think of our time frame on this picture. Ladd is scheduled to be reinducted in six weeks. I don't think this is any time to start making changes in our story line. Especially with an unhappy writer who, by his own admission, does not construct plot lines quickly. Right, Ray?"

Chandler was happy to nod in agreement.

"We gotta get this one in the can," Sistrom went on, "Ladd's high salary is killing us. He hasn't had a new release in almost a year and I don't think we should take any chances. Oh, maybe some cosmetic changes to appease the Navy. Maybe make the sailor AWOL from the hospital instead of just on leave. That would get their Medical Corps off the hook for releasing him too soon. But at this point I think we better keep the sailor as our murderer."

Dozier nodded and rocked in his swivel chair. "Okay, thank you." He cleared his voice, almost apologetically. "Now I'd like you all to hear what Billy has to say."

Wilder had been sitting still and quiet for a longer period of time than Chandler had thought possible. He was now about to make up for it.

"I'll make this short and sweet." Wilder sat on one hip on the corner of Dozier's desk and faced the *Blue Dahlia* staff. "The studio is heavily committed to doing three war projects. In all three we gotta have Navy cooperation to make the scenes go." He shrugged, pacing near the windows. "They got all the ships. There is no way around it. We have to have their cooperation. If we don't cooperate with them on this little pastiche of yours, Raymond, they might pull out."

"I was wondering what you were doing in here," Chandler deadpanned.

Wilder shrugged. "I'm doing my patriotic duty, Raymond." He had an exaggerated way of pronouncing Chandler's Christian name, almost as if he were talking down to a European child.

"That line doesn't sound quite right coming from you. . . ."

"Are you challenging my dedication to the war effort, Raymond?"

"One of those war films wouldn't happen to be your project, would it?"

Wilder grinned his secretive little grin. "One must go where the good stories are."

"I see. So you want us to turn what promises to be a meaningful film into an also-ran whodunit so that you can have free access to the fleet—"

"I'm thinking of the good of the studio. It's not just me, old bean." He leaned hard on the "old bean."

"And what if we say no?"

Wilder stood up and tested his cane on the carpet nap. "Would you like the names of the other two directors who might be affected by your decision?"

Dozier interceded. "I don't think that will be necessary, Billy. We can all read the trade papers."

Wilder briskly tapped his pants leg with his cane and made motions as if to leave. "I don't like playing the heavy in this piece. Maybe you should think on this—you know there has never been a successful war movie made that didn't have the blessing of the branch of service it was about. I think maybe I'm helping you in the long run."

"Ours isn't a war story," Chandler said. "It's a people story. Are you issuing licenses on those now, Billy?"

Wilder smiled and wagged a "naughty, naughty" finger at him. "Don't be bitter, Raymond. You must learn how the game is played. Some you win, some you lose."

"Oh, I know how the game is played. I had an excellent teacher. If we don't change the script to satisfy you and the Navy you're going to go tattle to Mr. Freeman. And you're going to take your two big bullies with you and—"

Wilder interrupted with a laugh. "Ah, such imagery. I can see you haven't lost that famous Chandler touch. Now all you have to do is put it to use on your script revisions. Well, I'm sure you have things to talk over. Good day, gentlemen."

Wilder made the most of his exit line and strode from the office as if on his way to inspect the troops.

Suddenly the room seemed devoid of energy. Dozier rocked and exchanged knowing smiles with Joe Sistrom. Marshall was busy checking the leather knee patches on his riding breeches. And Houseman was busy watching Chandler.

Houseman had reason to watch Chandler closely. If the project was going to fold now his own fortunes with the studio could very well be on the line, too. It had been Houseman who had initiated *The Blue Dahlia* for the studio. Since both he and

Chandler were products of British public schools they had struck up an easy friendship. And it had been Houseman who had persuaded him to turn what had originally been a book idea into a film vehicle for Alan Ladd.

The writer huffed and puffed on his briar pipe for several seconds then lapsed into a litany of the abuses he had suffered at the hands of Billy Wilder when they were working on *Double Indemnity*. Most of which was pretty old stuff for the people listening. Things like being expected to do menial chores for the great director: opening doors, adjusting venetian blinds so the light did not strike the great man's eyes. Next he compared Wilder's dictatorial tendencies with the evil political powers loose in the world at that moment, then he ended with a scathing indictment of Wilder's abundant sexual appetite.

"Mr. Dozier," he pleaded, "are we to sit still for this? Isn't there anything you can do about him?"

"Yes, certainly. There's a lot that can be done. And we're going to do it, too." Dozier rocked thoughtfully, then added, "Just as soon as he stops making hit movies."

He reached across his desk and picked up his copy of *The Blue Dahlia* script, which some unimaginative secretary had bound in a scarlet cover.

"This means we'll have to start shooting without a completed script. Ray, how much of the first act of this epic are we going to have to work on?"

"How should I know, when I don't know an ending for it yet?"

"First we better settle on a new murderer, hadn't we," Dozier mused. "We could make Veronica Lake's husband our murderer. What's the character's name?"

Sistrom agreed. "He's the heavy of the piece anyway. The audience would enjoy seeing him get it in the end. What do you think, Ray?"

Chandler shrugged. "If you can puzzle it out, what do you need me for?"

This only added to the strained feelings that were building in the room. After a few more seconds of unproductive silence Dozier said, "Why don't we give you time to kick this around, Ray? Let's see . . . tomorrow is Sunday. Why don't we get back together Monday, around ten?" He made a note on his desk calendar. "Just keep this in mind. Timewise our backs are to the wall and we won't have the luxury of a lot of exterior location stuff."

"What's that supposed to mean?" Chandler asked.

"Oh, take this love scene on page seventy-two"—he thumbed his script—" 'Beach—twilight.' We could spend three days trying to get this right. But we have Ladd and Lake together in the hotel room scene just before it. There's no reason the love scene couldn't just be added on there. We could shoot it in one afternoon. You see—"

"Mr. Dozier," Chandler put in, "there's a dead body in the hotel room."

"So?"

He looked around the office in disbelief. "Anybody, when was the last time you spoke sweet nothings in a woman's ear with a decaying cadaver in the same room?"

"Believe me, we can get away with it," the film's director assured him. "We'll shoot the two of them in over-the-shoulder close-ups. With mood lighting and a little music, our audience will have forgotten all about the body."

"But I won't," Chandler said. He said it in a normal voice, but no one in the room seemed to hear.

$2$

$\mathcal{S}$ince around the second year
of the war the studio dining room had taken on the militant
name of commissary. It was an unpretentious structure, not un-
like any lunchroom in any company with a large number of white
collar workers. And like other companies, the walls were deco-
rated with samples of their best product: black and white head
shots and memorable action scenes involving the current crop
of stars, all displayed behind uniform pinewood frames that were
mounted on piano hinges, which made it easier for the publicity
department to update the product.

The only pictures that were exceptions to the uniformity
rule were three large oil paintings of past C. B. De Mille productions, which hung in places of honor. They were displayed
in heavy ornate wood frames that might best be described as
Yosemite Rustic. In fact, if there was a coordinating motif to the
place it could be called that. Or maybe *The Squaw Man* remembered. Whatever the original intent, the place had become a
pleasant incongruity in light of the studio's current trend for
slick modern looks to their productions. A case in point was the

*Double Indemnity* promotional shot that had recently been put up: Fred MacMurray and a blonde Barbara Stanwyck, in the famous white sweater, clinking tumblers of whisky through their cigarette smoke as they contemplated murder. Still the incongruity didn't seem to bother anyone, least of all Raymond Chandler, who couldn't help looking at the picture with a touch of pride each time he came into the place.

The real fascination of the commissary, though, was not in its decor but in the history that was said to have taken place within its walls. Deals made, practical jokes played, hearts broken, careers made and others sidetracked. And even more so in the history that was yet to be made.

A giddy euphoria danced in the place. It was 1945, the Depression was over, the war was finally going well. More people were seeing more films in more theatres than ever before. You could not buy a new car and you made do with half-soled shoes because there was a war going on. But the picture business had been declared an essential industry, and it was full speed ahead. The public's appetite for entertainment seemed insatiable. Rumor had it the studio had reached the point where it was impossible to make a film that did not make money. Over the course of the year the studio would employ sixty-eight writers and grind out over seventy new releases. There was a sense of excitement and suspense in the air. Plans hatched over the commissary's Daily Special were usually set in motion within the week and everyone's favorite all-purpose expression was, "Get it in the can."

The studio was a place unique unto itself. Within its walls it was the movies that became real, while the outside world, with its gas rationing and its body counts, became the illusion. Except for the appearance of an occasional man in uniform, the only hint that a major war was going on was to be found in the red, white and blue banner that hung over the main exit: SAVE FILM AND WIN THE WAR.

Although the commissary was open to all, it had a strict social pecking order that the regulars learned to observe. Producers and their distribution friends were seen only long enough to duck into the closed dining room reserved for them; also among the missing were the muscle folk on the other end of the social ladder—the carpenters and gaffers and grips, who dined elsewhere, out of their black lunch boxes with thermos bottles in the lids. They had seen it all before and couldn't be bothered. But the rest seemed to enjoy making appearances. The contract players had their gathering area, as did the publicity people, the lighting directors, and a few cameramen. There were even certain tables that everyone understood were reserved for actors or directors who were entertaining visiting members of the press.

And there was a large table in a choice alcove that was "off limits" to everyone but writers and their invited guests. It was choice because it afforded a good overview of the entire commissary, the door to the producers' private room as well as the main studio street outside. And it was just private enough to allow them to deliver their wisecracks about the passing scene in full voice, without being overheard by other tables.

Billy Wilder had done much to set the conversational tone of the table with his acid barbs and European cynicism toward life's foibles. Now that he had moved up in the world and was directing his own stories he had stopped gracing the table with his presence. But several of the writers felt compelled to see that his spirit lived on. And no one escaped their barbs for long.

It had taken Raymond Chandler several months to adapt to the lively pace of the place. After a spotty career as an executive in the somber oil business, followed by almost ten years as a semi-recluse while he established himself as a mystery writer, the writers' table at Paramount nearly threw him into culture shock. But his abilities were apparent from the first day. There wasn't much around that table that was held sacred, but true talent certainly was. He was older than most of the other scribes, which gave him something of the stature of a father confessor or elder statesman. And eventually he adjusted to the rapid repartee, giving as well as he got.

But after the bout that morning in Dozier's office Chandler had been in no mood for kidding around. In a blind rage, he had gone back to his lime-green cubicle in the writers' building and spent a half hour pacing his threadbare Kelly green carpet. Finally a fellow writer stuck his head in the door and told him it was time for lunch. Still he didn't snap out of his self-inflicted trance until he found himself standing at the writers' table holding a lunch tray containing a bowl of mashed potatoes, coffee, and two desserts of tapioca pudding.

"Oh damn."

"What's the matter, Mr. Chandler?" A young man at the table asked.

Chandler slumped into his seat. "I hate tapioca. I must be losing my mind."

The young man hopped up. "Here, let me take them back. I'm going back anyway. Can I get you anything else?"

"Oh, a salad. Anything."

The young man scooped up the puddings and was on his way with the briskness of a new waiter.

"Who is he?" Chandler asked Robert Preshell, his nearest neighbor.

"McGrath. Don't know that I've heard his first name."

"Is he a writer?"

"He has the office next to mine. We share a secretary, but I'll be darned if I know what he's working on."

From the opposite side of the table, H. Allen Smith was peering over his glasses and smiling at Chandler. "That's definitely the sign of a writer hard at work—going through the food line and not knowing what you've put on your tray."

"Correction," Chandler said. "It's the sign of a punch-drunk writer. I feel like I've just gone twelve rounds with Joe Louis."

"I thought your screenplay was set. Did Dozier get his nose out of joint about something?"

"No. Billy Wilder beat us over the head with the Pacific Fleet. My baby is lying broken and bleeding out there in the gutter."

"How'd he get hold of your script?"

"Dozier showed it around, apparently."

Smith laughed. "You'll have to do like Billy does. Don't have a finished script until the last week of shooting when it's too late to do anything about it."

"I think he's meddling in this just to get even with me. I don't bow and scrape well enough to please him," Chandler growled. "Can you imagine what he'd do if someone messed up one of his projects? What wouldn't he do?"

"Please," Smith overacted, "not while I'm eating cafeteria

meatloaf. Billy's not so bad though. Why, once I completed an entire compound sentence in his presence."

Young McGrath returned with a chef's salad, which he set before Chandler. He refused Chandler's attempt to reimburse him for the price difference but then launched into a favor request of his own.

"Please, let me bounce an idea for a joke off you."

"I'm not much of a judge of humor," Chandler protested.

"Well, I mean all of you, collectively."

The writer's table served as a virtual cornucopia for new jokes, but the race definitely belonged only to the swift. Anything less could be disastrous for the teller. Now young McGrath took his life into his own hands with the announcement that he had a corker to share. It seems there was this drunk who accidentally bumps up against this very formidable professor, see, and the man tells the drunk, Sir, you are drunk. The drunk says, Oh yeah, well you're ugly, but tomorrow I'll be sober.

Chandler laughed, but when he realized he was the only one doing so he cut it short. Laughter was like drawing blood in a duel.

Someone else at the table said the joke was already well traveled and gave chapter and verse from an old W. C. Fields two-reeler where it had first appeared. Before McGrath had time to realize he had egg on his face the discussion had already switched over to the proper length for a good punch line, then back again to W. C. Fields's unique brand of humor. You had to be on your toes at all times.

During a brisk argument about which actors could tell jokes and which couldn't, some generous soul tore the government seal off a new bottle of rye whisky and started passing it around the table. It was coming on to Saturday afternoon when traditionally not a great deal of work would be turned out; most of the men got started on their jolly time by dribbling a polite shot into their coffee cups and passing the bottle on.

Chandler handled the bottle when it came to him but passed it. But he didn't take his eyes off it. Then, when it was almost beyond his reach, he lunged for it with eager fingers and poured himself a very generous shot.

The table's topic of conversation took another violent swing when Harry Tugend showed up and started complaining loudly and at great lengths about his strange problems with a well-known middle-aged actress.

"I'm a married man with a wife and kids. What do I need this kind of grief with her?"

"What's the matter, Harry?" The table never lacked for straight men.

"Here I am, talking to her," Tugend went on, "trying my best to get the woman to be in my picture and all the time I'm trying to keep from being raped."

"You mean you think the woman's a nymphomaniac?"

Tugend scratched his ear and thought about it. "Well, I suppose she could be one if you could quiet her down a little."

This broke the no-laugh rule with a vengeance and most of the eyes in the commissary turned and strained to see what was so funny. Billy Wilder and his producer-partner Charlie Brackett were walking through the place just then, on their way to the producers' dining room. Wilder and Chandler accidentally made eye contact. Wilder smiled and walked close enough to call to Chandler, "Chin up, old bean."

Chandler only scowled back at him. Wilder tipped his cane in a salute for Chandler's benefit and disappeared. Chandler raised his cup and drank deeply.

It started that easily. No wrestling with his conscience. The first drink of the day. Or was it the umpteenth drink of something he had started the night before? It went down warm against the throat and hit mashed potatoes. That meant it would take a while for the exciting flush to come. The flush like a baby orgasm that would get him going. Get him up, up where Billy Wilder and the sick script couldn't get to him. With his low tolerance for the stuff it wouldn't be long in coming. He closed his eyes to wait for it but when he did he saw Cissy there, in the morning sunlight, sitting on his bed. He opened the eyes again and tried to see nothing but lettuce leaves. Then someone was talking to him—

"What's this I hear about Howard Hawks buying the rights

to your book *The Big Sleep*?" It was Seton Miller, one of the quickest wits and best gossipers ever to grace the table.

"Well, Warners bought it last year. Hawks has been directing, I hear."

"You don't sound very happy about it."

"Hardly. My agent sold all my rights for a mere seven thousand dollars." Chandler drained his cup and looked around the table for signs of the bottle. "I'm convinced that writing fiction is one of the classiest ways of starving to death yet devised by man. I can only go to the well so many times. And speaking of the well . . ."

The bottle reappeared and was passed his way. He helped himself and went on. "I tried to talk them into using Cary Grant for my detective, but they're using Bogart instead."

"He was great in *The Maltese Falcon*."

"Oh, Bogart's all right. The problem is, now if you take Bogart you gotta take the current light of his life, what's-her-name Bacall. They tell me they are doing a lot of new shooting, padding the part of the older Sternwood girl for her."

"Listen," Tugend put in, "I've seen her in person. She can use all the padding she can get."

"Yeah, I know what you mean," McGrath said. "I saw her in *To Have And Have Not*. Do you think she did the singing in that or did they dub her voice in with somebody else's?"

"My God," Miller screamed, "you mean you think somebody actually went out and looked for a voice like that?"

It wasn't only actresses. Women in general did not fare well at the writers' table. Chandler often wondered what was said about Cissy when he was not present.

The conversation turned to the physical attributes of two starlets who had recently come up from MGM and Chandler dropped out of the chatter and into his own private world. He could see what was happening to himself, what the rye was doing, almost as if he were a disembodied spirit watching someone he hardly knew from the inside. First came the quick easy verbiage, the grammar and syntax moving toward American sloppy, but now and then something brilliant emerging. Next would come the deep philosophical pondering. Maybe a little biting cynicism thrown in, just to impress the critics. Then would come . . . what came next? He couldn't remember. The conversation had changed yet again and he was being paged.

"Hey Ray, you got a mention today in the Rambling Reporter column," Seton Miller was saying. He had a copy of *The Hollywood Reporter* next to his lunch. "Listen, 'with very little ballyhoo from the studios, writers the likes of James M. Cain and Raymond Chandler are giving us mean realistic stories with originality and bite.' "

"I see my problem now," Chandler cried sarcastically. "Too much originality. From now on I'm sticking to the Jerry Wald school of film writing. I wait till all of you have gone home for the evening then, I rifle through your desks for ideas."

"Ahhh, yesss," someone mimicked W. C. Fields, "I'd sell my soul for one good plot."

"Now we're back to Billy Wilder again."

"Good plot? Why would any Hollywood writer want a good plot?" Chandler asked. "Suppose you had one; you turn it over to a producer who thinks he's God Almighty with two pair of pants. And he turns it into the same formula story this town has been doing for fifty years. Any similarity between it and high drama is purely coincidental."

"My my, but aren't we testy today," Preshell marveled.

Chandler smiled. "I've just been given the assignment of writing a tender love scene in a hotel room between Alan Ladd, Moronica Lake, and a day-old cadaver—or should that be 'among'?"

"Mmm, it has possibilities," Preshell mused. "I think you oughta give the body a couple lines just to make it interesting."

"It would never work." Miller frowned. "How could the audience tell the difference between the stiff and Veronica Lake?"

"She'd be the one whose lips don't move when she talks."

Chandler shook his head. "You know you guys are beginning to make sense. Which can only mean I'm no longer sober or not drunk enough." He drained his cup again and set it down gently, as if he were having tea with the king and queen. Then he sighed.

23

"Do any of you ever have the feeling we are reliving the days of the Roman circuses and we're frantically juggling words in the air so civilization won't end? Here we are at the heart and soul of motion pictures, the only new art form that has evolved on this tired old planet in a hundred years and what are we doing? Are we reflecting life? Are we showing the way to a troubled world? No. We're making illustrated cartoons for half-wits. We're filling in the bubbles over the heads of Dick Tracy and Tess Trueheart. Damn it." Chandler slammed a narrow fist onto the table, trying to show ferocious anger, but it didn't quite come across.

"You know what I'd like to see? I'd like to put a real dead body in that room over there." Chandler pointed at the door to the producers' private dining room. "Have it sitting up to the table ready for lunch with a nappy tucked under its chin. I'd like to see what that bunch would do." He snorted a bitter laugh at the thought of it. "By God, they'd pee in their collective pants. That's what they would do."

Chandler sat back and smoldered awhile.

H. Allen Smith, across the table, was studying him with his crafty smile. "You know, you remind me a lot of your detective, Philip Marlowe."

"Me? Hardly. I'm no Philip Marlowe."

"Ah, but you are in a way. You're both idealists. Marlowe is down on Los Angeles because the people here don't conform to his own stylized notions of how they should act. And you are down on Hollywood because our themes aren't up to your standards. Ease up a little, Ray. There's nothing wrong with a little good escapism now and then. We don't have to do a new *Greed* every other week."

"How about once a year? Would that be okay?"

Smith shrugged, then leaned his square head forward to get Chandler's private ear. "I'm just trying to give a bit of friendly advice. Idealists in this business have a bad habit of slicing their own throats. I'd like to see you stick around awhile."

"I'll remember to wear my mumffler."

That did it. When he started stumbling over words, he knew it was time to shut up, which he did for a time. Then the girl with the coffeepot came around pouring refills. She splashed his cup full again and Chandler went into his own version of a W. C. Fields line.

"Godfrey Daniels, somebody put pineapple juice in my pineapple juice."

Getting a laugh at the writers' table was almost as prestigious as an Academy nomination.

hen the table crowd had thinned and he felt it safe to navigate on his own, Chandler rose and started with slow dignity back to his four walls and blank writing paper. At the foot of the commissary steps he found young McGrath waiting for him.

"Oh, Mr. Chandler, can I see you for a bit? I got an idea I think you'll be interested in."

"Certainly."

"You want to come over to my office?"

"Let's see. You share a secretary with Preshell, don't you."

"Yeah, I do."

"Would that be Francine?"

"Yeah, it is. Why?"

"Why don't we meet in my office instead?"

McGrath opened his hands in surprise. "You don't want to walk by my secretary's desk?"

"Do you want to meet with me or not?" Chandler snapped.

"Sure, okay. It's just, I thought . . . I have a bottle in my office."

"Bring it along."

"You got any mixings?" McGrath asked.

"Young man, in my lower desk drawer I keep a midget bartender by the name of Harry Cohn. If he can't mix it, nobody can."

McGrath laughed obediently and ran on ahead.

Before his Hollywood contract Chandler had spent almost nine years on the wagon. Nine years in which he had gone from a boozed-out has-been of an executive at Dabney Oil to about the zenith of what any mystery story writer could hope for on this earth. They were the lean Depression years when penny-a-word publishers were king and a seventy-five dollar check in the mail was justification enough for a block party. But Cissy had hung in there with him and together they had developed his unique style of writing: the highly personalized storyteller with a moral code and virtues the reading public liked. Chandler had carried the craft of mystery writing to the door of literary excellence and more than a few critics were demanding it be opened for him.

Such a heady record of career rejuvenation had left Chandler with a profound sense of invincibility. And now, when the social and professional life in the writers' building at Paramount seemed to demand that he tipple a few, he decided he could handle it. Why not? It seemed to help his spontaneity. Film work required a certain fluidity and he told himself that deep in his heart he had learned his lesson. Never again would he lose control of himself.

Back in his cubicle he absently repeated the word "fluidity" to himself several times as *The Blue Dahlia* script went into his middle drawer and the lower drawer opened. It was fun and games time.

McGrath came in carrying a bottle but no script. So, this was to be another idea-bouncing session. Hollywood writers, Chandler had discovered, talked a thousand words for every one they wrote.

After their drinks were ready, McGrath tipped back in one of the four steel chairs in the room and propped his feet on another one. He was probably around thirty, good looking with sandy brown hair and quick blue eyes. And he was a wiggler.

There seemed to be some part of his anatomy in motion at all times, which probably explained why there wasn't an ounce of fat on him. He rocked, sipped at his glass, and shook his head, which meant he approved of the drink. It was the kind of nervousness that told Chandler the boy had been wound up some place other than casual Southern California.

"Oh, by the way, Francine sends her regards. I didn't know you two knew one another."

He was fishing, but Chandler kept his eyes on the glassware. "Are you stuck on a story line?" he asked.

"Ah no, not really. It was another matter I wanted to put to you."

"Oh. What's that?"

"I'm assuming I can speak in confidence here."

"I don't know why not."

McGrath did a quick check in the hall, reclosed the door carefully and returned to face Chandler with a smile. McGrath always seemed to be marveling at some clever idea just below the surface, but now his performance was bubbling over.

"I suppose you've heard about some of the practical jokes that have gone on around this town over the years."

"Most of them, I think."

"You heard what the Marx Brothers did to Thalberg's office down at MGM . . . and about all the dead Christmas trees that got dumped on the lawn of that Twentieth Century producer last January . . . "

Chandler nodded.

" . . . and about Sadakichi Hartmann and that Fowler group, they got John Barrymore's body out of the mortuary and took it over to Errol Flynn's house and threw an old-fashioned wake."

Chandler nodded again, hoping to get the young man to his point. "This town seems to have a death fixation."

"It laughs at it. That's what it does. It laughs at it."

"So, you want to do a story about practical jokes in Hollywood?"

"No," McGrath giggled and shook his head broadly. "I want to pull one off."

Chandler shrugged. "So?"

"I want to pull yours off."

"Mine? What are we talking about?"

"Don't you see? A joke's no good unless it has a point to it. An angle. And you've got the perfect angle. You got a story line point to make. You want to prove that nobody feels like playing patty-cake when there's a dead body in the same room."

Chandler closed his eyes so he wouldn't have to watch McGrath bobbing and weaving. Why wasn't this guy in the Army? He'd be very good at dodging bullets.

"McGrath, I think you're assuming I know what you're talking about when in fact I don't."

"I'm talking about your plan to, as you put it, 'make those producers pee in their collective pants.' "

Chandler blinked and sipped his drink. "You mean you want to fix up a mannequin and put it in—"

McGrath giggled, "No no, I mean a real stiff. A real live dead body."

"Ho-ly mother of . . . what are you talking about?"

McGrath leapt to his feet to quiet Chandler down. "Listen. Now listen, it can be done."

"Not with my help it can't."

"It's such a perfect set-up. Its just begging to be pulled off. And I have access to a body—"

"Listen my young friend, toting a dead body around for a joke is against the law."

"Oh, what law is that?"

Chandler puffed, "I don't know what law. But you can't do it."

"It's only a misdemeanor."

"McGrath, do you realize what would happen to you if you got caught? They still talk about the Fatty Arbuckle scandal around here as if it happened yesterday. I don't know about you, but I rather need this job."

"But we're not going to get caught."

"You're damn right *we*'re not. Why don't you go out to Universal where they make all those graveyard and mummy epics."

" 'Cause they got no sense of humor out there. At Paramount this'll make a name for us. They'll be talking about this for eons. Is it going to kill you to hear me out?"

Chandler found his glass empty and immediately started to replenish it. McGrath took this as his cue to continue.

"Look, at three o'clock this afternoon, approximately two hours from now, there's going to be a big meeting with most of the top brass of the studio. It's going to be in the producers' dining room. A lot of military and a couple people from the State Department are scheduled in. Billy Wilder didn't want it held in a screening room. He wants to play down the Hollywood business."

Chandler had been shaking his head through most of it, but with the magic words "Billy Wilder" he stopped shaking and started listening.

"What's Wilder got to do with it?"

"He's the one making the presentation."

"What presentation? What's this all about? And how come you know so much about it?"

"For the last five years it's been my business to know things like this." McGrath had traces of authority in his voice but instead of explaining he went on. "Our government is getting ready to occupy Germany when the war in Europe is over. That means we gotta set up a whole new government. Police, street sweepers, everything . . . including a Ministry of Culture. That's where Wilder comes in. He talks Kraut. He used to be in the film business over there and now he wants to be one of the movers and shakers in the Ministry of Culture. He's got his name in to be motion picture chief of psychological warfare or something. I imagine he'll sell the government on the idea of taking a lot of Paramount films over there and dubbing them. . . ."

A tight little smile began to appear on Chandler's thin lips and his eyes were dancing. "Sooo. That's why Wilder's cozying up to the military. Things are beginning to make sense."

McGrath painted the scene complete with gestures, like an unemployed director. "Now picture that group of mucky-mucks walking into the room and finding a body sitting up at the table, maybe a pencil in his hand and a bowler hat tipped down over his eyes? Can you picture what that would do to the meeting? What the State Department would think of the show biz types then?"

"Lovely," Chandler cooed, "simply lovely. What a just retribution for what he's done to me." But then his expression fell. "Unfortunately there's no way you could get in there without being seen."

"Oh yes, there is. There's a corridor right off the kitchen that leads from the dining room to the parking area for service trucks. It's for outside caterers when the producers throw a special party."

"It sounds like you've been casing the joint."

"Not at all," McGrath smiled. "It just happens I paid my way through USC's School of Journalism by working for Albert's Catering Service. After lunch on Saturdays that commissary is like a morgue. Believe me, I know."

Deep in thought, Chandler made three neat interlocking water rings with the bottom of his glass, then said, "Speaking of a morgue, you said something about a body."

For the first time since he'd entered the room, McGrath sat quietly. He sighed and smiled easily. He wasn't selling anymore. Now he was planning.

"The morgue is exactly right. You see I've got this friend that I met when I was working the midnight police blotter beat for the morning Hearst paper. Every morning they make the rounds of the flop houses and wino hangouts where the city's bums sleep. They used to pick up three or four dead ones regularly. Probably more now with all the new transients hitting L.A. It would be an easy thing if one stiff got lost in the paper shuffle."

"You get around, don't you?"

"I know this town inside and out. And I'm gonna make it pay off, too."

"My, my, such ambition in one so young."

"Listen, in this town you gotta work hard and fast. About every six or seven years a whole new layer of newcomers land on our doorstep with ideas and plans of their own. And they remake the place in their own image. And if you're not quick on your feet and know where you're going, you get buried in the layers. It's a town of layers, don't you see."

Chandler steered him back to the plan at hand. "What makes you think your friend would be willing to help us?"

McGrath smiled and rubbed his hands. "My friend, you see,

is star struck. He even hangs out in a little restaurant up the street hoping to rub shoulders with studio people. He wants to be an actor so bad he'd sell his soul for a . . . screen test at Paramount."

"And you're in a position to get him one?"

"Well, no. But Larry doesn't know that."

The two of them giggled and leaned over their drinks. From a distance and with a bit of imagination they could have passed for Walter Huston and Barry Fitzgerald plotting over the pool table in *And Then There Were None*.

4

he events of the ensuing hour became something of a blur in Chandler's mind. The next thing that had any impact on him was in a building with too much marble and porcelain. There were people arguing and the echoes of their voices were grating on his ears.

"When? I wanna know a date first. When will I get the test?"

It was McGrath's friend Larry Curtis bickering with McGrath about the use of a body in exchange for a screen test, and their voices were bouncing off all the walls. When Chandler could finally focus on the young man, he was disappointed. He'd expected Larry Curtis to be a handsome, virile leading man type. Instead, he had unbelievably close-set eyes, a pockmarked face, prematurely thinning hair, and a stooped posture that seemed to fit his present profession as a morgue attendant. With Hollywood's penchant for typecasting, Chandler knew the young man's only hope for a film career would be playing Benny the Weasel in a few gangster movies. Hope springs eternal.

McGrath wasn't having any luck getting Mr. Curtis to cooperate, in spite of the well-embroidered story he was feeding him: The studio needed the body for a scene it was shooting that very afternoon, McGrath was insisting, and they needed a real body for authenticity. Naturally a big studio like Paramount couldn't put in such a request formally, but they certainly paid their debts and Larry would not be forgotten. Curtis only shifted his suspicious little eyes between McGrath and Chandler.

Chandler had been introduced as the film's producer and for his part in the charade he leaned in the doorway of Curtis's office cubicle scowling like a producer and trying to act as sober as possible. Much of the ensuing argument was lost to him since he had all his mind could handle playing his mute part and keeping his knees locked straight.

Curtis's reluctance to cooperate, it seemed, stemmed not so much from his unwillingness to sneak a body out of the place as it did from his lack of confidence in McGrath. A very astute man, Mr. Curtis. Finally, by some fluke the conversation swung around to movie stars, and when Veronica Lake's name was mentioned Mr. Curtis's eyes lit up. McGrath, not a man to miss an opportunity, played his artificial ace. He promised not only that he would supply an introduction to the actress, but he would personally see to it that Curtis would play opposite Miss Lake in his screen test scene.

For some miraculous reason this bit of news seemed to allay good ol' Larry's reservations about McGrath's honesty and before long the two younger men were headed for the lockers.

"What age you looking for?" Curtis asked.

"It doesn't matter. Just so it's fresh and not too heavy."

McGrath pulled keys out of his pocket and tossed them in Chandler's direction as he walked by. "Here, pull the truck around to the loading dock."

Truck? What truck? Chandler picked up the keys from where they had fallen and went outside to look for a truck. To his amazement there was an Albert's Catering Service panel truck parked where he thought they had left McGrath's car.

Chandler, not a good driver under the best of conditions, finally got the strange vehicle started, inched it through the gate at the rear of the large medical facility and aimed it at the first ramp he saw. When the front of the car made contact with the dock's large rubber bumpers the engine died.

Someone called out, "What are you way over there for?"

Chandler focused his eyes toward the distant sound. McGrath and Curtis were standing at another loading area thirty yards away. Between them was a medical cart with an object on it, covered by a sheet. The sight of the white sheet shocked Chandler back into the reality of what they were doing and he started to panic, which took the form of freezing him in place. When it became obvious Chandler was not going to move the truck to them, McGrath and Curtis started wheeling their burden toward him.

In a few seconds there would be a body directly behind him in the truck. Chandler needed fortification. He reached under the passenger's seat for the bottle he knew would be there. He may not have known what car he was in, but he knew where the bottle was.

The large rear door swung open and, as the clumsy transfer was being made, two other people dressed in white came by and joked about the sign on the side of the truck. Curtis said it was the City of Pasadena's new way of saving money. Everybody laughed and the body was shoved in unceremoniously, like a sack of potatoes.

"There you go," Curtis said. "Just don't get his head lower than his stomach."

"Why not?" McGrath had to ask.

"The contents of his stomach might roll out. You don't know what stink is until you smell half-digested rotgut wine."

Chandler groaned and put his head on the dashboard. McGrath opened the door and hurriedly scooted into the driver's seat. But before they could get underway, Curtis was at the window reminding them of his screen test.

"I'm off duty Mondays and Tuesdays. You think we could set it up for this coming week?"

"I don't know," McGrath confided, "I'll have to check Veronica's schedule and let you know."

"What kind of flowers does she like? I'd like to give her something for helping me out."

"I'll have to get back to you on that."

"Call me tonight. Don't forget now," Curtis warned.

McGrath finally got the truck rolling out the gate and began tapping a happy rhythm on the steering wheel. "We got a great one. It has a tie and a dark suit. The suit's a little dirty and beat up, but that makes it all the better. I couldn't come up with a derby but a brown fedora will make it just as funny. You okay, Mr. Chandler?"

"I'm beginning to think this isn't such a good idea."

"We can call him Clarence. Larry says he's got a tattoo on his arm, a heart with 'Clarence loves Virginia' over it."

"Please don't say that. I don't want to know," Chandler groaned. "I don't know why I thought this would be so funny. We better take it back. It's so bright outside. Somebody is sure to spot us."

McGrath wiggled contentedly in his car seat and tapped on the steering wheel. "Everything is going great. You'll see."

Chandler rolled down his window and sucked at the fresh air. This only made him dizzy so he returned to his bottled friend under his seat for a little reality relief. It helped. Very soon he was back floating along without benefit of the car springs. The longer the drinking bout lasted the harder it became to maintain that pleasant edge. But for right now it was still working. After what seemed like two minutes of silence he smiled at McGrath.

"We switched cars on the way over to the morgue, did we?"

McGrath looked quizzically at him. "Of course we did. Don't you remember?"

"Of course I remember. I was just wondering about switching back." The last thing he wanted to do was admit he had lost track of some time. That, he knew, was serious. He looked out the window and tried to memorize passing streets to get his consciousness working. They were traveling west on Beverly. It wouldn't be long before they would be heading north to Melrose, then they'd be back at the studio. . . .

"Mr. Chandler, do you mind if I ask you a rather personal question?"

"I never know how to respond to that. What's the question?"

"Your wife's a bit older than you, isn't she?"

"So?"

"Well, I was just wondering what it's like—in bed and all—with a much older woman."

"I may be tight, but I'm not that tight. You've got a lot of gall."

"Listen, don't get sore. I got a reason. I've been seeing a lot of an older—well—a much older gal. It started out all business but one thing has led to another. She's getting pretty serious. I was just wondering if there were any pearls of wisdom you could drop my way."

Chandler studied his face to see if McGrath was playing him for a sucker, the same way he did the hapless Larry Curtis. But there seemed to be traces of genuine feeling there and it might be safe to open up a little.

"I think a lot depends on the woman. If she wants the same things the man wants. Then it has a chance."

"But do you think there could be . . . does love keep on going? I guess is what I'm asking."

Chandler closed his eyes to think, but he was immediately met by his own private Cissy, standing before him. It wasn't the bathrobed Cissy from the kitchen on Drexel Avenue, but the young one with the cornflower-blue eyes, the real blonde hair without traces of age or hairpins. She always came to him in a pastel chiffon thing, very modest, but so soft and delicate the traces of her nipples could be made out. And underneath the chiffon was only the special ivory-colored garter belt with the lace that smelled of lilac and the sheer midnight-blue silk stockings. He knew they were there because that was the way he wanted it, in his mind.

It had taken him a long time to realize she didn't exist and never had. Even stoned, he knew that much. She belonged only to that special land where knighthood was still in flower. Where truth and duty and honor and even purity grew on trees. It was the same distant fallow land that had sired the mind of Philip Marlowe. The girl with the cornflower-blue eyes and Philip Marlowe. He hoped they would be very happy there together.

When his eyes opened again he realized young McGrath was still waiting for an answer.

"Does love still exist? McGrath, I didn't know what love was when I married. I knew lust and desire and I called it love. I'm convinced most men marry their illusions. The love only came later, much later, when there was a price somebody had to pay. And she paid it, without blinking an eye. That's when you start to see the wonder and the glory. She's the beat of my heart. She's the voice heard softly at the edge of sound."

He couldn't remember if he believed all that himself anymore, but the trips back to the land of knights made him talk that way. And it seemed to be making a favorable impression on young McGrath. They rode in silence for several blocks.

Then, as they approached the service entrance to the studio, McGrath suggested Chandler should duck down out of sight. He was too recognizable a figure at the studio and the guards might get curious if he showed up in a delivery truck. As Chandler did so, his eyes were caught on the white sheet in the back and he remembered with a start the task at hand. He thought of Ladd and Lake and the love scene with their hotel cadaver in his story and he made the odd connection with his own sweet talk with McGrath while in the truck with a cadaver of their own. He started laughing.

"What's so funny?" McGrath whispered.

"People. They're so fickle."

"Well, pipe down. We're at the gate."

The truck rolled to a stop and McGrath called to the guard, "Commissary delivery."

The guard didn't bother to rise from his sitting position in his little guard house. He called back, "Okay, you know where to go."

"Sure do."

The truck rolled on through the gate, and Chandler continued laughing.

5

McGrath hurried the truck along the tall hedges that hid the commissary service area from a little garden the execs used on occasion and swung into place at the commissary back door. No problem so far. Then he went inside to see if it was all clear. When he returned he was pushing a four-wheel, stainless steel cart that normally held large coffee urns.

"Here, we can roll Clarence on this."

"Please don't call him that. Is anybody in there?"

"Just two kids mopping up out in front. They'll never notice."

Chandler, fortified with the last few drops from their bottle, studied himself like a boxer as the truck's back door was opened. McGrath did most of the work. Fortunately for the queasy Chandler, the sheet stayed in place as the move was made; he had only to lift "it" by its heels. They then bounced across the doorsill and down the hallway, their speed and excitement increasing with each step.

At last they were there. McGrath put his shoulder against

the door to the producers' dining room. It normally swung freely, but now all he got for his efforts was a teeth-rattling jar. Damn, the thing was locked. He shook the handle until Chandler pointed to a typewritten note thumb-tacked to the door frame. McGrath squinted at it and read, " 'In case we haven't reached you by phone, our afternoon meeting has been canceled due to the illness of Mr. Freeman. Sorry for the inconvenience.' Damn."

Chandler growled, "Didn't you know Mr. Freeman got a cold last night at a preview?"

"No, of course I didn't know."

"Well, why didn't you? I thought you knew everything." His mood was flipping about now from one extreme to another. "What are we going to do now, genius?"

They started slowly back down the corridor pushing Clarence along, both of them stricken with grief over the loss of their great joke. They had just about decided there was nothing left to do but return Clarence to his spot in the city morgue when suddenly someone appeared at the screen door at the end of the corridor. The tall blond figure stood in the bright afternoon sunlight and cupped his eyes against the screen door, trying to look in.

"Hey, anybody in there?"

"Oh, good grief. Palmer," McGrath whispered. "Go down there and stall him. Don't let him in here."

"Who, me? Me?" Chandler stammered.

His nerves had made his body go rigid and his mind go blank. But McGrath pushed him forward forcefully.

"Yeah, what you want? You can't come in here."

"I don't want to come in," the man insisted. "I want somebody to move this panel truck."

"Move truck? You can't come in here. No."

Chandler stood in the doorway trying to block the man's view, but he also gave the man a good view of himself.

The man laughed, "Hey Mister, you're drunk."

"Oh, drunk am I, eh? Drunk? Well listen, tomorrow, tomorrow you're gonna be ugly. No wait a minute. That's not right. . . ."

"Look, Jocko, I got the mayor and two city councilmen

40

behind the hedge over there. We're trying to take publicity pictures."

"Well, take 'em. Who's stopping you?"

"That truck is stopping us. We can see it right through the hedge, and we're getting a bad reflection. Now are you gonna move it or not?"

"Okay, okay, don't get huffy. I'll move it in two shakes."

It finally dawned on Chandler to close the door on the man. He did so and in a moment the shadow of the blond man moved reluctantly away from the translucent window in the door.

"Who is that guy?" he asked, heading back toward McGrath.

"It's Lyle Palmer. He does newspaper stuff for the studio. Gimme a hand."

"Hey, what you doing?"

McGrath had the wooden door to a large refrigerator locker open and he was moving trays and things about inside. "We're gonna put Clarence in the cooler for safekeeping."

"We can't do that. That's a food storage area."

"He's not gonna eat any, you know. You got any better ideas?"

As Chandler tried to think, he heard distant noises back in what must have been a pantry area of the kitchen. They were trapped for the moment. "Okay, what do we do here?"

There were large trays of diced Jell-O squares sitting in the cooler. Apparently the kitchen staff was toughening them up for Monday's lunch crowd. McGrath and Chandler began moving things about and shifting trays until there was space enough to slide Clarence in.

"Whatever you do, don't get him upside down," Chandler warned.

As the two of them struggled to get a grip on Clarence, the sheet slipped down, exposing most of the dead man's face. As their run of luck had it, Chandler ended up looking eyeball to eyeball with the sad little wino face. Chandler got woozy and planted himself against the opposite wall. McGrath was quick and wiry enough to take up the slack. He got Clarence into the fetal position by himself, hoisted him into the shelf next to the Jell-O and finally got the door squeezed closed behind him.

41

"Okay, he's in," McGrath panted. "You gonna be all right?"

Chandler only groaned.

"Tell you what. Why don't you go on back up to your office, Mr. Chandler. I'll go out and see Palmer and see how much longer they're gonna be. I'll give you a call when we can move Clarence."

Chandler made no argument against this arrangement and hurried out of the building, using the main entrance as McGrath had suggested.

A breeze from the west had come up and he loosened his collar and breathed deeply. The walk and the fresh air started to clear his head and he found himself muttering things like "What am I doing?" and "I must be insane" by the time he reached the writers' building.

"Oh, Mr. Chandler, there you are." It was Simone from behind her switchboard. "Your wife called for you but I didn't know where you were."

"Is she all right?"

"Oh, yes. She just wanted to tell you that she went out to lunch and had a very nice time."

Although Simone was always friendly and helpful to him, Chandler had the nagging suspicion she was like a French concierge who dutifully reported the activities of her writers to the powers that be. He thanked her for the news from his wife and started up the stairs to his office.

"Mr. Chandler, are you all right?" It was Simone, again, who was watching his progress on the stairs.

"Yes of course, my dear. Quite all right."

He had been extra careful not to stumble or sway. He wondered what possible defect he was displaying that might have given him away. Then he realized it was taking an uncommonly long time to negotiate his way to the first landing. But he finally made it all the way up and into his office. No lock on the door. Writers, apparently, were not to be trusted behind locked doors. He would agree with that.

He sat at his desk and took out *The Blue Dahlia* as if he could do some work, but he never got the cover open. He was an intelligent man with something of a literary reputation to uphold and a wife to . . . a wife to care for. What ever possessed him to be a part of such a stunt? Was he going to destroy this career, too?

It was during this period of mental flagellation that he thought he heard what could have been a gunshot. The writers sometimes heard a backfiring Model A along Melrose Avenue or six-gun fire from the Western set over at RKO or even gunshots from their own back lot, so it wouldn't have been unusual.

Trying to get some of yesterday's coffee heated up on the small hotplate Chandler heard a soft knock at the door.

"McGrath? That you?" he called.

"No sir, it's me, Clarence."

Chandler started screaming and spilled cold coffee down the front of his trousers. Clarence, the studio guard, opened the door to see what the trouble was.

"You all right, Mr. Chandler?"

"Oh, Clarence. Clarence, it's you. I thought . . . I spilled some coffee. . . ." Chandler tried to laugh.

Clarence came into the room and helped Chandler into his desk chair. "You want I should call a doctor?" he asked. He touched the wet stains on Chandler's pants. "Why, that's cold. I thought you burned yourself. What is it, Mr. Chandler?"

"What are you here for? What do you want?"

"Well, what was it you was screamin' for?"

"Nothing. I was . . . Nothing. You scared me, calling out your name that way."

"All I said was I was Clarence."

"Don't say that. You don't have to keep telling me. I know who you are. What is it you want?"

"Oh, we had some Mexicans loose on the grounds, running around by themselves. We finally got 'em coraled, though. They said they was Leo Carrillo fans and they was lookin' fer him. He ain't even at this studio. We finally got 'em all kicked out."

The live Clarence's syntax was giving Chandler a headache. He leaned over his desk and rubbed his temples. "What makes you think I know anything about Mexicans?"

"Oh, it's not that. We was trying to figger out how they got on the lot in the first place and somebody said they saw 'em comin' outta the writers' building. Some a' the windows on this building look out on the city street, you know. We just wanted to check all the windows."

Clarence walked to the second-story window and looked out. "There's a little bitty ledge out there, but I don't see how that could 'a helped 'em. One a' them was pretty fat. Well thanks, Mr. C. Sorry to disturb you an' all." He tried to make his exit a casual one, but at the door he couldn't help shooting a quick suspicious glance Chandler's way.

After the guard had gone, Chandler went to the men's room down the hall and did what he could about cleaning himself up. He put cold water on his face and the back of his neck, which didn't seem to do anything but aggravate the headache. He had never had headaches or bad hangovers before when he was drinking, but then neither could he remember trying to stop a binge without letting it run its course.

He checked his watch and was surprised to see a half hour had passed since he'd come back from the commissary. What had happened to young McGrath? Judging from the noise level in the hallway, the building was nearly empty. A typewriter clattered away someplace downstairs. Probably a secretary, judging from the proficiency. No sound from the other end of the hall, where a group frequently gathered to swap dirty jokes. If there were other writers about, they were silent behind their closed doors.

Back at his own office, Chandler found that a note had been slid under the door. "Meet me you know where" was all it said. It was in a quick scrawl on a three-by-five slip of paper. He had half a notion to leave word with Simone that he was ill and sneak home. But there was something in his makeup or public school training that wouldn't let him do it. He borrowed two aspirin tablets from Simone and trudged back toward the commissary like a good scout.

The main entrance he had recently exited was locked, which didn't surprise him, so he went around to the back, expecting to find the truck and McGrath waiting for him. But there was no sign of life at all. This was a puzzle but not of great concern, so he waited and rubbernecked around a bit outside, half expecting McGrath to show up in his usual excited manner. When this didn't happen he tried the back door to the commissary kitchen. It was open, but there were no sounds from inside. No kitchen crew. The only noise he could pick up was the humming of the large refrigeration unit.

He eased himself inside and called, "Is anybody here?" Nothing. He was just about to try McGrath's name but his eyes were drawn to the door to the cooler. How odd. Why hadn't they noticed that before? A corner of the dead man's coat had caught in the doorjamb just below the latch. He'd wait and let McGrath take care of it when he showed up. But where was the man? He didn't like the idea of standing around this close to the remnants of a botched practical joke. What could possibly be holding the man up? He took the note out of his pocket and read it again: "Meet me you know where." He turned it over in his mind and tried to think of how he might be misinterpreting the message, but he kept coming up with zero. This was the only "where" he could possibly think of.

Someone would be coming back to lock up the facility for the day. He couldn't stay there indefinitely. He walked to the back door, ready to leave, but then turned and looked at the cooler. His penchant for neatness would not let him go with that bit of cloth sticking out that way. It should be easy enough to open the door a crack and stuff the jacket corner back inside. He wouldn't have to look at anything inside.

The latch had a long handle designed to be pulled straight out, which in turn snapped the locking mechanism free quite suddenly. Chandler, who was a mechanical ignoramus, tried to ease the door open. The door handle did what door handles will do and the cooler door sprung out at him like a jack-in-the-box. It happened with unexpected force as well for the body. Chandler found himself struggling to prevent it from rolling out. He heaved and pushed against the loose form for all he was worth, his eyes averted and his mouth tightly closed for fear of some kind of oral contamination from the dead. But that didn't prevent him from grunting and crying out in all his agony.

Finally he got the body returned to its original upright sitting posture and was just about to close the door again when he realized something wasn't quite right. What had happened to the sheet? What he was feeling on the body didn't feel like it

45

had before, when he had helped McGrath load it into the freezer. He had to take one quick look. No sheet. But no, it was there but . . . it was covering something behind . . . almost as if it were covering something . . . and there were two . . . but that was impossible.

Chandler forced himself to look up at the face of the uncovered body. He gagged, then cried out. It was McGrath. McGrath wedged up on top of the body under the sheet, a neat little bullet hole in his temple. And there was blood, dark red blood that had come from the oozing red circle, and blood from the open mouth. Chandler slammed the door shut and closed his eyes tightly. But he could still see the grotesque image in every detail. The ashen grey skin as if all traces of color and life had been sucked out of it through the mouth and the little oozing circle. The circle with a nice symmetrical ring of black flecks around it.

Chandler hurried over to the large stainless steel utility sink and threw up his lunch. Then he dry heaved nothing until he hurt all the way down to his crotch. It was like his bout with the flu in 1918, his heart was pounding and his body shook from the chills so badly he wondered if he was going to fall down.

He had to get out of there. He had to stop thinking of what he was thinking. He had to have a drink. No, no, that was what he mustn't do. It was what he wanted, but he mustn't. He had to start thinking for himself now, about what he was going to do.

Hand over hand along the countertops he made his way toward the back door and got it opened. Still no one about. Two quick bells sounded in the distance. Some production crew had just finished a scene, probably in the back lot. He pulled himself together and headed out the door. The soundstages nearby seemed quiet except for a few carpenter types coming and going. There would be no more visits to the writers' building. He headed right for his Packard.

But as he passed the row of old bungalows that marginal producers and assistant producers used, he was hailed by his friend with the old school tie, John Houseman. Houseman was young and eager and no doubt anxious about his own position and he would want to talk story with Chandler, which was the last thing in the world Chandler wanted to do just then. He eased himself into the shade of the adjoining soundstage, leaned against the wall, and waited for Houseman to catch up.

When he did he flinched at the sight of the writer. "Raymond, are you all right?"

"Yes, I'm all right. Why do you ask?"

"Have you taken a fall?"

"No, I haven't fallen down. What a strange thing to ask me."

"But your shirt," Houseman pointed. "Is that blood?"

Chandler wiped at the smear he found on his tie and shirt front, only making it worse. "Nose bleed. It just started without warning. It must be the tension. Must get home . . . get cleaned up."

Chandler started walking but found Houseman stayed right at his side. "Look, old man, I'd like to help you with this new story twist. I think it can be licked and we can still end up with a credible story line. . . ."

"Yes, right. I'd like to hear what you have to say. Tomorrow. Give me a call in the morning."

Houseman was giving Chandler the fish eye, the look all alcoholics learned to recognize all too well. "I'll be happy to come along with you now. It wouldn't take long to say what I—"

"Tomorrow will be best. Give me a call in the morning."

Chandler started walking faster, letting Houseman know the conversation should end at this point. He got to his car, finally, and started it up. He could see Houseman in the rearview mirror so he was on his best behavior as he turned his big car around and got out of there.

He got to Melrose and turned west before he started breathing halfway normally again. Then he tried to think logically about what had happened. But nothing would come. He would go home and then things would start to clear up. Once he was home he would know what to do. It was all gibberish in his head now. Things like an old line from one of his books. It was his detective Philip Marlowe talking: "I was right: Dead bodies are heavier than broken hearts . . . dead bodies are heavier than broken hearts."

Chandler wondered what profound wisdom he ever imagined there was in that line.

6

can't believe you did all that." Cissy cooed as she stroked his forehead and hair. "I remember when we couldn't persuade you to look at your own mother's open coffin."

He had come home, set his wife down on their old wicker settee, put his head in her lap, and had told her everything. But she wasn't reacting properly. He sat up, put his glasses back on, and studied her.

"Cissy, didn't you hear what I said? There's a dead man with a bullet hole in his head over there in the food cooler. How do you think I got this blood on me?"

She examined his shirt more closely. "It looks more like gelatin stains to me."

"All right, maybe it is. There was a lot of Jell-O in the place. I must have bumped against it. . . ."

There was a look in her eyes he hated. He had promised himself a thousand times she would never have to feel that way again, but there it was. When she tried to smooth back his cowlick he grabbed her hand.

"Listen to me. I'm not hallucinating. This business really did happen. Yes, I'd been drinking. I admit it. If I hadn't I never would have gone along with the scheme. But I'm not that far gone."

"What's the name of the man you went with?"

"I don't know his first name. Just McGrath."

"You don't know his first name and yet you go off with him to get a body . . . all right. I'm sorry. I know you didn't mean it. . . ."

"Stop talking like that. Don't you know what it does to me? We're beginning to sound like out-takes from *Stella Dallas*. It's done. That's what we've got to worry about now. It's done and what are we going to do?"

"Why, go to the police, of course."

"Have you really thought that through, I wonder?"

"Why not? You haven't done anything."

"Except Houseman saw me looking like this and coming from the commissary. And that publicity guy, ah Palmer, I think, he saw me standing in the kitchen hallway. They have me nailed to the spot."

"But you had no grudge against the man. You're always telling me the murderer has to have a motive. . . ."

"And even if I can clear myself of involvement in murder there's the business of being involved with a very bad practical joke. It sounded so logical, so very funny at the time. I kept imagining how the telling of it would go over at the writers' table." He pulled at his own hair and started pacing the room, but his head wasn't up to such activity and he had to sit down again. "It's bound to come out in the investigation. I hardly think they are going to overlook the extra body. The studio will say good-bye to me in short order. And then what happens to your treatment?"

"This is no time to be thinking of that. We'll have to get by on your books. We did it before."

"But you're getting worse. You know you are. I can't give this up without a fight. We've got to think this through. There must be something we can do."

An idea struck him and he moved to the phone as quickly as his throbbing head would let him and looked up the number

49

for the city morgue. A laconic operator got him the number, then he sat watching the clock and waited while someone at the other end looked for Larry Curtis. Time didn't work right when he was drinking. When he didn't want it to, it flew by. But when he watched the clock it never seemed to move. Finally he heard the familiar nasal voice.

"Curtis, you remember me, Mr. Chandler? I was just in to see you with Mr. McGrath—Listen, I've run into some trouble with the body. I need some help—Can you meet me at Paramount?—It's more than that—Mr. McGrath can't talk to you— Well, because he can't—It's just you and me now and—You're out of what? What's that supposed to mean? Listen, don't give me that technical mumbo jumbo about all your bodies accounted for. You and I know where this one came from and—What about Moronica Lake, er, Veronica Lake, and your screen test. You're not forgetting that, are you?—I'm sorry, you can't talk to McGrath—To be honest with you there's been an accident— Come on now, Larry, in this business we gotta help each other out. Can't you get an ambulance or . . . don't hang up. Listen."

It was just as well that Curtis had hung up on him. Chandler was shaking so badly he had to stop and reorganize anyway. He was coming down from his alcoholic high too fast. He knew he'd have to have something—a parachute somebody had called it— to ease the transition. He excused himself, saying he needed to get cleaned up. But before he could get into the bedroom and his hidden bottle, Cissy called out, "I put your bottle on the buffet in the dining room."

Without saying a word, he came back into the dining room, took a tumbler from the buffet, poured himself two inches, and then made a production of recapping the bottle before he drank. Cissy came into the dining room and sat at the table, but not so close that he would get a sense of being smothered. She knew precisely how to play it.

"I'm not hallucinating, I swear," he repeated. Then he waited while the shaking subsided. "I can't lose that job now. I can't. But what happens Monday morning when the commissary opens and somebody wants Jell-O. . . ."

Now it was her turn to shake. At first he thought she was crying, but then he saw she was trying to hold back her laughter.

"I'm sorry, dear. It really isn't funny. But I just had the mental picture of some poor unsuspecting pudgy cook—he would have to be pudgy—opening up the refrigerator and being besieged by the two bodies. . . ."

He caught the infection very quickly and was soon roaring helplessly, finally having to rest his head on his typewriter cover for support. The tension of the day seemed to roll away with each guffaw.

But all the laughing had a detrimental effect on Cissy and their momentary gaiety turned to sober concern as she lapsed into a coughing spasm. At first it was light, but it grew in intensity until she seemed to be in danger of losing consciousness. Chandler got her water and the small inhaler designed for asthmatics that had helped her in the past.

He half carried her back to the couch and after several anxious minutes she was finally able to breathe easily while lying down.

"Sorry, dear," she smiled. "Lunch out with the girls . . . must have . . . too much."

He was not by nature a good nursemaid. Usually it was she who was nursing and caring for him. But he knelt beside her and watched her with such a doleful expression of love and frustrated concern she wanted to do something to shake him out of his pain. She covered his burning eyes to make him stop staring at her.

"What a dear you are, my Raymio. What a dear."

He wanted to hold her in his arms but only held her hands lightly and kissed each palm.

"So you want to do something to get us out of this mess," she said slowly. "Well dear, there is really only one thing to do."

"And what is that?"

"You silly. I'm surprised that *you* have to ask."

He suddenly changed his mood and started straightening some scattered magazines on their small end table. "Let's not be childish."

"Childish? That's a strange thing to say," she teased.

"I am not Philip Marlowe. He's a character in a book of fiction."

It hadn't been the first time she'd made such a crazy sug-

51

gestion. Maybe every wife wanted her man to be more dashing, more he-man than he was capable of being. And maybe most men can imagine themselves that way in weaker moments when they aren't thinking too well. There had been times when Chandler had taken off the glasses and squared his jaw at the fuzzy world and pictured himself as the man of action. But not today. At fifty-six you get to know who you are. You know it takes two days of bleeding over a typewriter to come up with the clever repartee it took Marlowe a split second to deliver. It was out of the question.

In an attempt to terminate the line of thought Chandler went into the bathroom, stripped to the waist and washed himself at the sink. In the bedroom he found that Cissy had already put out a clean shirt for him and was sitting on the bed, quietly waiting.

"I wasn't planning on dressing again." He went to the closet and pulled out his old paisley bathrobe.

"It's only three o'clock."

"I know what time it is," he barked. "And you are going to bring another attack on if you aren't careful."

He went to his writing spot at the dining room table and got as far as taking the dust cover off his typewriter. Cissy had followed him.

"Do you want something to eat?"

"You know I can't eat now."

"Well, I'm going to make a pot of tea."

In the kitchen, while she waited for the water to boil, Cissy listened for the sound of typewriter keys, but nothing could be heard except the distant traffic on Santa Monica Boulevard.

It was still quiet ten minutes later when she brought in the tray. "The longer we wait to report this, the worse it's going to look, Ray."

"The L.A. chief of police hates my guts, you know."

"It could be worse. It could have happened in Santa Monica."

They exchanged smiles. Santa Monica was the model for his fictional Bay City, where it was frequently hard to distinguish the police from the underworld characters he had created.

She poured two cups. Chandler cooled his down with his friend from the buffet behind him.

"Just for the sport of it," she began carefully, "I mean treating it as if it were a story line, what would be the first thing Philip Marlowe would do if he were faced with such a case?"

Chandler knew what she was up to, but went along with it, just for the moment. Maybe it was the act of sitting at the typewriter that helped. Anyway, some thoughts started forming. "Well, he would have one ace in the hole. Chances are good that he would probably be the only person, other than the murderer, who knew what had happened. Until Monday morning, when that condition would be bound to change, he would have the luxury of knowing a little bit more than the murderer thought he knew. . . ."

He wasn't quite sure where all of it was leading and his voice dropped off. Cissy only nodded and waited.

"The logical thing to do of course would be to know as much as possible about McGrath, know his enemies. . . ."

"What kind of writer was the man?" she asked.

"I have no idea. He seemed to be knowledgeable about the newspaper business, but I've never heard of any screen credits . . . yet he had a regular office assignment and a secretary assigned to him."

"The secretary could no doubt fill us in on the man. Do you know who she is?"

Chandler shuffled papers so he wouldn't be tempted to look at her. "I have no idea."

"But it shouldn't be hard to find out."

"Simone, our phone receptionist, would probably be of more help."

"And the man must live someplace. Perhaps he has a wife and family."

"I don't think so. For some reason I got the impression he was single. But you know, I can see where he would be a man who could attract enemies easily. He was ambitious. He prattled on about how he knew how the town worked and how he was going to make it pay off. I don't think he would hesitate stepping on a few toes to get where he wanted to go."

"If he had a newspaper background maybe he was doing an exposé of some sort and he was murdered because of the murderer's need for secrecy."

They contemplated their tea for a time while they searched in silence for other ideas. Then Chandler grunted a laugh and rubbed his shoulder.

"Our murderer would have to be quite strong. McGrath was not all that heavy, but it would have been a Herculean task hoisting him onto that cooler shelf. That also opens the possibility of there being more than one, doesn't it?"

"Or he could have gotten into that position while he was still alive," Cissy offered, "and then shot."

"Now really, darling, who in their right mind would ever do a thing like that?"

"I don't know. I'm just bouncing around for possibilities."

"Well, that's one I think we can safely scratch."

She raised an eyebrow and cooed softly, "Who in their right mind would put a morgue body in there in the first place?"

"Thank you, my dear, for that vote of confidence."

"Oh Raymio, I know what kind of condition you were in. You don't have to defend yourself to me. I simply mean not a great deal of this is making a great deal of sense in the cold light of day so just about any irrational explanation might be our answer."

Chandler gave a cynical snort and rubbed his eyes. "That's the trouble with reality. It's frequently irrational. If I did stories the way life truly was, I'd never get them published. I suppose that's one reason I was attracted to the mystery format in the first place; everything gets tied up into neat little packages in the end. Far neater than real life could ever hope to be. The world is . . . the world is a dirty place, full of selfish, grasping, ignorant people who perform seventy percent of their activities in secret. A place to be avoided whenever possible."

"That's your tea talking and you know it," she tried to tell him.

"Is it? I wonder. I wonder if that isn't the reason I have to be three sheets to the wind in order to carry on an intelligent conversation with a stranger." He forced a fist against the short stack of writing paper in disgust. "Here's my reality. Oh Cissy, who do we think we're kidding with these games? I'm not Marlowe. I'm Caspar Milquetoast. I have the luxury of knowing how all Marlowe's stories will end before I write them because I write them backwards. And I'm too old and tired to play cat and mouse games now."

"But Philip Marlowe is inside you. Everything he stands for, every concept and value. It was all in you before it was ever in a story."

"There's no trick to talk of values. Any fool can sit down at any typewriter and write of values. What is it we're arguing about? I can't be something I'm not. You wonder why I'm so suspicious of happy endings. Well, it's because there are so few of them in life. It's unrealistic."

"Maybe it is, but isn't that what we should be striving for anyway? Isn't that what you and I started our . . . for . . ."

Her coughing had come back. She tried to ignore it at first, but it was too much for her. She got up and headed for her asthma aid which they had left in the living room. He started to help her, but she waved him away with about as much anger as she had ever displayed.

He watched as she got the inhaler, took two deep drags on it, then plopped herself down into the easy chair. She had tried so hard for so long to keep herself young in appearance and manner for his benefit, but her true age was beginning to exert itself, especially under stress. Each movement seemed to call attention to the details. The widow's hump at the base of the neck, the sharp angle of the wrist, now at odds with the graceful curve of youth it had replaced. And the greyness, the loss of vibrancy and sparkle in the eyes, the hair, the skin. She was a walking example of his argument against happy endings.

He put a new sheet in the typewriter and tried to prime the pump by typing: "My name is Raymond Chandler. I have a twenty-six week contract with Paramount Studios Inc. at one thousand clamolas a week to write screenplays of their choosing. I haven't a care in the world. Everything is coming along just peachy, except for the moment I have forgotten the name of the project I was working on. My name is Raymond Chandler and I need money."

Sometimes it worked and sometimes it didn't. He took the sheet out and dropped it in the circular file. For no apparent reason except to get away from the typewriter keys, he walked into his bedroom, leaned against the dresser, and looked at himself in the mirror. He wasn't too far behind Cissy himself, but at least there was a certain vitality there, behind the red-rimmed eyes. Then he noticed a newspaper clipping that had been wedged into the corner of the mirror. His wife was in the habit of cutting out articles from magazines and newspapers to keep him abreast of her reading interests and to keep their running conversation well oiled. Cissy's note in the corner of the story said: "You remember Bobby? He used to deliver our paper when we lived over on Highland." An arrow ran down to the smiling face in an airman's uniform. Robert Clifton III had been awarded a Distinguished Service Medal for something in Europe.

Chandler did not like to read about heroes and war. He had had enough of it in the Real War.

His eyes moved automatically to the small picture that he kept behind his cuff link box. It was a larger version of the one he had carried with him in his own war. It was of Mrs. Cissy Pascal, another man's wife, before she belonged to him. The forbidden love that had sustained him during those boring months of training and waiting and the weeks of paralyzing panic in the trenches. A face that could sustain dreams with ease, the face that was responsible for too many bad poems with too much posturing and sentiment. It was an image belonging to a different era. A face fit for the locket of a Victorian romantic with consumption.

Chandler sighed. He took off his robe and reached for his shirt. First the left sleeve went on, then the right. Then, as he ruffled the front to loosen the white pearl buttons from the grip of the starch, he found himself wondering what the Knights of the Round Table wore under their metal breast plates.

As he expected, Simone was alone at her switchboard, doing some finishing work on her long nails. The producers not currently in production had already left for the day and those in production were too busy with other matters to keep track of wandering writers. And Dozier, who was supposed to be in charge of them, never adjusted to his role as watchdog, consequently the kennel on Saturdays was frequently empty. But Chandler looked around and listened just to make sure. Then he leaned across the counter toward Simone.

"Hello, my dear. Looks as if you've been left all alone."

"Oh, oh, Mr. Chandler." He had startled her twice. Once for being there and again for being in such good shape. "Mr. Houseman tried to reach you earlier."

"What time was that?"

"Around two-fifteen, I believe."

"I think I've already seen him."

Chandler wasn't very adept at small talk, but he chuckled and leaned sideways against the counter, trying to act casual.

"Say, listen, you know everything that goes on around here. What's the story on this young McGrath?"

"You mean Corky?"

"That's a grown man's name?"

"I think it's Charles, actually, but that's what he goes by. What about him?"

"What kind of stuff does he write?"

She shrugged. "That's a good question."

"Well, who does he call? Who calls him?"

"He gets a lot of calls, actually. . . ." She tapped her temple with a red fingernail.

"From . . . ?"

"From several of the powers that be, actually."

"But what about any writing assignments?"

"Well, yesterday Mr. Putnam left a message for him. He has a plot outline overdue and Mr. Putnam wanted to know when it would be in."

"Who's Mr. Putnam?"

"Why, he's in charge of the cartoon department. Didn't you know that?"

Chandler gulped. "McGrath wrote plots for cartoons? This studio's cartoons?"

McGrath's prestige, what there was left of it, was slipping fast in Chandler's estimation. Most theaters expected cartoon shorts to be sent along with a studio's features to fill out the bill, but Paramount never bothered to put the adequate money or effort into such financially marginal areas, hence the cartoon department always seemed to be in a state of flux and something of an industry joke. The wrong kind of joke. Jesse Lasky, in defense of his studio's product, was reported to have said, "Our cartoons are nothing to be laughed at."

Simone was frowning at Chandler. "What do you mean, he 'wrote'? He still does, doesn't he?"

A stupid mistake, slipping into the past tense like that. Some secret-keeper he was. He decided to ignore the slip.

"You think that's his only current assignment?"

Simone shrugged, then adjusted her headphone and dialed a number. "What say we ask Francine?"

"No, no, let's not bother with Francine."

58

"It's already ringing."

"I'd rather not involve her, do you mind?"

"Why not? She's his secretary."

Chandler got the distinct impression he was being toyed with. There were traces of a Parisian twinkle in Simone's eyes. But as she waited for a response to her ring, her smile faded. "That's funny, she doesn't answer. She's supposed to be in." Simone checked a schedule she had taped to her directory file. "She's supposed to be there. . . ." she repeated with a frown.

"Looks like you'll have to start locking the back door. Say, ah, you wouldn't have McGrath's home address, would you?"

This abruptly changed Simone's attitude. It seemed an innocent enough question to him, but it elicited a quick vicious look from her. She flipped her directory to the M's and read in a loud formal voice, "315 Hobart Avenue." She turned her back and pulled a couple dead plugs on her board.

Chandler wondered what button he'd pushed to get such a reaction. Maybe it was just one question too many. He thanked her ʼnd left.

Outside he leaned against the cool green stucco on the north side of the building and wrote the Hobart address in a small notebook. Maybe Marlowe could keep such facts in his head, but his creator couldn't. What to do now? Should he head right to Hobart? It seemed logical the murder was studio related, so perhaps the thing to do would be to stay on the lot and nose around. But how and where? And what could he possibly ask anyone without throwing additional suspicion on himself?

He was still mulling this over as he walked over to the publicity department. It was a small, cramped complex of cubicles where people seemed to be confined to their own little prison cells made up of paper stacks, teletypes, and typewriters. All the glamour in this business seemed to get splashed up on the screen; there wasn't any left over for the serfs and their hovels.

Chandler interrupted the receptionist in her proofreading and asked if he might have a word with Mr. Palmer.

"I'm sorry, Mr. Chandler, but Mr. Palmer is still at his luncheon appointment with the mayor and the council members. Could someone else help you?"

"Was that luncheon here on the lot?"

"Yes, sir, over at the De Mille patio."

"Maybe they're still over there. Any possibility of that, you think?"

She checked the clock on the wall. "Oh, I hardly think so. They're probably on their way back down to the City Hall by now."

"And Mr. Palmer would be with them?"

"I'm sure he would. He left his car down there so he could ride in the limo with the mayor. I take it this is something only Mr. Palmer can handle for you?"

Chandler smiled and tried to do his British casual. "That's right. Just a personal thing. You might ask him to give me a ring when he can. Perhaps tonight at home if he doesn't mind."

"Yes, Mr. Chandler. I'll give him the message."

Next he walked over to the rear of the commissary and took a second look at the hedge next to the driveway. He didn't know there was such a thing as a De Mille patio, but he found the gate through the hedge and there it was. More of a wide place between buildings than a real patio, but the graceful flagstone and nicely manicured lawn and shrubbery made it into a pleasant area for a small garden party. Three small metal tables were still set up with what looked to be the remnants of a catered luncheon. Near the section of hedge that backed up to the commissary delivery area stood a large floral horseshoe with a banner reading 30 YEARS OF ENTERTAINMENT, CONGRATULATIONS PARAMOUNT arced across the front. The guests had all left but some of the studio's maintenance people were busy tearing down the papier-mâché decorations and trimmings.

Chandler noticed one hand-printed name tag next to one of the place settings that hadn't been cleared yet. It read "Councilman Gilbert Terry." He sauntered over to the trash barrel and found three others he recognized: Mayor Fletcher Bowron, Councilman J.J. Bodecker, and a Mr. Bob Alworthy. Alworthy, if his memory served him correctly, was an assistant to the mayor. Apparently the studio staff attending the luncheon did not rate their own name tags. At least he couldn't find any more in the short time he had for poking around in the barrel before the maintenance people got restless.

He sat down on one of the lawn chairs and jotted the names in his little book, next to Mr. Lyle Palmer's. He did it more as an exercise in something familiar to do, rather than with any hope that it might prove germane to his problem.

Next, he looked at the hedge and tried to re-create what must have happened. He studied the area where they had been taking the pictures and he could imagine the problems the photographer must have had with the well-labeled panel truck just on the other side. There were several bare patches in the hedge. Let's see . . . Palmer had come through the gate and made his complaint known to them. Then, after he, Chandler, had stumbled and fumbled about with Palmer at the back door, McGrath said he was going back over here to talk to Palmer . . . but was that before or after he moved the truck?

And that was another thing. What had happened to that damn truck? It didn't belong on the lot, so someone must have reported it or moved it off the premises. But who? It didn't seem logical that McGrath would have had time enough to move the truck to a distant location, come back and leave the note at Chandler's room in the writers' building—which was about a five-minute walk at best—then get back to the commissary in time to get killed and stuffed into the cooler like so much unwanted baggage.

The truck, of course, could have been hidden in any of the many soundstages. They all had large doors and flat entry flooring. But if it were in a soundstage, that would seem to imply preconceived planning on someone's part. Getting those large doors open and closed didn't appear to be an easy task. But there again someone would have been sure to see the thing coming and going.

He'd try to corner the guard Clarence before he left and ask about it.

Then there was the problem of the gunshot. Some people surely still must have been on the patio. Why wouldn't they have responded? A silencer, of course. Or could they have assumed, like Chandler did, that it was part of a scene?

Chandler was perspiring from sitting in the hot afternoon sun. The small patio didn't allow for much air circulation. He went out to the main street and found one of the studio-owned bicycles that seemed to be everywhere. He put his suit coat in the bike's basket and proceeded to peddle up and down between most of the large soundstages nearby, hoping to get a glimpse of the catering van. The shadowy caverns between buildings cooled him off a bit, but there was no sign of the missing truck.

A couple of secretaries who knew him came out of the editorial building and stopped to watch the sight of Mr. Chandler on a bicycle. This made him feel a bit foolish. Everything seemed so normal. So everyday routine. Where were all the clues? He kept thinking something out of the ordinary should be happening. There was a murdered body over in the commissary and no one was paying any attention.

He peddled to the main gate and looked for his friend Clarence. The live one, that is.

"Clarence, did you get all your Mexicans rounded up?"

The guard laughed. "We hope so, Mr. C. Sorry to trouble you like I did."

"No trouble," Chandler said and brushed a pants leg to show he was all better. "Say listen, have you or any of the other guards seen anything of a delivery truck with Albert's Catering written on the side of it?"

"You think it's here on the lot?"

"It was earlier. Over by the commissary."

"They'd a' used the delivery entrance. What you wanna get the truck for?"

"I put a cufflink of mine down on one of their trays and I think they might have gone off with it," Chandler said with a straight face. "Any chance the truck might still be here on the lot?"

"Just a sec. I'll check with Henry over on that gate." Clarence went into his booth and made a call. While he waited he told Chandler, "We log everything in and out you know. If they's still here we can—Hello, Henry. Say listen, there was a Albert's Catering in earlier today. Any chance they still on the lot?" He smiled at his favorite mystery writer while waiting for Henry's response. "You sure? 'Bout a hour ago you say? Okay, thanks." He hung up and shrugged. "Sorry, they's already gone. You wanna use my phone and give 'em a call?"

"Thanks, no. I think I'll call from my office."

Chandler turned his bike around, then had another thought. "Do you keep track of people that come and go just as you do trucks?"

"Oh no," he laughed, "that'd take all our time. Just studio guests is all. We got a list a' visitors' names and we check 'em off as they show up."

"Anyone other than the mayor's entourage come by today?"

"Oh, just the usual." Clarence scanned his clipboard. "Four different flesh peddlers to see the casting director, a writer and his agent to see Mr. Dozier, but they never showed, and then Barbara Norman and her chauffeur was in—"

"The silent film actress?"

"Yeah, you remember her?"

"She was a favorite of my wife's."

"You should see that ole yellow car of hers if you ever get the chance. It's a Doozy. I mean, it really is a Doozy." Then back to his clipboard, "And that's about it. Kinda quiet on Saturdays usually."

"Billy Wilder was scheduled to make a presentation to some government people. None of them on your list?"

"No no, that got canceled this morning. None of 'em showed."

"Canceled this morning? Would you happen to know the time?"

"I wasn't on the gate when it got called in. I'd say around ten-thirty or so."

"I see. Thank you, Clarence."

"Sorry about your cufflink. Hope you can track it down."

"Thanks."

Chandler rode over to the rack next to his car and parked the bike. He climbed behind the wheel of the Packard and waited for a time, trying to assimilate what little he had learned. He envied Clarence for a moment, marveling at the man's sublime ignorance of the language he thought he could speak. And the man's innocence. Oh, to be free of the fetters of taste and original thought, if only for an hour.

But wishing didn't get the job done. He began to realize how little he knew about solving real mysteries. To construct a mystery novel he merely had to start from the solution and then hide a series of clues along the way to it for the reader to stumble over or ignore until it was explained to him (the editors at *Black Mask* had told him the majority of their readers were male and Chandler had gotten into the habit of thinking of his reader as a man). But now it would be another matter. He never was good at riddles. What chance did he have, realistically? Nevertheless, he'd gather up what information he could and worry about the rest later.

It finally dawned on him to make the call to the catering people, not of course about the cufflink but about the missing truck. There was a pay phone nearby. No sense in tempting Simone beyond her limitations. He walked over to the booth and fished a nickel out of his pocket.

When he got the number, a male voice came on the line and said something that could have passed for an Italian pasta recipe.

"Hello, is this Albert's Catering?" Chandler asked.

"Dat's what I say, isn't it?"

"Yes, ah, this is a friend of Corky McGrath's. Do you remember him?"

The voice gave a noncommittal grunt.

"Didn't he work for you at one time?"

"Yeah, sure. Mr. Hollywood. All da time it's Hollywood, Hollywood."

"That sounds like him. I was calling about the truck he borrow—"

"Truck? He take-a my truck? Da sum-a-bitch. I lose a job because I got no truck to pick up a da cantaloupe."

"You mean to say he stole . . . took the truck without permission?"

"Momento, momento." A slightly familiar female voice in the background was shouting at Albert. Albert covered the mouthpiece with something but the ensuing argument could still be heard if not understood. Chandler remembered seeing a small, round-faced woman hand McGrath some keys some place or other. Finally Albert came back on the line. "Scusa, my crazy wife she say to him, 'Okay, half a hour for da truck. No more.' But he no bring it-a back."

Chandler cleared his throat. "Do I understand you to say the truck is still missing?"

"No, Mr. Hollywood, he park it in a street. No bring-a da keys in-a da office. No tell us it's-a back. An' now I gotta no cantaloupe, thanks to him."

"You found it parked in the street? Outside your place? Did anybody see who . . . I mean, did you or anyone see McGrath bring the truck back?"

"You tink maybe I see him? I wring his crazy neck if I see him, da sum-a-bitch."

"I see. Thank you."

"Say, who is dis talking?"

Chandler hung up without answering that one. The conversation not only jogged his memory about how he and McGrath had picked up the truck, it also brought back traces of his headache. He smoothed out his forehead with his fingers and thought of the old World War I chestnut: "Ever since I came to this country I've had nothing but trouble with foreigners."

So what did the phone call give him? Whoever murdered McGrath was courteous enough to return the borrowed truck. That didn't wash. The driver would most certainly run the risk of being seen when he dropped off the truck. Why not just park it off the studio lot somewhere and let the police locate it after it had been reported stolen or missing? Unless . . . unless he thought by returning it that way he could separate McGrath's death from the truck's use for hauling the other body around. Old cirrhosis-of-the-liver Clarence. That second body was going to give the police fits. Only in Hollywood. Was it logical that the driver returned the truck just to throw the police off the scent? There were holes in that, too. Wait a minute. The car. They must have driven over to the catering place in order to pick up McGrath's little Ford. Chandler would like to know what happened to the car. Chandler would also like to know where the catering place was.

Back at his Packard he hauled the cloth car top out of its hiding place behind the back seat and struggled to get it snapped and latched into place on top. And while he worked, it occurred to him that he had actually taken some action and made a bit of progress—thinking on his feet for a change. It gave him a giddy feeling, as if he really were going to solve the case.

He revved the engine, the way they did in the Warner gangster movies, and hurried on past the guarded gate with only a quick wave to Clarence. Then he headed east, hoping Hobart intersected Melrose somewhere or other.

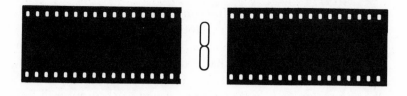

At the Western Avenue intersection Chandler had to stop for a long train of noisy cars to pass by. Most of the people in the caravan were yelling, pounding on door panels, or honking their horns. At first, he thought they were members of a wedding party on their way up toward Hollywood Boulevard for some cruising fun. But then someone on the street near his open window hollered out to the passing parade asking what all the excitement was about. A redheaded girl in a convertible called back, "The war in Europe is over!"

There had been nearly a week of hopeful rumors about the war's end, but so far the Germans had not been cooperating. Chandler turned on his car radio and flicked the dial about, trying to verify the girl's claim. General Patton, an announcer said, was freewheeling around Austria with his Sherman tanks while a Russian named Zhukov was kicking in the door to Berlin. And Swan Soap still promised to be mild to your hands. Apparently the redhead in the convertible had it wrong.

The only guide Chandler had was his old Dabney Oil Company street map, but the city had been growing so much it had become badly out of date. After some double checking and back-tracking he finally found 315 Hobart Avenue. He parked the Packard across the street under a flowering jacaranda tree with the intent of sitting in the shade and watching the house for a while. Precisely why, he wasn't sure, but he had had Marlowe do the same in *Lady in the Lake* and it had worked out well for him.

The day's heat was beginning to wane and directly across the street a plump lady in a plaid housecoat came down her porch steps and started her lawn sprinkler. She was upwind of him and now and again he could catch a whiff of the cool spray in his nostrils. Just enough to make him think of lilacs in Nebraska but not enough to remind him why. Each spring still brought with it a gnawing restlessness that settled somewhere above his third left rib and didn't leave until summer was half gone. Perhaps it was the unrelenting sameness of the Los Angeles climate that had started to grate at his soul. He wasn't sure. Not that he missed the chilling winds off the lake in Chicago or the bone-gripping dampness of England. But there was something about lilacs in the spring. A secret treasure, unknown to the City of the Angels.

Number 315 Hobart turned out to be the south half of a stuccoed duplex, probably a rental, judging from the rather spartan look of the small lawn and garden areas. The builder had trimmed the edge of the roofline with two rows of terra cotta tiles in an attempt to make the basic rectangle look Spanish.

Nothing out of the ordinary showed. Nothing, that is, except for the big, shiny black Buick in the driveway. Chandler was busy writing down the license plate number when someone came out of the duplex and got into the car. Chandler didn't know about it until he heard the screen door slam. By the time he looked up it was too late to get a decent look at the driver, who was already backing out of the driveway.

What to do? Should he follow the car or hang around and see what else the small duplex produced? Before he could decide, his writer's tendency toward reflective contemplation made the decision for him. The Buick raced down the street and headed west on Third.

He spent a few more minutes looking for more war news

on the radio, wondering how he could get into McGrath's place. When the sprinkler lady went inside, Chandler got out his sunglasses and reached to the back seat for his old Panama with the snap brim. He jammed it down hard on his head and headed for 315. He opened the screen door and rapped lightly. While he waited he pulled the mail out of the box and thumbed through it. Two pieces of interest. A telegram and a postcard. The card, printed in pencil, was from "Mom" in Phoenix. She said things had been slow in the hardware store last month and they wouldn't be able to loan him the two hundred dollars. He was to take care, and it wouldn't hurt him any to drop them a line. Chandler returned the card to the box, next to two circulars. The telegram he put in the side pocket of his coat.

When there was no response to his rap, he gently tried the door. It was locked, so he went down the driveway and tried the small side door. That was locked, too, but right inside the kitchen windowsill, in plain view, hung an old skeleton key on a dirty string. He slipped the stem of his pipe through a convenient hole in the screen and soon had the rusty hook off its eyelet, the window screen propped open and the key in hand. The key fit and he stepped into the quiet kitchen. It wasn't really illegal entry, he told himself. At least he could always say the door was open. Marlowe would be proud of him. Never mind his heart pounding like a sledgehammer.

Either McGrath didn't use the kitchen or he was a very fastidious housekeeper. Except for a tray containing three liquor bottles, the place was spotless.

The living room was a different matter. Enough windows had been left open in the flat-roofed building so it wasn't stifling, but there was still a certain oppressiveness to the dark atmosphere. For a moment Chandler thought he had stepped into a scene from one of his own novels. The art objects were something less than exotic and the Chinese decor was missing, but the heavy drapes and the low overstuffed furniture reminded him of the Geiger house in *The Big Sleep*. When his eyes adjusted to the low light level and he remembered to take off his sunglasses, his attention was drawn to a large colored Hogarth print that hung over the mantel of the fake fireplace. It depicted a wenching scene in a tavern, with a large gathering of male and female revelers. They all appeared plastered and several of the couples were in the fondling stages of sexual arousal; many hands were under the skirts and into the bodices.

Chandler wondered if McGrath knew enough about Hogarth to know he had done the work as a criticism of the morals of his day and not as a device to stimulate sexual desire in the viewer. He doubted it. On another wall was a smaller work but nonetheless provocative. It was a tinted photograph lifted from the European Hedy Lamarr film, *Ecstasy*. The teen-aged actress was romping in a wooded stream in her birthday suit. Judging from her expression, the ecstasy was just around the bend.

In the part of the room that used to serve as a dining area, there was a small rolltop desk. Chandler sat down next to it and pulled the chain on a floor lamp. The green and yellow glass in the lead beaded lampshade gave the room a slightly jaundiced appearance, like last week's newspaper.

Chandler took the telegram out of his pocket, eased it open and read: "Stop with the Chavez Ravine story—We are not paying for it—Neither will Times/Mirror—Why are you never home? Victor"

There were several copies of the *Herald Express* lying about the place. Chandler picked one up and found the masthead on the editorial page. The only Victor listed on the staff was an associate feature editor: Victor Hopkins.

He didn't have to look far for the phone. A line ran from the wall nearby and disappeared into the desk. He rolled up the lid on the desk and found a phone, buried along with a typewriter, under some half-written sheets of foolscap bulk paper, one in the typewriter and others cluttering up the place. Chandler was not the only writer in the world with a writer's block. He found the *Herald Express* number in a small address book.

While he waited for his connection, he couldn't help but take a peek at the work in progress in the typewriter.

"FULL SHOT—GRAND STAIRCASE—NIGHT—CANDLES LIT
The Queen with cape and bloodied sword descends.
Queen
Guards . . . Oh, where are the palace guards?
I must know . . . Are the cherry trees in blossom

yet? I must know . . . The dawn is coming . . .
The cherry trees . . . .

Prince Rupert
(enters from below)

The guards are asleep, my Lady.
(sees sword) Oh, my Lady, what have you done?


Chandler blinked and shook his head. Oh, McGrath, what have *you* done? Does Chekhov know about this? He knew it wasn't cricket to judge another's work still in the embryo stage but this had all the trappings of a melodrama from the Thirties. Or the Twenties.

Next to the typewriter, in a professionally bound booklet about thirty pages thick, he found the story outline for the script McGrath had been trying to piece together. It was written in a graceful feminine longhand and it did not spare the adjectives. Prince Rupert was not only "handsome" but also "suave" with a "lofty demeanor," while the Count Somebody was listed as a "cunning wretch." At least McGrath had kept to the spirit of the thing.

"Victor Hopkins here."

Chandler was jolted back from his eavesdropping on castles and queens by a gruff voice on the noisy phone line. He whipped off his eyeglasses and did his version of Cary Grant playing Philip Marlowe.

"Yes, Mr. Hopkins, I was inquiring into the series you people are planning on doing on the Chavez Ravine business."

The gruff voice lost a little of its authority with a cover-up type of cough. "We're not planning any such series of articles."

"Oh come now, Mr. Hopkins, I happen to know McGrath is working on it."

"Corky McGrath is not a staff reporter. I have no control over what he does."

"But you buy his stuff—"

"We have in the past. We've already turned him down on the, ah, matter you mentioned."

"What you mean is you sent him a telegram."

"What I mean is we aren't in the market. I can assure you."

"Mr. Hopkins, the only thing you are assuring me of is the story must be too hot for you to handle."

"Oh, quite the contrary, we've not been able to verify any of the charges so we think it must be just so much hot air. We can't pursue every rumor that comes along, you know."

"What I know is you're trying to dance me round Robin's barn."

"What a quaint expression. May I ask you what it is I may have said that gave you that idea?"

"Certainly. It's what you didn't say, Victor, that gave you away. Since when do Hearst editors talk to people on the phone for more than two seconds without asking their name. You're so anxious to show you aren't doing the story you're telling it to anonymous callers. Next you'll be taking out full-page ads in the Sunday *Times*."

"Look, friend, let's get to the point, shall we?"

"Yes, let's do. I don't care whether you do the story or not. I'm no shake-down artist. All I want to know is, who has McGrath been talking to?"

"How the hell should I know."

"Look, where did he get his marching orders?"

"Not from us. He came in with his own Megillah. We told him at the time we were interested if anything could be proved. But now we're not."

"Okay, what did he come in with?"

"Why don't you ask him?"

"I'd like to, but I can't do that."

"Why not?"

"Because McGrath . . . is no longer available for questioning."

"What? What's that?"

"I mean he's just, ah, shall we say missing."

Chandler tried to make it sound as casual as he could but the harder he tried the more he sounded like a Chicago hood understating his evil potential in order to strike terror in the heart of his mark. It was turning into a comic opera. The editor got in the act next and proceeded to play his part as the next victim. The voice that had started out as a basso profundo was ending up first-tenor tremolo.

"Look, now look. I can assure you we are not doing the story. The editor-in-chief . . . you can talk to the editor if you like. Or Mr. Hearst if you like. I'm sure he will tell you the same thing. Look, I only work here. You'll ah, you'll have to excuse me now. I've got a paper to—" Click.

Terrific. The tough guy routine always worked so well for Marlowe. What happened? Chandler didn't know any more than when he started. Well, no that wasn't quite true. He knew there was a genuine fear on the part of one, probably two, large if not necessarily crusading newspapers, to keep something quiet. That could mean it would be big enough to murder for. But who would be behind it? And what the devil was Chavez Ravine?

9

Chandler was still meditating on his ineptness on the phone when the first indication he wasn't alone, a low female-type moan, floated out from behind a door in the back part of the house. How incredibly stupid he felt. He had been so excited about his job of breaking and entering that he hadn't bothered to put two and two together. The man who'd left in such a hurry must have left a friend behind. Maybe the pictures and the setting weren't for McGrath's entertainment alone—why hadn't he had sense enough to search the house first?

The moaner sounded again, as if rousing from sleep. Chandler still would have time to head for his car and watch from relative safety there, but that was not the way Marlowe would play it. He pulled the chain on the lamp next to him and waited in the semi-darkness of the room, trying to think of what he was supposed to do or say to start getting some useful information.

Bed springs squeaked, furniture bumped. When the bedroom door was finally swung open Chandler's heart was at his throat. Her long dark hair was mussed and fell forward over most of her face, but what was left was enough. The hip action and the way she had of carrying her shoulders up high and thrust back were unmistakable. She was nude except for black nylon stockings and a red garter belt. She sashayed her way across the room and started searching for something in the general vicinity of the couch. Under an end pillow she found her brassiere and proceeded to put it on as if in the privacy of her own bedroom, making sure her ample breasts got properly seated. Her panties she eventually found on the floor next to the couch. She wasn't stable enough to stand on one leg at a time so she sat on the arm of the couch and got them hoisted into place.

Chandler, always the social gentleman, waited until she had shimmied into her slip before he announced his presence.

"Hello, Francine."

The poor girl came unglued. She screamed and bounced back against the wall, knocking the Hogarth cockeyed. Then she fell onto a chair just long enough to snatch up her dress, which had gotten buried between a pillow and the backrest. She yanked it free like a lion tamer working a bull whip and made a dash for the bedroom.

"Francine, it's me," he called, futilely.

She slammed the door after her. Then, as an afterthought, she opened it again and looked out to make sure it was who she was afraid it was, and slammed the door again.

"What the hell are you doing here?" she yelled.

"Francine, come out. I've got to talk to you."

"No."

Chandler adjusted the south-facing venetian blinds to bring in more light in the room and watched the driveway for a moment. He thought perhaps there was another door in the back and Francine would try to slip away, but nothing happened. Then he noticed her high heeled shoes and purse next to the front door. The amorous details of her afternoon tryst could be reconstructed by the location of her clothes in the room.

"Your shoes and purse are out here," he called. "Come out. I wouldn't be here if I didn't have to be."

Still no response. He went back to the rolltop and started looking for Chavez Ravine. Judging from the partially filled slips of paper lying about, McGrath had hundreds of story ideas bouncing around in his mind. But he had difficulty following through on anything. Most of what Chandler found consisted of half-baked film set-ups; young man with undiagnosed illness meets lady horse doctor, et cetera. They were situations, not plots. The poor boy died never knowing how to build a second act.

The closest Chandler could come to a line on Chavez Ravine was an unusually large number of Spanish-sounding names in McGrath's small phone book. What could he be onto? A Mexican Mafia? He put the book in his side pocket and was continuing his search when the bedroom door opened again.

Her hair was now combed and she had become very sullen. Her cotton summer dress, featuring giant orange and yellow birds of paradise flowers, flattered her figure. She walked, without using the swing set, to the table where Chandler had put her shoes and proceeded to put them on. The extra three inches in height seemed to add to her reserve.

There was a certain hardness to her expression that Chandler had never seen before. He wondered if it was a result of her current predicament or if it had become a built-in part of the superstructure. And he wondered if he was to blame for it. There had been a time back with Dabney Oil when he had served as the father figure for a sweet young secretary with a different expression. All very innocent and fun. But a shaker of martinis and a motel north of Oxnard had taken care of that.

"I've gotta catch my bus," the new Francine announced "What do you want?"

Her bluntness was almost a relief. He didn't want to stir up old embers if he could help it. "Tell me what you know about Corky McGrath?"

She twisted her head at him in disbelief. "You got to be kidding. Here and now?"

"Believe me, it's important."

"Can you think of one good reason why I should do anything for you?"

"I suppose I can't." He cleared his throat, nervously. "I did get you in the door at Paramount . . ."

"Thanks a lot."

" . . . although I didn't ask you to transfer to the writers' building."

"I thought you'd want me to. Just goes to show how wrong a girl can be, doesn't it?"

"I got you the job because you needed a job. Now, Corky McGrath—"

"Corky McGrath is a first-class, A-number-one wiggle wart with wandering hands. What do I know? I do typing for three guys."

"What do you type for McGrath?"

"I'd been typing a screenplay, but I quit."

"Why'd you quit?"

"Because I found out it's all on spec. We're not supposed to do any work on speculation. Only stuff producers have okayed."

"What kind of screenplay was it? Did it have a title?"

"Oh, I forget. 'The Queen Reigns,' 'The Fortunes of Royalty.' Something like that. He changed the title every week. I need a drink. You need a drink?"

What a stupid question. He closed his eyes and went on, "Didn't McGrath have any regular writing assignment?"

"If he did, he didn't share it with me. I take that back. I did a two-page story line for the cartoon department. That's about his speed, if you ask me."

"Does Chavez Ravine mean anything to you?"

"What is this, a Mexican geography quiz?"

"It's important."

"The only Chavez Ravine I know of is down by Elysian Park. Greasers live there, and nice white girls don't go there."

"Did McGrath ever mention it to you?"

"Say, what's with all this McGrath business? No, he never mentioned it to me. Why should he?"

"He was writing a newspaper article about something down there."

"Well, bully for him. McGrath can drop dead for all I care."

"Francine, did you know this is Corky McGrath's place?"

"Here?" She pointed at the rug. "You mean here? He lives here?"

Chandler nodded. Francine had to sit down and hold her

head. "My God, what a mess my life is. Now everybody will know. . . ."

Chandler grimaced at what was to come but was powerless to stop it. She started sobbing quietly at first. Then she built it into a swearing session with a few punches into the armrest of her chair for good measure. Then she brought it down again with quiet tears. Finally, she said, "You know when I started at Dabney Oil I was a virgin?"

"Yes, I seem to recall your having mentioned that."

She snorted. "You seem to recall. . . ."

"Come on, I'll give you a ride home."

"I need a drink."

"Your friend left the tray in the kitchen."

"My friend . . . the son-of-a-bitch told me he rented this place for us." Two more slaps to the armrest's midsection. "Well aren't you going to fix me something?"

"I'd rather not, if you don't mind." His voice gave him away and he knew it. "Shall we go . . . ?"

"So . . . you still get the ol' cravings, too, after all this time."

"No, not really. Only sixteen or seventeen hours a day."

She laughed. "Well, if you're not going to be a gentleman. . . ." She rose and headed for the kitchen. All her machinery was now in working order. At the doorway she gave him a quick glance to see if he was watching. He was. She smiled and disappeared.

Chandler spent the time tidying up the rolltop and listening for the sound of sparkling liquid drops gurgling and splashing their way into a glass. He held out his hand and looked at it, to see if it was moving on its own. It wasn't noticeable.

When Francine emerged from the kitchen she was carrying two drinks. She set the extra one on the coffee table and proceeded to make herself comfortable on the couch.

"There we are now. . . ."

Chandler moved uneasily about the room. "What time did you and your friend get here today?"

"Let's not talk about him now. Come sit down."

He didn't. She still wanted to chat.

"How come you started with this mystery writing business? I thought you wanted to be a poet."

"I decided to give T. S. Eliot his chance."

"You know I read one of your books. *Farewell, My Darling.*"

"*Lovely,*" he corrected. "*Farewell, My Lovely.*"

"Oh yeah. Sorry. I read it because I thought maybe you put me in it. Only now I'm not so sure. Which one was supposed to be me? The good girl or the bad girl?"

"Which one you want to be?"

"The good girl, natch."

"Okay, that was you."

"Just like that, huh?"

"Sure. Don't you see yourself in the part?"

She seemed to take it as a philosophical challenge and grew very serious. Then she bolted down a good two fingers of her drink and stared at the remains.

"Tell me something," she asked. "And I want the truth."

"I'll try."

"Can you honestly tell me you don't care about me anymore?"

It was eye avoidance time. Chandler had been pacing the room but now he stopped, seeming to develop a keen interest in the quality of the fabric in the window drapes. "The answer to that, my dear, is an orphan without a future."

"Oh, stop now with your cutesy little poetry answers. I think you owe me that much."

"But the answer is still going to come out the same. I'm going to stay with my wife. If I can."

"It's always been her, hasn't it? You were just playing me for the good time, weren't you?"

"No, not true. But she was the one who was there to pick me up after our Dabney fiasco. I don't know why I went off the deep end and I'm sorry if I took you with me. But the job was . . . I couldn't do it anymore. Not one more ledger entry. Not one more voucher signed. I can see that now. And she could see it, too, long before I could. That's the wonder of it. She's been my sounding board when I needed story help, and my silent partner when I needed the quiet. I don't expect anybody to understand, but it was as if my writing was the fuel that warmed her hands. It was the two of us all the way that did it. That made the books come alive."

"That coulda been me. I could do all that for you."

He smiled and shook his head. "No, babe. You have a lot of attributes, but critiquing dialogue is not one of them. You're better at creating it. And other things."

"You know half the time I don't know what the hell you're talking about."

"Neither do I, dear. Neither do I."

She clutched at her drink and downed it as if it were going to supply her with some needed answers. She didn't appear to find them. "And what about me? What's going to happen to me?"

"She's ill, Francine. She's got a lung thing the doctors can't cure. The tissue keeps hardening. . . . Can't you see what I'm facing? I took her away from her husband. I promised her a life that I haven't . . . been able to give her. I can't leave her. It isn't in me. My father, the swine, left my mother and me to a life of humiliating poverty. I can't do the same thing to her: I have to be able to live with myself."

"So you're going to piss your life away because you feel sorry for her. She's an old lady, for God's sake. Well, what's going to happen to me?"

"I don't know. What usually happens to girls who leave their panties under the living room sofa?"

Her face seemed to age before his eyes. "You son-of-a-bitch. Whatever made me think you were different?" She snorted and covered her eyes with her hands. "It doesn't have to be this way, you know. I still got the hots for you. Isn't that a riot? With this other guy, I close my eyes and pretend. . . . I'm spilling my guts to you. Doesn't that mean anything?"

"Francine, it isn't what I want, it's what's going to be. It's been nine years, and I still can't look at a Jack Daniels label without thinking about you, but I'm telling you it just isn't going to happen again."

"What a compliment. I think I'll start a diary. That one needs to be memori—mem—remembered. Get the hell out of here."

"Come on, I'll take you home."

As she rose he reached for her purse to hand it to her. She snatched it away from him and announced, "I gotta go to the can." In an afterthought, she came back and kissed him hard on the mouth, then hurried away. She smelled of Irish loam after the potato harvest. For one instant he was a boy again, lying in the damp furrow and he didn't care about anything. He had reached out for her to draw her back, but she had already gone. It was good she went when she did because his resistance was worn down to the nub. And then he was so taken with his own reverie that he missed the hidden significance of her gesture.

With Francine in the bathroom he breathed deeply and forced his mind back to the business at hand. Whatever else the bedroom was, it was also the place where McGrath used to hang his hat and he'd better have a look. As he walked back to it he muttered to himself, "I must be cruel in order to be kind. I must be cruel . . ." He hated melodrama and tried to avoid it like the plague in his writing. But life kept dealing him these dead-end hands. Was that it? Or was it just that he couldn't see beyond them?

The scene with the girl had shaken him and he had to remind himself what he was here for. He had come to the house to find out about the young would-be writer, not to gain more insight into his own shortcomings.

The bed was surprisingly neat. Maybe she had tidied things up a bit. Chandler's search was of no help and only served to point out McGrath's meager living conditions. There was one clean shirt left in the only dresser in the room. And in the closet, two pairs of slacks, a seersucker suit, and one corduroy jacket with a torn seam in the right sleeve. Apparently the best clothes the man owned were the ones he had on when he died. The closest thing to Chavez Ravine Chandler could find was a dog-eared Spanish/English paperback dictionary on the nightstand next to the bed.

He was just about to go through some pockets when Francine let out a scream. At first he thought it was another temper tantrum, but then he heard glass breaking and something hitting the bathroom floor.

"Francine?"

The only answer was another moan of pain. He moved

81

tentatively to the bathroom door, half hoping it was locked, but it wasn't. He pushed it open slowly. She was sitting on the floor staring at her left arm which was bloody from a small gash just up from the wrist. Her drinking glass was broken on the floor next to her and his first impression was she had cut herself accidentally. But then he saw the two-edged Gillette razor blade in her right hand.

10

By the time Chandler walked out of Hollywood Presbyterian Hospital it was going on eight o'clock. The nurse's aides had given him some damp paper towels and he did the best he could at sponging up the blood on his leather seats and on the floor mats.

After his mother's lingering illness and death he had thought his days of caring for women in distress were over, but apparently not. They had stitched up Francine's wrist with little difficulty and were keeping her overnight for observation. Now the question was, would she try it again? The fact that she had left the bathroom door unlocked and that she had yelled so readily would indicate it was more an attention getting device than anything else. But anytime someone takes a sharp instrument to themselves, drunk or sober, it has to be taken seriously. What would happen when she checked out tomorrow? Or next week, or next month?

It was dark when he got back to 315 Hobart. The five minutes of twilight Mother Nature allotted for the Greater Los Angeles area had come and gone with no one but a few happy city wrens any the wiser. At least they were celebrating something as they fluttered in the sprays of water on the soggy lawn. The sprinkler lady had forgotten to move her hose and water was now spilling over the curb like a miniature Niagara Falls. Chandler was sorely tempted to go up and turn the water off for her but decided he had other good deeds to attend to. He wondered where reporters kept their notes. He wondered why McGrath's corduroy jacket had a torn sleeve. And he wondered what the bourbon and water left on the coffee table would taste like.

There were more cars parked on the street now and he had to drive half a block past the place to find space for his Packard. The big car did not handle gracefully in small spaces and, while he was making his third attempt at parking, he became aware of the young people in the car behind who seemed to be enjoying his antics behind the wheel. Once he got parallel to the curb they applauded him with good-natured cheers. Chandler checked them over in his rearview mirror. He had only the street light to go by, but they appeared to be three teen-age Mexicans in an old Chevrolet who had chosen this quiet side street to do their drinking. What were these people doing this far west, anyway?

As he approached the McGrath place from the south he noticed light coming from the living room area. He stopped on the sidewalk and tried to remember if he had left any lights on. He was pretty sure he had not. He walked very gingerly down the driveway and tried to scan the room through the white sheer curtains and blinds. The ceiling light in the dining area was on and there were faint noises coming from that general area, as if someone were going through the desk drawers.

Chandler hesitated to get too close to the house for fear of being seen, but his curiosity was killing him. He was wondering what Marlowe would do next when he heard the distinctive sound of the rolltop desk being closed. Then the light went out. Would whoever it was be leaving? And if so, would it be the front door or the kitchen door? He stood in one spot and turned around twice trying to think where he might hide or what he might say if the party should suddenly appear at the kitchen door. When he was on his final pirouette, the front door opened. Chandler backed his nervous body into the bushes next to the house and watched as a diminutive man trotted down the sidewalk and around the side of a large foreign looking car parked just to the south of the duplex driveway. The man was in a hurry but there didn't seem to be anything sinister or secretive about his movements. He carried something under his arm. Something about the size of the professionally bound story outline Chandler had seen in the desk. Maybe he hadn't examined that book carefully enough.

As the man opened the door of the large car, the interior light shone on his face. He was an Oriental in a black chauffeur's uniform. Probably a Jap who had become a Filipino on December seventh, four years ago. Rumor had it Los Angeles had plenty of them. The man tossed his hat and the book into the car and climbed in. It took several revs on the starter before the old giant of an auto came to life. By then Chandler had worked his way toward the curb and was trying to make out the license number. There was no taillight next to the license and he couldn't see the number, but the car was distinctive enough that he'd have no trouble following it. It was a very ornate old yellow Duesenberg. Probably not another like it in the county.

The car backed up, gears meshed as it ground its way down the street. Chandler hurried to his own car and wondered why the Duesenberg seemed so familiar to him. He hadn't seen one like it since his brief visit to Paris during the war.

The Mexican youths in the Chevrolet had gone, leaving behind five empty beer bottles neatly lined up on the curb. The empty space would make it easier for him to get his car out.

The yellow car was moving slowly enough for him to catch sight of it just as it reached Wilshire Boulevard and the late Thomas Ince's house, sitting on the corner of Hobart and Wilshire.

The sight of the Ince house took him by surprise, and it shook him. He knew it was there. It was one of the first landmarks Chandler had had pointed out to him in the City of Angels. But it symbolized something he wasn't ready to face. Poor Ince. Another man from the motion picture industry who had made the error of crossing swords with a powerful newspaper man. In his case it was fatal. Was this a good night for omens, Chandler wondered?

But back to the matter at hand. The car turned right and

85

headed for the ocean. Chandler stayed about a block behind, feeling happy about his first tail job.

Then it hit him. Doozy. "It's a real Doozy," was the way Clarence the guard had described the silent actress's old car. The old car that just happened to be at the studio that noon. Doozy, Duesenberg. Some American slang really did have a logical origin.

The traffic along Wilshire was fairly heavy. Farmers from the valley did most of their shopping Saturday nights. The blackouts the stores had suffered during the first part of the war were ancient history now and the stores along the long road were lit up for business. Pickups and '36 Fords abounded. Square-shaped ladies in print dresses and small felt hats with flowers led middle-aged men in double breasted suits and odd fitting straw hats, cut to look like fedoras, in and out of doorways. Now and then a pair of thin sailors up from Long Beach bobbed by, searching for things they weren't going to find on the brightly lit boulevards.

As his car and the Doozy rolled west the stores took on a more sophisticated look; straw hats and print dresses were among the missing. They were approaching the high-rent district. Just off the boulevard on either side were three- and four-story mansions built in the twenties. Old oil and new motion picture money. The kind of people that didn't go window shopping on farmers' night. But the kind of people that could afford to hire private detectives. The kind that Marlowe had had a love-hate relationship with for many years. Chandler was happy about the scenery change, but his heart was beating a bit faster.

The Duesenberg swung off onto a small side street and Chandler had to do some fancy lane changing in order to follow. By the time he gained the street, called Lorraine, he had lost the car and had to rubberneck at each driveway to find it again. There was one extra-large property that sat right on the corner of Wilshire and Lorraine and when he finally got to its driveway he slowed to a halt. Up the twisting inclined roadway, about sixty feet away, sat the yellow car in front of a brick building, which was either a large garage or the stables for the Lippizaner stallions. The chauffeur was already out of the car and had started pushing it. The car started pivoting. Apparently it was on some sort of turntable that could be operated by a small Oriental. After the car had pivoted 180 degrees he got back in and backed it into one of the open stalls. The large garage door closed automatically on a motorized winch and swallowed the Duesenberg and the Oriental in one gulp.

Behind Chandler another car flashed its lights and he drove up the block to get out of its way. He made a U-turn when he could and headed back toward the large dark estate on the corner. He parked and slid over to the passenger side of the seat, took off his horn-rimmed glasses and rubbed his nose.

Would what he was thinking play, or wouldn't it? Clarence had said an old actress what's her name Norman owned the Duesenberg. McGrath had talked about an older woman in his life and the story outline certainly sounded like something a Duesenberg owner might come up with. Now then, why had the chauffeur gone to the house on Hobart to get the story outline out of the desk? It would seem to imply that the old gal knew that McGrath was no longer with us if she sent her man to collect her belongings. Why? So she would not be implicated? And how could she know about it . . . if she wasn't involved with the murder?

He needed a drink. He didn't care what they said about alcohol dulling the senses, he got better ideas, or he had more energy to search for them, when he had something going. He felt under the seat of the Packard to see if there was anything there he'd forgotten about, but came up empty.

Once out of the car he took a deep drag on the cool night air. The large, dark houses on both sides of the street and the hints of finely manicured lawns put him into his personal valley of insignificance. When you can't afford a gardener for your two-by-four yard, it's easy to ridicule the rich. But not so easy to confront them. Cold sober. He sauntered up the drive thinking of logical reasons why he might be there. Excuse me, but my car broke down. I was looking for Wilton Place. Would this by chance be it? And you didn't by any chance kill Mr. McGrath in a fit of old-age jealousy, did you?

There was a large entrance gate at the sidewalk level, but judging from the tree branches and other foliage growing through the iron bars it hadn't been used to keep out the hoi polloi in some time. In fact, most of the foliage in the place appeared in need of attention. Halfway up the drive toward the garage the road divided, with the new branch going off toward the main house and making a neat little circle around a fountain that contained about half of Michelangelo's statuary from his Florentine years. There were lights burning in the house, but it didn't look as if they were expecting guests. He decided the garage looked much more inviting. He wasn't sure why, but he wasn't ready to approach the house yet.

There were lights burning in the garage, too, and Chandler went up to the door that closed on the Duesenberg and stood on tiptoe to look into the interior. There were only three cars in the inside besides the monster, which almost made the place look empty. A white, streamlined open job with teardrop front fenders and chrome tubes running out of the hood and into the fenders, a little Dodge four-door, probably the maid's or butler's, and a Model B Ford coupe.

There was something disturbingly familiar about the Ford with its one bench seat. Chandler moved two doors down to get a better look. On tiptoes again he could see the C ration sticker in the corner of the windshield. He remembered now, McGrath had a C card for his car. He had been bragging about it on the way down to get the body. And his windshield sticker had a tiny corner torn off it, too. Just like this one.

Hard evidence. Here was something he could go to the police with. But could he? What could he really prove? That someone at the house knew McGrath, perhaps. That was about all. How and why the car got to the garage from the catering place could be open to multi-interpretations. It would just come down to his word against someone else's. Someone with money.

As he lowered himself from his position on tiptoe his legs started shaking. He gripped his knees to get control back, but it wasn't helping. Things had been going so well. He was even beginning to feel like the aggressive type. He was moving and doing. Not just sitting at the typewriter contemplating his navel. But how could he hope to do more in the state he found himself in? He forced his legs to move. He was a spastic puppet.

By the time he had talked himself out of his brief moment of confidence he found himself out of breath and standing at the curb next to his own car. He had to figure out some plan of action. Maybe some way of getting them to tip their hand. Maybe some way of worming his way into the old girl's confidence. But he couldn't face her in this condition.

There was a cocktail lounge not far away noted for its exotic mixed drinks. A very friendly place, and they were not adverse to supplying him with something for the road when he needed it. He got his big car going and asked himself out loud, "Now, which way to La Brea?"

It was going on ten o'clock when he reappeared at the Lorraine house, but he was loaded for bear. He swung the Packard up the drive as if he owned the place, then angled off toward the house and around the fountain which, up close, showed itself to be an eyesore. The statuary was covered in dirt and the pool was bone dry. Maybe he should have asked the sprinkler lady from Hobart to come along. She could have had that fountain overflowing in jig time.

Just as he was pulling to a halt, he heard something scrape against the right side of his car. Upon examination he found the porcelain figure of a Negro boy in a jockey uniform standing on a pedestal at the curb. The figure's right arm, which should have been reaching out to hold the guests' horses, was now lying in the gutter, a victim of Chandler's miscalculations as to the width of the Packard. He picked up the arm and walked confidently up the steps. Putting a hand to his mouth he puffed and tried to smell his own breath. Not a whiff of Bacardi and grenadine, he told himself. He'd had three. If Philip Marlowe's favorite drink didn't do the trick, nothing would.

He counted five tones on the elaborate door chime melody, then pulled it a second time just to make sure he heard correctly. He marveled at how alive and attuned to all his senses he felt. Just to prove his point he peeked through the glass panel next to the front door.

A large butler type appeared from somewhere in the inner depths, fastening his vest buttons as he approached. The door opened just far enough so he could fix both eyes upon the intruder.

"Yes?"

Only then did it dawn on Chandler he had forgotten the last name of the silent actress Clarence had mentioned that morning. Barbara something. "I need to speak with Barbara."

"I beg your pardon."

"Come on, Jeeves, open up. I have to talk to Barbara."

"And who, may I ask, are you?"

"I'm Inspector Cramer from the Thirty-Second Precinct. Well?"

"This is Miss Norman's residence."

"And she's in. Right?"

"One moment, please."

Chandler permitted the door to be closed on him, then turned and looked out at the night and rocked on his heels, as he had seen a policeman do in real life once. He had the goods on her and he intended to wrap up the matter in no time. He smiled at the large Italian cypress trees standing like guardians about the drive, the cool jasmine-flavored night air, the gentle forest glenlike silence that hung over the place, and he wondered if, by some twist of nature, the elements could possibly know how clever he was. He reached for the hip bottle he had bought for the road and took one small sip as a reward for being smart.

The door finally opened for him, just as before, and the butler intoned, "Madam will see you for a moment."

"Fine."

But the door didn't open further. "May I see some identification, please."

"You certainly may."

Chandler pushed on the door and at the same time handed

the startled butler the porcelain arm. That held him in neutral long enough for Chandler to get into the outer lobby.

The first thing that struck his eye was the large marble staircase. He strongly suspected it was on loan from the National Archives building in Washington just for tonight's performance. About twenty feet above him on the first landing stood the lady of the house. She was still tall and straight and looked like she was ready to do the queen's role in her story. The flowing gown had a white fur piece at the top of it that made it look suspiciously out of date. She touched a dramatic hand onto the two-foot-wide marble parapet and spoke.

"Yes, may we help you?"

Chandler recognized the voice by type. It was husky, almost manly, from too many highballs and cigarettes. Or too much stage work. He studied her carefully, but could not recall ever having seen her on the silver screen. Only her old stills. He moved across the floor of the large entranceway, which was made of marble squares of black and white, like a giant chessboard. He stopped on black bishop seven to speak his piece.

"Good evening, ma'am. I'm Lieutenant Cramer, working out of the stolen car detail and I would like to ask you some questions if you don't mind."

"Are you laboring under the impression I am in the habit of stealing automobiles?"

"Miss Norman, if you are not a car thief then I am sure you won't mind cooperating, will you?"

"Please don't bandy. It hardly fits the time or occasion, does it?" She deadpanned the line without moving a muscle. Her skin seemed to be without a wrinkle or blemish, almost childlike in appearance, which made Chandler wonder how it was he knew beyond doubt she was old.

"We have information regarding a Model B Ford coupe that has been stolen and a car fitting that description was seen entering your estate. Is that direct enough for you?"

While he was talking, he noticed her looking up to the ceiling and shuffling slightly to her right. After she stopped he realized she had moved into a more favorable light.

"Surely there must be some mistake. Aren't there many autos that might fit that description?"

"No mistake, ma'am."

"What was the license number?"

"I'll ask the questions, if you don't mind."

"Lieutenant, how are we to know if this one is your car if you don't tell us the license number?"

"If what one is my car? Are you admitting you have such a car?"

She took a handkerchief out of her sleeve and waved it as if to clear the air of her little faux pas. Or to have time to think. "What car? How should I know what car? I'm not the one who has lost a car."

"I thought you were about to suggest I compare my information against a car you have here in your garage. Now who's bandying, Miss Norman?"

She looked off pensively toward her key light and, with one fingernail, stroked her jaw line, about where a jowl should be. "I find this conversation extremely tiresome, officer. I do hope there is a point to all this."

"Is it absolutely necessary that we carry on this conversation at such a great distance?"

He didn't wait for an answer but started up the steps toward her. She held her ground well, as if she were used to close-ups. His legs felt strong. Even powerful. He could do no wrong, he decided. He didn't stop until he was on her level and three feet away. She was made up and heavily powdered but still didn't look all that bad. Ten o'clock at night and dressed for company. Was she expecting him?

"There now, that's better isn't it?"

"Lieutenant, have you been drinking?"

"A martini with dinner. Now about the auto. Would you mind if my men had a look around the place?"

"My daddy once told me if this situation ever arose I was to ask for something called a search warrant."

"Must we get into that? I do know a judge who is an insomniac. It would be a nuisance but a simple matter. I don't imagine the car would go wandering off while I'm gone, do you?"

"It's hard to say," she cooed. "Suppose the owner should come looking for it?"

"Do you really think that likely?"

"Strange things do happen in this town, Lieutenant."

He smiled to match hers and shook his head slowly. "Not that strange."

"You mean you think the owner is . . . dead?"

"Why, whatever gave you that idea, Miss Norman?"

"Just a blind guess. I mean what other logical reason would cause a person not to claim their property? I know. You want to ask the questions."

She was getting to be too much for him. He couldn't think of anything halfway cute to say so he laughed and leaned on the balcony railing. "For a girl who doesn't like to bandy, you do all right." He took off his glasses and polished them for dramatic effect. Then softly, "How did you know he was dead, dear?"

"How who . . . ?" She changed her mind and started with the hanky waving again, then nervously reached into a pocket hidden in her gown and came up with a miniature bell, which she started ringing. There was a glassy look about her eyes and Chandler feared for a moment she had slipped a cog and the bell ringing was part of a hex, meant to make him disappear. But then an upstairs maid appeared on the upper landing.

"Yes'm."

"Lillian, please call Gilbert and have him come up to the main house. This gentleman seems to have taken an interest in our automobiles."

The maid disappeared and the actress returned to her version of a genuine smile.

"I don't suppose I could interest you in a drink, could I?"

"I'll take a raincheck. We never drink on marble stairwells. It's part of the detective's code."

"My, but aren't we the clever one."

"What were you doing at Paramount around noon today?"

She blinked. "This isn't about a missing auto at all, is it?"

"It's all tied together. Do you want to tell me?"

"What do most actresses do at studios? I was seeing a man about a film."

"Did you get the part?"

"What are you, a casting director now?"

"No, but I've jailed a few of 'em in my day. Who did you go to see?"

"Ernst Lubitsch."

He shook his head. "Try again. Lubitsch is a sick man."

She drew in her breath as if she had been struck. "No, no, he's not. That's a filthy lie." The smile had disappeared, too.

"I know he's not with the studio now—"

"How do you know that? It's not true. There have been promises made. Promises in this house . . ." She looked toward the upstairs as if searching for the very spot, then back down again to her tormentor. "But what would you know about such things? You and your type. You spend your days living in the gutter with the vermin of the world, turning over rocks to watch the bugs scurry. What would you know of the arts?"

"I know this much, dear. I know Ernst Lubitsch wouldn't touch that project of yours with a ten-foot pole."

"My project"—she bristled, made a point of looking further down her nose and started again—"my project is so far above your kind you wouldn't know what to do with it."

"Oh, I know what should be done with it, but the fire season is upon us and we're not supposed to burn our garbage."

He had finally gotten to the tender area. She reached out to backhand a slap to his face but it was delivered in slow motion, almost as if she was in rehearsal and she was saving her good stuff for when the cameras were rolling. He caught her hand and smiled. She pulled away with a gesture that Sarah Bernhardt had a patent on.

"They put you up to this, didn't they," she cried.

"They being . . . ?"

"So, the police are working for the studio now, is that it? Well, let me tell you, a promise is sacred to me. I do not forget. They may play their little games. I know what they are up to but I can see right through them. They are afraid of greatness. Little men with little minds that send desperate little men to do their bidding." She gave Chandler the up-and-down, in case he didn't know who she was referring to. "Any script needs a touch-up here and there. It's only a first draft. I will not be dismissed like this."

"I know you didn't see Lubitsch. Who did you finally get in to see?"

"Are you telling me you don't know?"

"That's right, I don't."

"I wasn't born yester"—she cleared her throat on that one—"I'm not a fool, Lieutenant."

"No, I'm quite sure you're not. You impress me as being quite intelligent. And maybe just a bit ruthless and vindictive, given half a reason and half a chance. Maybe just ruthless enough to get rid of your scriptwriter if you thought he had turned you into a laughing stock."

She did her thing once more with the hanky. "Don't be silly, I have not dismissed my writer."

"Why don't we go down to the station and tell that to the precinct captain?"

"Of all the silly things to say. You're going to arrest me for firing my scriptwriter?"

"Come on, dear, don't play dumb." He took her arm for a brief instant before she jerked it away.

"There will be no need to touch the person."

"Fine. You want to talk. Talk."

"Talk about what? You seem to be laboring under some false impression. Can't you see the studio has been lying to you? If they sent you here just to harass me it won't work. Ah, here we are. . . ."

She started down the steps to welcome her chauffeur, whom the butler had just ushered in. Chandler put a hand on her to stop her.

"I'll handle this."

"You'll handle nothing. Don't paw me. Gilbert, please show this man the garage and any of the cars we might happen to have out there or on the grounds."

"Yes'm. What car are you interested in seeing, sir?"

"A Ford coupe with a C ration sticker on the windshield."

"I'm sorry, sir, but we don't have any car of that description on the premises."

"Listen, you little Jap, don't give me that stuff—"

"Jap? Did you hear that? He calls me a Jap. Where do you get off calling me a Jap?"

While all this was going on, the butler continued up the stairs.

"Excuse me, Madam. May I have a word with you in private?"

"No, you may not," Chandler barked. "What's on your mind, Jeeves?"

"It's about the inspector, Madam . . ."

"What inspector is that, Thompson?" Madam wanted to know.

The butler gestured slightly to Chandler, "Why this inspector, Madam."

"Inspector? Didn't you tell me you were a lieutenant?"

"That's right. Lieutenant Inspector Crawford, of the Thirty-Second Precinct," Chandler said proudly.

"I'm Chinese-Hawaiian on my mother's side, I'll have you know." The chauffeur was edging up the steps to join the party.

"Well, bully for you."

"I'm just as American as you are. More. More American."

Chandler was trying to ignore the little man. The butler cupped his hand to speak privately to Madam. Chandler bent forward to listen.

"I took the liberty of telephoning the police, Madam. There is no Thirty-Second Precinct in Los Angeles."

"Short doesn't make you a Jap you know." The Oriental who wasn't Japanese fumed.

"I can explain your problem, Jeeves." Chandler tried to smile but it was getting hard to do. "I'm with the Beverly Hills Police. That's where you made your mistake."

Barbara turned back to the Lieutenant Inspector. "I thought you said your name was . . . something else."

The butler edged behind the Madam. "He told me his name was Cramer . . ."

"That's right, I'm Cramer," Chandler sputtered, "but only on my mother's side."

" . . . and I'm certain there are not thirty-two police precincts in Beverly Hills," said the butler, who was beginning to look more and more like a bouncer. "Sir, I asked you once for your credentials. Now I'm afraid I must insist or we shall call the police."

"What kind of charlatan's game are you playing, sir?" Barbara Norman demanded. Then, her theatrical airs restored again after this brief respite, she pointed to the front door. "Out. Get out of this mansion and never set foot on this private estate again."

Chandler squared his shoulders. "Does this mean I don't get my free drink?"

The butler firmly took his arm and started down the steps. Chandler decided to make one last effort. He wrenched free and grabbed at the woman.

"You did it, didn't you? The three of you together killed him. The big guy hauled him up into the cooler and—"

The chauffeur lunged from the steps below and tried to tackle him around the waist, but Chandler's midriff bulk was too much for him. Chandler wedged an arm into the chauffeur's bear hug to loosen it, stood him up and kneed him so he fell hard against the railing.

"Let that be a lesson, my good man." Chandler dusted his hands. "Never resort to violence unless you are prepared to—"

Out of the corner of his eye he caught a glimmer of the butler making a move. He turned just in time to catch a big fist directly on the bridge of his nose. To his amazement it didn't hurt a bit. Perhaps, like Superman, he had become immune to the slings and arrows of this world. He looked back down at the chauffeur to see how he was doing. To his further amazement the little man had gotten a Herculean grip on the railing and brought the entire marble stairwell, railing and all, up over his head and slammed the works onto Chandler.

He smiled as he closed his eyes. Just as he'd thought; the whole thing was a prop. They hadn't fooled him for one minute. . . .

12

His next brush with reality was in the the form of two yellow-green eyes studying his face intently. The sound of rhythmic purring and the uncivilized kneading of little black paws on his chest told him he was among friends. He closed his eyes again and tried to work the cat into the plot he had been working on in his sleep. Perhaps Taki would be the missing link, the final solution to his problem of what to do about a body that had somehow gotten itself attached to his first-person-singular detective. It seems they both had been eating from a common, Chinaman's bowl—the detective and the body—when somehow the two of them got stuck together, the food being a white, fluffy adhesive substance that looked suspiciously like tapioca pudding. And try as he might, the detective could not free himself. Now then, how to get the cat involved. It's always a good idea when stuck on a story line to introduce another element. But what could the cat do? Maybe he could get it to eat the tapioca away. But the cat wouldn't touch the stuff. Smart old Taki. All he wanted to do was tug on the chest strap of the detective's arm holster.

"Shoo. Get away, Taki."

It was the voice of reason. Chandler was jolted back to the other world with the realization that his nightmare, except for a few minor details, was all too true. Taki hopped off her perch and Cissy came into view with the familiar red drink. His "morning tonic" as she used to call it when it was still a novelty.

Chandler slowly got himself into position to take the glass. He could tell when he moved he could not stretch out his arm as he had the morning before, so he kept his free hand near his hip and waited for her to put the drink in it.

"What time is it?"

"Almost nine. Sorry to disturb you so early, but there are some things you'll want to get started on. That is, if you're still interested in pursuing this thing."

"What do you mean by that?"

"Well, the way you came in last night, I thought perhaps you had chucked it all."

Chandler sipped and tried to pinch a memory out of his aching head. "I'm afraid I don't remember coming home. Is the car all right?"

"You didn't come home in the car. Two Mexican boys delivered you to the front door—"

"What?"

"That's right. I did the best I could with your clothes but you weren't very cooperative."

"Are you sure they were Mexicans?"

"Well, they looked it, and they talked in that muffled way they do."

"What did they say?"

"Not much. Is this where you live, et cetera."

"They didn't threaten you or say anything about what they would do . . . ?"

"No, of course they didn't. They were joking about the whole thing. I took it you had hired them to bring you home. Didn't you promise to give them five dollars?"

"Not that I recall."

"They said you did. I gave them three, all the small bills I had. That seemed to satisfy them. They thanked me and left."

He felt like shaking his head to clear it, but quickly decided it would be an unwise move. Deep in thought, he sipped again at his drink then pulled his head away. "You put an egg in this, didn't you."

"You've got to have something on your stomach besides the booze."

"Will you let me manage my own drunk? This might be the last time I'll have the . . . dubious pleasure of enjoying one for the next twenty years."

He got to his feet and closed his eyes until the two thousand mynah birds in the attic had stopped screeching. When he could, he reached for his glasses and put them on. For some reason, they didn't seem to fit properly. And the rumpled figure in the mirror told him he had slept in his shirt and pants. He excused himself and headed for the bathroom. Cissy followed with his bathrobe and waited in the hall, but kept the door open a crack so she could continue their conversation.

"There's a man from Warner Brothers who has been trying to reach you. He said he'd call back. A Somebody Eagle?"

Chandler yawned, then decided, "I don't know anybody named Eagle."

"Maybe that's not it then. I know it was something like a bird of prey."

"Hawks? Howard Hawks?"

"Yes, that's the one. He said he had to talk to you about your story line. Is this something else I should know about now?"

"He's the one who's directing the film of *The Big Sleep*. Tell him to get in touch with me in the county jail."

"Don't be like that."

"They bought it. Let them stew over it. I don't have time to worry about it now."

"Okay. Then your Larry from the morgue called."

"He did? What did he want?"

"He said two elderly ladies from Iowa had appeared on his doorstep ready to take their brother Clarence back home for burial. He's got to have Clarence back right away."

Chandler appeared at the door in his Jockey shorts, the left side of his face already lathered in Burma-Shave. "Would you say that again?"

She did. "And he wants you to call him at his home after nine. I wrote down the number. . . ."

He literally ran for the phone in the dining room, found the number on Cissy's note pad and dialed with nervous fingers. "This might be the answer to our problem . . . if we can only get onto the studio lot today. . . ."

But his fondest wish was not going to be granted. He finally managed to rouse the young morgue attendant from sleep, but Larry proceeded to deny he had called and talked to Mrs. Chandler the night before and did not want to do anything about retrieving the body as he had said he did. Chandler argued with him, just as before, but got nowhere. Finally he said, "I got a bad connection here. Would you mind saying that again?"

That said, he held the earpiece up for Cissy and whispered, "Is this the same voice that called last night?"

Cissy listened for a moment, then announced, "He hung up."

"Did you hear anything? Was that the same voice that called last night?"

"Oh, yes. I'm sure it was."

Chandler scowled and worked on his front cowlick. "Tell me again what he said last night."

"He was quite upset and wanted to talk to you as soon as you got in, just as I told you. Then, much later, when he called again, he still wanted to recover the body and you were to call him at nine this morning."

Cissy wiped the shaving cream off the phone, then helped her troubled husband into the bathrobe she was still holding.

"Are we both going crazy, or is it just me?" Chandler mused. "None of this is making sense. Unless someone has gotten to our young friend, Larry, and frightened him . . . First an editor at the newspaper and now . . . But how could there be a connection? And what could make everyone suddenly clam up like this?"

"Why don't you shave? You look ridiculous."

"You seem to be taking all this very calmly."

"I have a third message for you . . ."

"My, but you were a busy little thing last night, weren't you."

"  . . . and then I have another idea we should follow up on."

He started for the bathroom. "Come in and tell me about it while I shave."

"No, no. Over breakfast."

"Now, you know I can't eat in this condition."

"Just a little cold cereal."

"You want me to be sick?"

"And do you want to end up in the hospital being fed through a tube again? Now, that's what I call sick."

He started to talk back but noticed she was turning slightly blue. She moved stiffly into the living room and reached for her trusty inhaler next to the couch.

Chandler came in and watched her gasp for air. After she had started to breathe more easily he asked, "Are you going to be okay?"

She nodded. "Too much talk. I'll lie here a minute." She raised her arms to increase her breathing ease and covered her eyes with the back of one colorless hand.

Her ultimate weapon. No, no, that wasn't true. She wasn't using it to get her way. He knew her too well to suspect it. When he had finished shaving, he fixed a Spartan breakfast tray for the two of them and brought it into the living room. He put the tray on the end table and sat on the floor near her.

"Okay, I'm going to do the best I can with this," he declared. "Now, what's this other message all about?"

She raised her head and reached for her orange juice. "Thank you, Raymio. You're very sweet to do this."

"Your wish, my command." He smiled and tried to look as if he had developed an appetite for cold cereal.

"Your friend John Houseman called and asked if he could come by this morning."

"Oh. Poor John. He's convinced he'll be let go if this Alan Ladd project doesn't get off the ground. Maybe I should bow out of it for his sake."

"What good would that do him?"

"They might be able to assign some other writer to the project."

He gulped down two spoonfuls of shredded wheat and pushed the bowl away. "What did you tell him?"

"I told him ten-thirty would be fine. I can call him back, you know, if you're not up to it."

"I suppose I better talk to him. Now, you said something about another idea. . . ."

"Oh, yes." She raised herself on an elbow. "Maybe you've already thought of this. Didn't McGrath say he was going out of the cafeteria to talk to the studio publicity man about the truck?"

"That's what he told me."

"Has it occurred to you to talk to him?"

"I tried to reach him at his office yesterday. I hesitate to call him at his home on Sunday. I don't know the man."

Cissy smiled and stroked his hair. "Always the considerate English gentleman . . ."

"What is that supposed to mean?"

"I mean I think they over-educate you in some of those highfalutin public schools over there. John Houseman is the same way. He wouldn't dream of just appearing on our doorstep to talk to you."

"I wouldn't expect him to, either."

"That's what I mean. Here we are in desperate straits and you wouldn't think of calling the publicity man at his home. . . ."

Chandler pushed her hand away from his hair, letting her see his displeasure. She laughed and put it back.

"I'm sorry, dear. I think it is one of your more endearing qualities. Don't be angry."

"It's a matter of decorum. There's a right way and a wrong way to conduct your life. It's not that I 'wouldn't think of calling him,' " he mimicked.

"Yes, dear."

For some thirty seconds they sat in silence and listened to the tick of the clock on the dining room mantel.

"All right, where is it?" he asked.

"Where's what?"

"Where's the publicity man's phone number?"

She laughed and dropped her head back down on the couch pillow. "It's on the second page of my pad by the phone. His name is Lyle Palmer."

"How'd you happen to know that?"

"His secretary told me when I called them yesterday afternoon."

Chandler laughed at himself and got to his feet. She extended a hand as a peace offering. He kissed her fingertips and started for the dining room and the phone. He got the number off the pad, ready to dial. He picked up the phone, but then had second thoughts and recradled it. "I think I'll dress first," he said, and headed for the bedroom.

A half hour later he reappeared in the dining room. He was dressed in his Christmas tie and the hound's-tooth check sport coat that Cissy said made him look like a Hollywood writer. He could hear her moving about in the kitchen behind the swinging door. He scowled at the telephone as if it were a pet cat that had been misbehaving, then went to the buffet and got out his reinforcement. When he pushed the door of the liquor cabinet closed it made more noise than he expected. The dishes in the kitchen sink stopped rattling.

After the rush-flush from the first morning drink hit him, he sat at the phone and started dialing. After three rings the businesslike voice of Mr. Palmer came on the line.

"Hello."

"Mr. Palmer, this is Raymond Chandler speaking. I apologize for introducing myself over the phone this way but—"

"That's all right, Mr. Chandler. Believe me, I know who you are. I think I've typed your name on at least five hundred press releases in the last six months. What can I do for you?"

Chandler chuckled in an attempt to make the matter sound like a joke. "I have a very convoluted problem here. I won't bore you with all the details, but I'm trying to account for the movements of Charles McGrath yesterday at the commissary. I understand you two know each other."

"Oh, indeed we do. Say, what was that all about? I presume that was you at the kitchen door yesterday, wasn't it?"

"Ah, yes. Yes, it was. It was all part of a practical joke that had gone awry. I think you'll hear all about it in time. But what I'd like to know is, did McGrath come out and talk to you or move the truck after you asked to have it moved?"

"Yes, he did move the truck out of our way."

"Do you know where he parked it?"

"I have no idea. It couldn't have been very far away because he came back over to our gathering very quickly."

"Your gathering? I take it that was a public relations type of gathering?"

"Yes. The studio's anniversary on the Melrose lot. We thought it would be nice to have the local dignitaries there. The mayor and the city councilmen gave us a plaque."

"How did Corky McGrath fit into that group?"

Palmer cleared his throat, which sounded like he was thinking about his response. "Mr. Chandler, I don't know what your relationship is with McGrath, but I think I should be frank with you. My, er, association with Corky has been something less than pleasant."

"Please don't feel you need to spare my feelings."

"Fine. Corky McGrath really did not belong with our group at all. But once a newspaperman, always a newspaperman, I suppose. I suppose he thought he could horn in anywhere. Fortunately our ceremony was over with and we were just wrapping up with some picture taking."

"What did he do, exactly?"

"He made himself at home at Mayor Bowron's table."

"I don't understand. Without being invited?"

"Well, he seemed to know Councilman Bodecker and the mayor's aide, Alworthy."

"Bob Alworthy?"

"Yes. You know the man?"

"Yes, I do. He wrote me a rather biting letter last year on behalf of the mayor. He was complaining about my description of Los Angeles in my book, *Farewell, My Lovely.*"

"It's the truth that hurts, eh?"

"Did McGrath know the two of them?"

"He seemed to. They were thick as thieves when I left."

"Left? What do you mean? I thought you rode back downtown with the mayor's party."

"Yes, I did. But first I ran the picture negatives and the story copy over to my secretary. She was to type it up and get it out for the late afternoon papers."

"Did you happen to talk to either Alworthy or the councilman on the way back downtown?"

"Neither of them made the return trip in the limousine."

"They didn't? Why not?"

"Your guess is as good as mine. When I got back to the cars somebody said they'd made different arrangements. I never gave it another thought."

"So you didn't see them or Corky McGrath again?"

"No, come to think of it, I didn't. It never occurred to me to think the three of them may have left together. If they did, I'd certainly have to wonder why."

"Our friend McGrath gets around, doesn't he."

"Yeah, like a chicken with its head cut off."

Chandler laughed. "For some odd reason I'm getting the impression Corky wasn't best man at your wedding."

Palmer laughed. "That's a pretty safe assumption to make. Oh, I suppose he's all right in his way. He's a hard worker, I think, but I've never been able to figure out what it is he's working at."

"How long have you known him?"

"He used to run copy for us when I was still with the *Times-Mirror*. He said he was a journalism student at one of the local schools. I don't recall which. He was going to set the world on fire as the new Walter Winchell if he didn't get his nose lopped off first. He's the original buttinski."

"How'd he get his position here at the studio?"

"What position? What has he done?"

"Well, he's on the writing staff. Hasn't he done a script that you've promoted?"

"Not that my office knows about. He said he'd written a documentary for our Shorts Department, but that wouldn't give him any status in the Feature Film building. Of course it's possible he did do something else and I haven't noticed it on our work sheets. To tell you the truth, I'm surprised to hear he really is on the staff. He'd said he was, but I take most of what he says with a grain of salt. He even tried to put the bite on me the other day for a loan."

"Oh? That's interesting."

107

"He said it was for an investment, but I doubted that. He was going to triple my money in six months."

"May I ask how much he tried to borrow?"

"Five hundred dollars."

"Do you have any idea what kind of investment he had in mind?"

"No, I don't. As I say, I didn't believe him, so I didn't pursue it."

Chandler hummed into the phone. "Well, thank you very much for your help. I hope the next time we meet it will be under more pleasant circumstances than our encounter at the commissary kitchen door."

"You know, when I first saw the two of you in the kitchen I thought you must be arguing about a screen credit or something. McGrath's a great one for trying to swipe other people's material."

"Oh, no no. Nothing like that. I assure you."

"Well, I'm glad to hear it. People have been killed in this town over things like that."

Palmer said it with a laugh, but the comment sent a chill up Chandler's back. Just what he didn't need right now—a motive that would imply he was McGrath's killer.

"Oh, by the way"—Chandler decided to change the subject—"would you happen to know if Councilman Bodecker's district includes Chavez Ravine?"

"Chavez Ravine? I'm afraid I don't know where that is."

"How about Elysian Park?"

"Yes, yes. Now I remember. I'm quite sure that would be in his district."

"You know about the ravine, then?"

"I know it's pretty much useless land. I think the city gave it to the track layers for a place to squat after they finished laying the Southern Pacific line into town. Nobody else wanted it."

"Thanks, Mr. Palmer. You've been a big help."

Cissy had come into the room during the last of his phone conversation and now that he had hung up she presented him with a cup of hot coffee.

He showed her his tumbler. "Sorry dear . . . I beat you to it."

"It was the drinking that got us into this, you know. You really think it's going to get us out?"

"I'm proud of you, dear. You held off on the lecture as long as you could, didn't you."

The clock ticked on, like an impartial referee counting out the seconds of their rest period between rounds. She put the coffee on the dining room table, next to his work space. "Well, it will be here if you need it. Was Mr. Palmer any help?"

"Only if you want more questions. It appears our friend was onto something and needed some money to invest in . . . something." Chandler rubbed his nose and thought. "A reporter in the course of his work is privy to a lot of inside information that might be useful to him. . . . I wonder what our friend discovered?"

"Are you thinking he may have been killed by the parties that wanted something kept quiet?"

"It appears your thought about the silencing motivation was on the money. But silence about what? I wonder if my car is still over at Barbara Norman's house."

"Ray, I don't want you trying to drive around this town today."

"Maybe I won't have to."

"What do you mean by that?"

"Ask me after Houseman leaves."

He ran his fingers across his face again as if exploring it. "I wonder . . . I wonder why the bridge of my nose is so sore."

13

Houseman appeared on the Chandler doorstep promptly at ten-thirty with his usual friendly but formal demeanor. He carried with him a large leather briefcase and a small, gift-wrapped box. Chandler recognized the wrapping.

"It looks like you've been by C. C. Brown's confectionary counter, John."

"Yes, I remembered Cissy was rather partial to a particularly wicked dark chocolate mint. A little appeasement for my disturbing the household on your day of rest."

"She will love you for it. She's lying down right now. Come in and get comfortable."

The two men sat in the living room and got right to it. Houseman lifted a sheaf of formidable notes from his briefcase. "I can imagine how shattering yesterday's story conference must have been for you. I want to lend you whatever moral support I can. I feel partially responsible for the debacle with the Naval officer."

"How are you responsible for that?"

"I should have anticipated their complaint."

"Oh, nonsense, John. None of us could have foreseen that. It might have been nice if Mr. Wilder had told us what was coming and given us a little preparation time, but I'm beyond expecting any civil niceties from that particular source."

Houseman sounded a noise of agreement and shuffled some papers. "I thought perhaps it might be helpful to you if I discussed some plot change ideas that I've come up with and you tell me if you feel they have any merit. Just something to get the juices going again, if you are interested."

Chandler got up from his rocker and walked to the front window. He rubbed at the bridge of his tender nose and his eyes narrowed and started darting among the different objects on the street outside. Ideas were germinating but Houseman, from his angle, could not know that. Suddenly Chandler turned back to face the room.

"Very good of you to offer, John. Actually I do have a plot change idea of my own. It's still in the thinking stage right now. Perhaps you'd give a listen to it and give me your honest opinion."

Houseman smiled as if a heavy weight had been lifted from his shoulders. "Nothing would give me more pleasure, Raymond." He leaned back and waited to be dazzled.

Chandler sat again in the wicker rocker opposite his guest on the couch, and took off his troublesome glasses. "I've always had problems with the beginning of our story. It starts too slowly. Not enough suspense or story value up front. We've got three servicemen coming home. Two of them with problems. William Bendix has a plate in his head and may be psycho; Ladd has marital problems. The third guy is just sort of there. By the way, have they cast him yet?"

"We're thinking of Hugh Beaumont."

"I don't know him. You may want to change him anyway, when you hear what I'm thinking of. As the story now unfolds, Ladd eventually becomes a suspect in his wife's murder. And for my money, the audience won't get hooked until that point. But I want to add another dimension. I want our hero to be guilty of something. A small crime, or something he's rather ashamed of, so that he has something to hide. It creates another layer of interest and intrigue for the chase. It's the kind of twist

111

that Hitchcock does so well in his stories. The hero who is something less than totally innocent."

Houseman was frowning and rubbing his ample forehead. "Perhaps you could help me with an illustration, Raymond."

"Certainly . . . oh, John, would you like something to drink before we get too far into this?"

"Did I smell coffee brewing when I came in?"

"You certainly did. I'll be right back."

Chandler hurried to the kitchen with the gait of a much younger man and busied himself with cupboards and glassware. When he returned he had a nice little tray for his guest and a fresh drink of his own in a tall glass. He didn't bother to explain his morning drinking but went right on from where he left off.

"Please bear in mind that what I'm about to tell you still has some rough edges. I want you to assume that it can be blended logically into the story and the personalities involved."

Houseman listened attentively while dropping two lumps of sugar into his coffee and stirring. Chandler was in a gay expansive mood and sipped regularly between thoughts, as if his drink was Fourth-of-July lemonade.

"I'm thinking our third serviceman had been hospitalized like Bendix. The three of them are old friends and when Ladd and Bendix are to be furloughed, their friend—I'll call him Hugh—naturally wants to go with them. He seems perfectly healthy, and he can't understand why the hospital officials won't let him go.

"But the audience learns why in a scene with the staff doctors. He is suffering from some malady, maybe a piece of shrapnel lodged next to the heart, which is destined to take his life at any moment without warning. But of course the three GIs don't realize this. They live it up on their last night together and, when under the influence, they decide they've had enough of service regulations. Hugh goes AWOL and the three end up back in their old hometown. Now we have our hero guilty of aiding and abetting his AWOL buddy. See how this complicates the picture?"

Houseman was trying to wear an encouraging smile, but his heart wasn't in it. "It does complicate the picture, all right. But I don't quite see where we are going."

"We're going right on with the rest of our story. Ladd has an argument with his wife, just as he does in the existing script. She is subsequently murdered by assailants unknown. Only this time—and here is the twist—this time she is murdered in the same room where our friend Hugh has had his comeuppance with the grim reaper because of his shrapnel wound. You see, two bodies in the room. Now our hero is caught in a double web. He has to clear himself of the murder of his wife and he has to do something about the body of his friend. . . . John, are you with me?"

"I follow you, Raymond, but I don't see what it is he is supposed to be doing about Hugh's body. Does Ladd know that Hugh has died from the old shrapnel condition?"

"I'm not sure. Let's say he does."

"I don't see where this is taking us, Raymond. It appears to me to be muddying up what I thought was a very clear story line. Does this bring us any closer to deciding who our murderer is going to be?"

"No. I haven't gotten that far with it."

Houseman eyed the ceiling for a time. Then, "I'm afraid I'm not being very supportive, am I? I think my main concern is we are asking our audience to suspend credibility too many times. The wife's murder is in itself an incredible—or at least an unusual—event. Then our friend Hugh has an incredible health condition. And he happens to die in the murder room. Do you see my problem? There are too many 'incredibles' to be believed."

Chandler smiled at his own private joke. If Houseman only knew what "incredible" thing was waiting for them tomorrow morning in the commissary cooler. Then he lapsed into involuntary snickers.

"Raymond, are you all right?" Houseman had to ask.

"Yes. Of course. You're right about the story, John. You're absolutely right." He finally got his face straight again to go on. "But I'm going to ask you to humor me just a bit more. Would you do that? Imagine that we are able to satisfy all your objections. The story does evolve logically and our hero does find himself in the situation I've just described. Now I would like to ask you, what would you do if you were he?"

Houseman searched the ceiling again. "Well, let's see. . . .
There would be nothing I could do about my friend, Hugh, if
he were dead. I'd have to concentrate my efforts on my wife's
murder. . . . I think, being the reflective sedentary person I am,
I would have a strong urge to throw myself upon the mercy of
the authorities. Of course if I did that, we would have no story.
So let us say I have blond wavy hair and the twenty-eight inch
waist of Mr. Ladd. Then I would do what detectives have been
doing ever since the *Moonstone* caper—I would start searching
out the other suspects and looking for something in one of their
acts or statements that points up an inconsistency. Of course, I
don't have to tell a mystery writer such as yourself all this."

"No no, I'm interested in knowing how you would proceed
if you were our hero. And let's assume there is a need to hurry,
for when Hugh's body is found with that of your wife's, it will
further implicate you as the number one suspect."

Houseman smiled, "I like that, yesss. Our likable character
facing apparently insurmountable odds to reach a recognizable
goal."

"Will you stop already with the academic theories. Tell me
what you would do, for God's sake."

Houseman was taken back by the edge in Chandler's voice,
but managed to keep up the façade of calm cooperation. "Well,
let's see . . . I would have been away from my wife for perhaps two years . . . I would endeavor to ascertain who she had
been seeing and who might have a reason to benefit from her
death . . ."

"Yes, yes, I've been doing all that."

"There is the possibility of hiring some professional help."

"There's not time for that."

"Well . . . the time comes when one of our suspects starts
to tip his hand—"

"And supposing they don't tip their hand? Supposing things
just go on and on and you can't force the issue and time is
slipping by, what then?" Chandler was near tears.

"Have you exhausted all your possibilities?"

"Well, no, I haven't. But I'm getting into the high risk area
and I'm not so sure I'm the man for it. Maybe if I looked into
Clarence's background I might . . ."

"Clarence? Have I missed something here? Who is Clarence?"

"Excuse me. I meant to say Hugh."

"What do you mean by the high risk area? You mean it could be dangerous?"

"That's exactly what I mean."

"Great. The audience will love it. The more tight spots the better."

"To hell with the audience. What about me?"

"Don't you mean Alan Ladd?"

Chandler laughed. "Yes, of course. You see what a dedicated writer I am. I've immersed myself so totally in the part I can't separate my own interests from that of our hero's." He lapsed into giggles and shook his head.

Houseman started putting papers back into his briefcase. "I think I have made a judgment error in coming today, Raymond. Let me apologize for the intrusion."

"Intrusion? John, you aren't intruding. I'm glad you came."

"What you do on your time off is really no affair of mine. I'll see you tomorrow when you're . . . at the studio."

"You are assuming tomorrow I'll be sober."

Houseman smiled and gazed out the window. "History seems to be repeating itself for me, Raymond. I had the dubious pleasure of baby sitting Herman Mankiewicz while he brought out the first draft of *Citizen Kane*. He had a problem with the bottle, too. I don't know what it is about writers and drinking. . . ."

"It really loosens up the ol' inhibitions, friend, even if it doesn't do much for the plot lines."

"Yes, I see what you mean." He rose to leave. "About the story. Your new complications might have some validity in the hands of a Hitchcock, as you suggest. Plus, we have an actor of limited scope on our hands. He is very popular and he makes the studio a lot of money, providing we stick with simple good guy–bad guy story lines. And we don't have the luxury of time to experiment on this one."

"I see. I was just trying out an idea, John. A bad one at that. Oh, Lordy, I've only worked on three screenplays and already I'm sick of the formula. I guess it would be best if I dropped out . . . give you time to bring in another writer."

Houseman sat back down. "Raymond, if you pull out, I'm sure the studio will fold the project."

"Would that be so terrible?"

Houseman slumped in place and stalled for time by putting his coffee cup and the sugar container back on the tray. "No, I suppose not. Worse things could happen. I've made a decent living in the theatre in the past. I don't think I would have difficulty in catching on to something—"

"You think it would come to that, do you?"

Houseman nodded and smiled. "I can't get you to reconsider? With a standard formula script to work with, the only way this project could fail is if we don't shoot it."

"When you say it cannot fail, you mean the money of course."

"Yes, the money. And the job. I rather like what John Ford says on that account. He makes what they tell him to make and he does it their way, so that when a good project comes along, he can do it his way."

"Very astute." Chandler sighed and turned the drink about in his hand to view it from different angles. "But I'm afraid I was never cut out for factory work. I found that out at Dabney Oil."

"I see. . . ." Houseman said, but he didn't move from the couch. Chandler had been avoiding looking directly at him, but he did now. Houseman's pale grey eyes were ringed by lids that had turned a bright shade of red. The facial muscles indicated he was struggling for control and the right words.

"Raymond, I was rather in hopes our common background and point of view might influence your decision. I would be eternally grateful if you . . ." It didn't get finished, except with the body language. His fingers were twisting in an interlocking prayer grip. When he realized what he was doing he stopped and placed his hands on his knees, but he still didn't move.

"All right, John," Chandler finally said. "It may be beyond my capacity to complete this, but I'll do the best I can for you for as long as I can."

"Thank you."

"You better not thank me until you've heard my conditions."

"What do you mean?"

"I want some leeway in the way I write. By that I mean I

want to be able to write at home if necessary. And I want a studio limousine on call out in front of the house twenty-four hours a day. And I want—"

"Are you serious, Raymond?"

"Of course I'm serious."

"But why? I'm sure you understand I'd have to ask that."

Chandler held up his nearly empty glass as explanation. "I've started something here and I don't know when or if I can stop it. It's beyond my control at this point. I don't suppose the studio wants a soused writer wandering about the halls."

"But you can't write in this condition. Can you?"

"It's been known to happen. And I want the studio to foot the bill for a nurse who will come by twice a day and give me vitamin shots. I'll make the arrangements. It's not the drunk that worries me, but coming down after it. That's the hard part. The malnutrition and the rest."

"Raymond, I'm worried about your health. Look, please don't do this. My job at Paramount is not worth your risking—"

"It's going to happen one way or the other." He drained his glass to make the point. "But if you want me to work on the story, that's the way it'll have to be. I wish it could be otherwise."

"What's the limousine for?"

"To take me and the script back and forth as needed."

Houseman scratched at his left eyebrow in befuddlement. "This is the strangest situation. I will have to check with the studio. I'll call you in the morning."

"No. Today. I want the limo by today."

Houseman got to his feet, shaking his head and smiling. "And I used to think Orson Welles was a bit strange."

"Oh? I didn't know Welles has a drinking problem."

"He doesn't. His failing is pistachio ice cream."

After Houseman left, Chandler wandered into the dining room and noticed Cissy sitting on the telephone stool in the hall.

"How long have you been there?" he asked.

"I heard most of it."

"You should have come in. He brought you some of your favorite mints."

She rose and moved to a chair next to his work station. "I understood what you were searching for with the double death business, but why all that fancy footwork about continuing with the script? Poor John. I thought he was going to cry."

"It wasn't exactly an altruistic move on my part. I will work on it for as long as I can, that's true. But he saw me running from the commissary with blood on my shirt front. I'm wondering what he will say tomorrow morning when we have the grand opening of the commissary cooler. Maybe if he feels I'm doing him a big favor it might help to cloud his memory."

He sat at his typewriter and looked about. "Rats, I think I left my *Blue Dahlia* script at the studio."

"Oh, that reminds me, there was something in the pocket of the coat you wore yesterday. Could that be it?"

"Maybe. Don't get up. Just tell me where it is."

She did and he went out on the back porch and sorted through the pile of clothes Cissy had set out for the cleaners. He didn't find the script, but he did find the address book he had picked up at McGrath's. He had forgotten all about it.

Fifteen minutes later Chandler was still sorting through the pages trying to decide on a plan of action when Houseman called back with the studio's decision. He gave Chandler the number of the limousine service the studio used. They would be expecting his call.

14

The big car rolled east along Sixth Street. At eleven-thirty in the morning the two riders seemed to have the city streets to themselves. The Negro chauffeur and the middle-aged, bespectacled white in the back. They could have passed for second-generation Pasadena money out for a Sunday drive amongst the common folk.

"This be Lorraine, mister. What house you say you want?"

"Turn right. The big walled place up ahead there."

Their long black Cadillac eased to a stop right behind Chandler's Packard, which was sitting at the curb. He knew it would be there; exactly how he knew was another story. Was it only last night? It seemed like a year ago. So long ago he had already lost most of the details.

Chandler got out and walked up to the entrance gate of the Norman mansion. The tree branches and shrubbery that had reached through the rusty iron bars last night had been trimmed back and the large decorative gate stood closed. The butler and the chauffeur must have had a busy morning. Chandler reached through an opening and pulled on a chain that looked like it was designed to grant some sort of action.

In a few seconds one of the garage doors up the hill swung up and the head of the little Oriental could be seen bobbing forward. Then the chest and then the bandy legs. He came down the driveway about thirty feet before he was close enough to recognize last night's counterfeit detective. He stopped and put his hands on his hips like an out-of-sorts British nanny.

"Say, Mister, didn't we teach you anything last night?"

"I just came by to pick up my car."

"We're fresh out of Ford coupes. Now be on your way."

Chandler forced a laugh. "I mean my convertible here on the street. How's the lady of the house today?"

"She's finally quiet. Let's leave it that way."

"That was quite a hysterical performance she put on, wasn't it?"

"Yeah, almost as good as yours."

"It's Gilbert, isn't it? Did I hurt you last night?"

"Did you hurt me? Of course not." He moved his shoulders like a boxer limbering up. But judging from his rolled up sleeves and the perspiration stains on his shirt, he had already had his morning workout wrestling with the foliage.

"Good." Chandler smiled. "I wouldn't want there to be any hard feelings. Tell me, what were you doing over at McGrath's place last night?"

"Ix-nay, buster, you're off limits." Gilbert turned and started up the drive.

"Who told you not to talk to me?" Chandler asked. When that drew no response he called, "How'd you know my name was Buster?"

"It ain't. It's Chandler," Gilbert sneered over his shoulder, "and you should know there are only sixteen police precincts in this town."

"Thanks, I'll remember that. Nice chatting with you, Togo."

The little man spun around and did his nanny imitation again. "You pull that chain again and you'll be counting the precincts in person. Now beat it."

Back at the limousine the driver was holding the back door

open for Chandler and trying to act as if he hadn't heard the exchange at the gate.

"Where to now, sir?"

Chandler put a steadying hand on the car roof and looked at his middle-aged, well-dressed chauffeur. "I think we're in for a long day. I suppose I should know your name, shouldn't I. It isn't Clarence, is it?"

"No, sir, it's Arnold. Arnold Billings."

"That's good to hear. Well, Arnold, I want you to drive very slowly back to my house and I will follow you in this beauty right ahead of us here. Just one moment . . ."

Chandler reached into the back seat of the Cadillac and picked up a paper sack he had left there. But as he moved toward his own car Arnold caught hold of the sack.

"Sir, maybe this better stay with me, just in case. . . ."

"In case what, Arnold?"

"In case the Bealer Boys comes cruisin' by an' happen to think maybe you be drunk." He tightened the lid on the bottle in the sack and put the evidence in a pouch in the limousine's back door. "It'll be there for you later, sir."

Chandler acquiesced. "Arnold, I think I'm going to like you."

"Yes, sir, I'm a likable fellow, a'right."

The two-car caravan moved slowly back to Drexel Avenue, making the trip without incident, except for one technical flaw while parallel parking in front of the house. Try as he did to prevent it, one of Chandler's tires insisted upon hopping the curb and coming to a stop only on the sidewalk.

"That be fine, sir," Arnold called to him, over the roar of the big Packard engine. "Let's not fuss about little things."

He finally got Chandler and his paper sack reunited again in the back seat of the Caddy, then asked, "Where to now, sir?"

"Hollywood Presbyterian Hospital. On the double-quick."

"You be thinkin' a' checkin' in?"

"No, no, Arnold. We have miles to go before we sleep. Lead on, Macduff."

"You want I should tell your missus where we bound?"

Chandler blinked at him in confusion. "Oh, 'bound'! Like

'bound for the promised land' you mean? Great Scot, I'm talking jive. No, no. Let's not worry the poor dear. Don't spare the horses, Arnold. The fair maid of the garter awaits."

Last night he had halfheartedly promised Francine he would pick her up by noon and give her a ride home. Unfortunately, it was now going on twelve-thirty as they approached the hospital. But as he was about to mount the front steps of the large brick building, by luck he spotted her flowered dress at the bus stop just north of the ambulance entrance. He walked up behind her and studied her dark hair and thin shoulders. When she wasn't primping and posturing for the opposite sex there was still an innocent little girl quality to her looks. The quality that had made Chandler want to take care of her, like a father to a daughter. Traces of that old feeling rushed back to him now as he watched her, and it was with reluctance that he called her name.

"Hello, Francine."

She scowled at him through the sun's glare, and the hardness came back into her expression. It was almost enough to break a body's heart.

"I was beginning to think you weren't going to show." She got up and followed him down the street like a lost puppy. Then she noticed the car and her face brightened. "Hey, I've always wanted to ride in one of these. Where'd you get it?"

"It's on loan from the studio. Get in."

Judging from the way she bounced into the back seat she was fully recovered from her adventures of the night before. A three-inch wide bandage on her wrist served as the only reminder.

Chandler gave Arnold her address in the Hollywood hills, then closed the glass partition between the seats as the big car pulled out. When Francine had finished running her hands over the upholstery she cuddled up to her old boyfriend. Her Mother Earth aroma was still with her. The baking on the sun-drenched bus stop bench had brought it to full flower.

She rubbed her nose against his cheek. "We could take a spin out to the ocean, you know. Whataya say?"

"I can't, Francine. There's no time. I guess I needn't ask how you are."

"Oh, I'm fine. I slept like a log. I think it helps to get some blood drained out now and then."

"Don't be flippant about it. You had me worried. You still do. I wish you'd tell me that nothing . . . else . . . like last night is going to happen."

She shot a glance at the back of Arnold's head. "He can't hear us, can he?"

Chandler tapped the cover of the intercom tube. "Not while this is closed."

"It was the drinking," she said casually. "I can hardly remember what I did. I'm okay now."

"And what happens the next time you get sloshed? I'm into problems deep enough already. I don't want any more blood on my conscience."

She frowned at him. "More? What's that supposed to mean?"

Chandler winched at his choice of words. "Nothing. Forget I said it."

"Say, what's going on, anyway? What's all the mystery about McGrath?"

"You sure you don't already know?"

"No, I don't know any more than I told you last night. Is there something wrong with him?"

"A fellow from the publicity department tells me that Corky McGrath worked on a documentary script for the studio. And it's my guess you did the typing for him. Didn't you?"

She thought about it, but her expression didn't change. "So?"

"So you didn't mention it last night."

"My God, is that a crime now? I forgot about it."

"Okay, it slipped your mind. What was the documentary about?"

"Come on, Ray, I type stuff all day long sometimes. You get so you tune it out—you just type—unless it's a script for a love story. Those I read."

"Was it about the city of Los Angeles by any chance?"

"Yeah, come to think of it, it was. Civic betterment. Stuff like that. Why?"

"Do you remember anything else about it?"

"I asked you first. You don't give a damn about me, do

you? You just wanna pump me about this McGrath business. Well, what's happened? What's he done?"

"That's what I'm trying to puzzle out. What has he done that would make people want to kill him?"

"My God. You mean really try to kill him? Where is he, hiding out someplace? My God, I was in his place. *We* were in his place."

Chandler rubbed his temples. "Hold it down, will you? I'm right here."

"I know but, my God! Do the police know about this?"

"Look, forget about what I said," he smiled. "I'm probably exaggerating the seriousness of the whole situation. This is Hollywood, you know. Can't you take a joke?"

She looked quizzically at him, then laughed and took his arm again. "You need a drink, don't you. I can tell."

He smiled at her and tried to forget about his headache. Arnold turned off Franklin and started up the twisting series of streets that would lead them to Francine's apartment.

"You wanna come in for a while? My roomie is in El Monte at her folks."

"I can't, babe. If I put one foot inside your place, I wouldn't see the sun for two days."

"Just like the good old times," she smiled, but her expression quickly turned to a quivering pout. Maybe it was the thought of being let out and going into her place alone. "My good times are scarce, Ray. Damn scarce."

"Not half as scarce as healthy libidos on middle-aged alcoholics."

She reached two fingers up under his shirt cuff and massaged what she could reach of his forearm. "I'm a big girl, remember. I can take care of any little problems you might think you have."

He laughed and kissed her lips quickly. She wanted more, but he put his hand on her cheek and guided her head to his shoulder. Then he looked for the big brown eyes of Arnold Billings watching them in the rearview mirror, but Arnold appeared to be busy with the last curve in the road before the apartment house. The car rolled to a stop in front of the Arabian

Towers Apartments and everything was quiet for a moment. Just like any Sunday afternoon.

Chandler bowed his head. "The Arabian Towers, madam. Complete with minarets."

"Huh?"

He pointed to the two decorative towers adorning the front of her building. "The prayer towers where Turhan Bey calls the faithful to worship. I think I saw this set in a recent Abbott and Costello film, didn't I?"

"I guess I'm not in the mood for wisecracks."

"They keep saying the war will be over any minute," he said. "You'll be up to your knickers in men before you know it. Men your own age."

She gave a sarcastic grunt. " 'My own age.' That's great advice coming from you."

She heaved her chest as if she suddenly found a need for more air. She was waiting for him to make a move, but instead he looked out the window. "Look, we can see the Palos Verdes Peninsula today."

"Well, bully for the Palos Verdes Peninsula." She pushed the door open and got out.

"That's a crummy choice for an exit line, babe."

"Okay, you're the hotshot writer. So write me one."

"How about, 'I have my notes on McGrath's documentary script here at the apartment. Let me run up and get them'?"

She shook her head. "It'll never play. I don't keep notes."

"Then how about a smile and a simple, 'Thanks for the ride'?"

"Remind me next time to take the bus. It saves on the jawboning." She turned and slammed the door in one move.

Arnold thoughtfully waited at the ivy-covered curb so Chandler could watch Francine and her animated derriere mount the steps and disappear inside her baby blue Arabian Towers apartment building.

He hated to see it end like this. He hated her version of the tough girl chatter she had fallen into. He wanted to take her in his arms and rock her back and forth like a father . . . like a father. He snorted, scoffing at his own thought. As if he could do anything halfway with her. It was the booze, he told himself. He was spending his life trying to fix things the booze had broken.

The ride from the hospital had been a carbon copy of the scene last night. Even the angry little burst at the end somehow seemed a duplicate of the suicide attempt. Chandler looked out at the crystal clear view of the greater Los Angeles basin and wondered why he felt so claustrophobic. It was as if he were trapped in one of the dreary English novels he was force fed in his youth, where a myriad of characters express their opinions on thirty-seven topics and nothing ever *happens.* His admiration for Philip Marlowe was growing by the minute. At least he could be relied upon as a catalyst, to make things happen. If only he were here. A five-minute consultation fee would be less than twenty-five bucks.

He hadn't had a drink since they had stopped at the Norman house, two centuries ago. He found his sack and looked for Marlowe somewhere deep in the bottom.

Arnold rapped on the glass and Chandler opened his intercom tube.

"Yes?"

"This limo goes through a lot a' gas. Should I turn it off, sir, or will we be movin' on?"

"Do you know where I can get a gun?"

The thick black neck of the driver turned slightly, as if he were going to look into the back seat of the limousine at his passenger, then he thought better of it and talked into the communication tube, "This be Sunday, mister. Ain't no gun shops open today."

"I know what day of the week it is. That isn't what I asked."

"Guns is bad news, mister."

"All I want is a little protection. I wasn't planning on knocking over a bank. All right, press on, Arnold, by all means."

"An' where do we be pressin' to, sir?"

"Let us try Chavez Ravine, Arnold."

Arnold thought about that. Then he pushed open the glass panel that separated the front and back seats. "Where?"

"Chavez Ravine."

"Sir, do you 'member the zoot suit riots a' '43?"

"Indeed I do, Arnold. I was stone cold sober the entire summer."

"An' I was runnin' a yellow cab outa downtown L.A. Are we absolutely positive we wanna go to Chavez?"

"I never said I wanted to. But the time has come. I have to go. I think somebody up there killed a friend of mine."

The big car rolled hesitantly down out of the Hollywood hills and found its way to Western Avenue, a street in transition. Or a street with an identity crisis. It didn't seem to know if it wanted to be a residential neighborhood of single-story California bungalows or a commercial effort of small retail stores selling foot powders, dance lessons, Armenian brass, and Greek candy. After two regular houses, the list went on: caskets for animals, storefront evangelists, frogs for sale, stud dogs, orange peelers. Chandler decided that stucco was to blame. It was too easy to erect things in this climate. Some boards and chicken wire. More like movie sets than real stores or houses. The lack of functional consistency to the buildings and their surroundings only seemed to add to Chandler's sense of ambivalence and unreality. You didn't have to be looped to be in fairyland in this town. But some days it helped.

South of Third Street, a traditional mainline Protestant church was just letting out from services. As usual, no church bells tolled. It seemed all the city's belfries had traded in their bells for neon crosses.

Mingling with the well-dressed and pale worshipers was a swarthy young man dressed in East Indian attire and carrying an advertising sandwich board. Apparently he hoped to attract a number of the hungry Christians to "The Self-Realization Fellowship Restaurant" where the specialty of the house that day was to be a "meatless hamburger."

Wilshire and Western. A line had already formed at the Wiltern Theatre for the Sunday matinee screening of Betty Grable's latest musical. The marquee read: SPECIAL SNEAK PREVIEW: MOTHER WORE TIGHTS AND SELECTED SHORTS.

Chandler was still pondering the title half a block later when he realized they were still traveling south. He asked Arnold,

"Excuse me, but isn't Elysian Park more toward downtown?"

"Yes, sir, it is. But a fren a' mine got a hardware store down this way."

"You suddenly feel a burning need for some hardware, Arnold?"

"I mean the other kind a' hardware. Like you ask me 'bout before."

15

$\mathcal{S}$outh of Olympic they got into
an area of town that Chandler was not familiar with, but Arnold
seemed to know his way around. They pulled into a broad alley
behind some rundown storefronts and came to a stop in the hot,
dusty stretch between garbage cans and loading docks. Arnold
tapped the horn twice and got out.

From a second-story window over one of the shops a heavyset man dressed in his undershirt stuck his head out and waved,
"Arnie. Whatcha say, man?"

"Gotta customer for you, Linus. You open for binnes?"

"Be right down."

Chandler got out and moved into the thin stretch of shade
the two-story building offered. While he and Arnold waited for
the man upstairs to make his appearance at the back door of his
shop, two little Negro boys came running up. First they eyed the
car and then Arnold and Chandler. The white man they ignored,
but the Negro they could talk to.

"You be Deacon Billings, ain'tcha," the larger of the two
declared.

"Tha's right, boy," Arnold said.

The boy smiled. "I seed you in church."

"Tha's right," Arnold chuckled. While talking to the children, his voice had taken on a deep resonant authority.

"Where yo' white gloves?" the other boy wanted to know.

Arnold examined his hands for white gloves. "Oh, I only wears them when I be officiatin'.."

With that established to the boys' satisfaction, they turned their attention to the big car. After a quick trip all the way around it, they discovered they could create distorted images of themselves by bobbing up and down in front of the shiny grillwork.

Arnold laughed and called them back. "You boys like to sit inside and turn the steerin' wheel?"

They both nodded wildly.

"Okay, you watch the car for me but don' touch, an' when I come out I'll let you turn the wheel. Now you holler if any trouble comes, you hear?"

They heard.

The back door of the shop opened and the heavyset man stepped back to let the two men in. Chandler estimated the shopkeeper to be in his late sixties and, except for the sound of the Mississippi Delta in his voice and a few strands of kinky gray hair, he could have passed for white.

The shop appeared to be a dry goods store that catered to women who made their own clothes. Judging from the large bolts of material, floral prints were still the big seller in the neighborhood. Francine was right in style.

Linus swayed from side to side on tired hip sockets as he walked behind a counter in the back of the store. "What kinda merchandise you all lookin' for?"

Arnold looked to Chandler. "You wants a revolver? They's the most sure."

"How about a Smith and Wesson? Thirty-eight caliber." Chandler's knowledge and experience with guns was limited to names he had read in the pulps. Cissy would never allow a gun in the house, so the question of owning one had never come up before. Smith and Wessons, he had heard, were standard issue for the L.A.P.D.

Linus pulled open a drawer and started moving muslin-wrapped guns about. "I got a German Luger. They's real sure. First World War make, but it just came up last week. Got a twenty-two caliber barrel on it."

He unfolded the oily cloth and showed them the automatic. It was slippery to the touch and it slipped from Chandler's grasp and bumped heavily on the glass counter.

"Sorry. How does it work?"

Linus showed them how to free the magazine in the handle and how to load it.

"What about bullets?" Chandler asked.

"Now wait a minute, here now." Arnold put a hand on Linus to stop him from bringing out the bullets. "We don't really needs bullets, do we? You say you ain't gonna use it. Just for show, ain't it?"

"I said it was for protection."

"How about we just show it? Won' that do the trick?"

"It probably will, but you don't show a weapon unless you're prepared to use it," Chandler insisted.

"Tha's right," Linus nodded. "The law a' the West."

Arnold frowned, but the bullets came out anyway.

"He want a whole box I 'magin'," Linus said.

Chandler grunted in agreement and broke open the box to start loading. "What do I owe you?"

Linus looked to Arnold. "Did you 'splain to him we got no papers or nothin'?"

There was a carefully observed protocol covering such situations. Arnold, as the Negro employee, or direct contact with the white man, was the only one who was to talk directly with the Man in close conversation. Arnold looked at Chandler. "That be okay with you, sir? There be no papers."

"Yes, I guess so. What's the difference?"

"If you get caught with it, you gotta say you foun' it."

"I understand."

Chandler fumbled with the bullets, then finally got six loaded into the magazine, with a little help.

"Now, maybe he better try it out." Linus pushed back a curtain and exposed a small closet lined with railroad ties. In the corner stood an old dress form that had obviously been used for target practice before. There were wood chips and holes showing throughout the closet. Linus pushed the weapon in Chandler's hands so that the barrel aimed toward the target. Then he cocked the mechanism.

But Chandler's hands were shaking badly when he raised the gun at arm's length to fire. The target was only fifteen feet away from the counter, but it was doubtful if the shots would stay in the closet. Arnold groaned. Linus lifted the pistol from him and broke the speaking protocol.

"Here. Like this, sir." He stepped back, raised the pistol with both hands, then slowly dropped it to eye level and put two quick rounds into the dummy's midsection. Stuffing popped through the outer wrapping of the dummy and Chandler grabbed at his ears in pain. He did not tolerate loud noises well, especially with half a load on.

"She works pretty good, don't she?" Linus smiled. He uncocked the gun, put the safety on and handed it in Chandler's direction. But Arnold took it and slipped it in his own coat pocket.

"Why don' I hangs on to it for now, sir."

"That might be a good idea, after all."

After the two loud reports in the enclosed room Chandler was rapidly losing his interest in handling firearms. A price of twenty-seven dollars was determined agreeable to all and Chandler paid up.

Back outside, the two boys had multiplied to nearly twenty. Arnold, as promised, let the two who had acted as guards take their turns at the wheel. With Chandler in the back and the boys in the front with him, Arnold let the older one steer down to the end of the alley, then he patiently turned the vehicle about and gave the younger his turn going back up the alley. Outside the car the other boys raced along beside them, cheering their buddies on as if they were leading in some ancient chariot race.

When the boys got out they were immediately surrounded by their admirers.

"Sorry 'bout the dee-lay, sir. I hope you don't mind," Arnold said, once they were underway again.

"No. I got a kick out of watching them."

Arnold chuckled. "They be talkin' 'bout that for weeks."

"Tell me, Arnold. Your friend Linus said that automatic

we bought 'just came up.' What did he mean by that? Does he get them from Mexico?"

Arnold scratched his ear, "Well, no sir. 'Bout twyst a year the po-lice gathers up all the guns they collects from people, an' they put 'em on a barge an' go out in the ocean an' dump 'em."

"You mean to tell me Linus gets them off the ocean floor?"

"Frens a' his do."

"How on earth do they manage that?"

"They don' say. But I knows it for a fact."

"What an odd little business to be in."

"Well," Arnold shrugged and twisted his head in resignation. "When you colored, you do what you can do."

Arnold got them through the quiet downtown streets of the Los Angeles business section and up Bunker Hill past the seedy turn-of-the-century mansions Chandler liked to write about. A few of the elderly residents were already out on their shallow porches getting an early start on Sunday afternoon rocking. But Chandler closed his eyes and tried to rest. He was not interested in looking for background color or characters for another novel. He had more than enough intrigue to satisfy him for a long time to come.

Arnold indicated he wanted to say something, so Chandler pushed open the glass panel between them.

"Sir, we almost there. You wants to tell me what we supposed to be doin' up there?"

"I wish I knew. Let's drive around a bit for a look-see and maybe something will come to me."

"We gonna cause quite a stir in this car," Arnold reminded him. "Just in case you think we sneakin' up on somebody."

"I know, Arnold, I know. But when you are white and stumped, you do what you can do."

Arnold granted him a chuckle and turned up onto a tree-lined street that looked like an entrance to a run-down park. But as they started climbing, the road quickly turned from gravel to dirt. The leaves and dead bark from the eucalyptus grove they were driving through kept the underbrush contained, but the road had begun to resemble a cow path. Because of deep ruts caused by washouts from the past winter's rains the big car bumped its undercarriage as they tried to navigate forward.

They had traveled less than five minutes from downtown, but they might just as well have been in the hinterlands of Australia.

After the second scrape on the undercarriage, Chandler called, "Is this the only way into this place?"

"This used to be a pretty good road," Arnold said. "Should I turn back?"

"No, but take it easy."

The first sign of life they came across was six young dark-haired girls walking into the ravine ahead of them. They were all dressed in their Sunday best, complete with hats and purses. A couple of the older girls even wore gloves. They moved to the side of the road and watched with serious little faces as the big car passed by.

A little farther on, the scene was repeated, this time with a mixture of boys and girls. The boys were all in white shirts and still bore signs that their hair had been parted and plastered down about a half hour ago. Once again they moved aside and watched with the same blank expressions, as if they had all been trained to avoid smiles.

"I'm sure glad we got that gun," Chandler said. "That little one with the pink purse looks mighty sinister."

"Where you 'spect they been?" Arnold asked.

"You should know. Aren't you the deacon?"

"You s'pose they walkin' from that big Cath'lic church downtown? That's a good walk."

As they approached the crest of a hill, the Sunday strollers seemed to increase in age and the suspiciously somber looks the big car drew seemed a bit more severe.

Chandler remembered what McGrath had said about Los Angeles being a city of layers. He wondered how many layers of history he was unearthing with this trip. Maybe if they traveled far enough along this road they would come upon a family of Chumash Indians leaching the poisons out of a pot of acorns over an open fire.

Once over the crest of the hill they'd been climbing, they started to descend into a valley of what looked like a village in western Mexico. It was only early May, but the bare ground was already covered with the fine dust of summer—parched white and ready to fly onto the scrub oak leaves, the hood of your car,

134

the back of your neck, and into the lining of your nostrils with the slightest disturbance. The big car was only inching forward, but a three-foot high trail of the stuff was doggedly following them, like a troubled conscience.

On every halfway-level patch of ground the underbrush had been worn away and a house or lean-to had been put up. Each house appeared to have its own fenced off area where chickens or other farm animals were kept. Other fences outlined active and healthy looking vegetable gardens. The fencing materials consisted of some wire but mostly railroad ties, no doubt "borrowed" from Southern Pacific, or rough-cut sections of wood that had been ripped from dead scrub oak trees in the surrounding hills. The sight of telephone lines and an occasional dilapidated car were the only indications they were still in the twentieth century.

It must have been what the land was like in its natural state—before the white man came and dug his wells, before he swindled the water out of Owens Valley and piped it over the mountains. And before the real estate agents came with their tarpaper and stucco.

Chandler wondered what it was about the place that seemed to set it off from other poor communities. Then he realized there had been no grading or land preparation for the area. Here and there the uneven ground had been terraced with the help of the ubiquitous railroad ties, but it still looked like a civil engineer's nightmare, with everything laid out according to the natural slopes and bends of the valley. The houses varied from middle-class, two-story frame structures all the way to corrugated metal huts. But in spite of its drawbacks, there did seem to be a functional logic to the place.

They came to what appeared to be the central area of the community. It was a flat, dusty stretch about fifty yards across. The major attraction was a series of rusty mailboxes, which sat like a wall of yawning pelicans waiting to be fed. Chandler had Arnold pull up next to them. With the purloined address book from McGrath's desk, he got out and started looking for names on the boxes that matched those in the book. It wasn't an easy task. Half of the boxes were for Rodriguez or Lopez or Garcia. Too common to be easy matches for the book. Finally, he found a match that was too unusual to be mere coincidence. Ottavio T. Tapia. And it was on a yellow and white box that seemed to be a cut above the others in appearance.

By then, some of the older church goers were coming by and Chandler approached them.

"Excuse me, ladies. Could you tell me where I might find Raymon Tapia?"

The older girls were prepared to hold their silence, but one of the younger children pointed to a two-story yellow house that sat on a knoll some two hundred yards away. "He's up there."

"Thank you. I suppose he's home, is he?"

"Mr. Tapia is always home," the same girl blurted out. One of the older girls took her by the hand and the group moved away without further exchanges with the strangers.

As they drove up to the house, Chandler was somewhat relieved to see the quality of the residence he had picked, since he wasn't too keen on the thought of hobnobbing with shack dwellers. The eaves showed traces of the gingerbread trimming of the 1890s, but the place was in good repair.

They pulled up close to the front of the house. Arnold got out and held the back door of the car open for his client.

"Arnold, do you want to go up to the door with me?"

Arnold politely declined. "I think I best stay here with the hubcaps, sir."

Chandler nodded and mounted the steps alone, like a condemned man on his way to the gallows.

Chandler was sweating freely as he got to the porch, but he attributed it more to his nerves and drink than to the weather. He carried a packet of Sen-Sen for such occasions. He shook out two tiny squares, got them seated in each cheek, then cranked the bell that was built into the front door.

It wasn't until that moment that he noticed the small flag hanging in the front window. It displayed a white field trimmed with blue, and in the center of the white field was a five pointed gold star. The home of a serviceman killed in the war. This wasn't the smartest move in the world. He was just about to beat a hasty retreat when the door was swung open by a thin, middle-aged Mexican woman with an apron over her best black dress. Apparently he had interrupted her kitchen activities. The aroma of frying pork chops drifted out from behind her.

"Yes?"

"Hello. Is this the Ottavio Tapia residence?"

"Yes. This is the Tapia house."

"May I speak with Mr. Tapia, please?"

"What about?"

"I'm a friend of Charles McGrath." Since this did nothing for her, he went on. "I'm trying to find out some things about him and I was given to understand your husband would know him."

"You mean my father. What you want from him?"

Before he could think up an answer for this, they were interrupted by the father's voice rattling off a *Que pasa*-type thing in his native language. The daughter turned back into the house and answered him in kind. The only thing Chandler could pick out was the name McGrath, which seemed to set the old man off in an angry outburst. The daughter listened patiently for a moment, then turned back to Chandler.

"I don't think we can help you. My father is in no mood to talk about him."

"He does know him then? Please. It is quite important."

The woman scowled while she considered what to do next. "I have food cooking. Who are you?"

"My name is Raymond Chandler. I'm a writer at the same place where Mr. McGrath works."

At the mention of his name her expression changed. "You are Raymond Chandler?"

"Yes, that's right. . . ."

"The one who writes the detective stories?"

"Yes."

She turned back to the father and rattled more Spanish. Chandler was stunned to hear his own name and the name of his fictional detective mentioned in the midst of the gibberish. The father's voice grunted something and the daughter turned back to Chandler with a smile as the door opened wide for him.

He was ushered into the small parlor which looked more like lace-curtain Irish than Mexican. An ornate, dark mahogany platform rocker and settee sat proudly by the grilled fireplace. Doilies and antimacassars in all the right places. And, of course, the obligatory picture of Jesus, showing off His bleeding Valentine heart, watched quietly over the scene.

And next to a window sat Ottavio Tapia, a grizzled little old man, confined to a wheelchair, or what passed for a wheelchair—a homemade device combining a simple kitchen chair with the wheels of an ancient baby perambulator. The old man, in spite of his years, looked like he belonged on horseback, following a herd of cattle, rather than in a femininely appointed sitting room. His forehead was white, but his ears, cheeks and nose were almost the shade of roof tile. A straight shock of unruly steel grey hair twisted off to one side as if he had just taken off his sombrero. And his beard looked like it had been growing without interference for about three days. He waved a stoic greeting and pointed Chandler into a chair near his roll-about affair.

The daughter excused herself to attend to her kitchen problems leaving Chandler to try to make conversation with the old man. It took him about three sentences to figure out Mr. Tapia only spoke Spanish. The old man fumbled through a well-stuffed magazine rack next to him and came up with a small magazine that he wanted to share with his guest. It was a well-worn issue of *Black Mask* in Spanish. Chandler smiled and nodded. The old man found the right page and showed it to him again. Chandler finally figured out it was his short story of "The Lady in the Lake." He wanted Chandler to write his name on the first page.

Then he rolled himself over to a table and got down a faded picture of what looked to be three vaqueros on horseback in open Western country. The scene had some significance to the old man who rambled on and on about it, but its meaning totally escaped the gringo.

Finally the daughter came in and rescued Chandler. Father and daughter bickered briefly over the picture. The daughter didn't want to have the picture discussed, but the father kept pressing it at Chandler and pointing.

"You must excuse my father. He wants you to know the man on the left there is his father. And the one in the middle dressed as a man is Senora Maria Rita Valdez. You have heard of her?"

Chandler said he had not.

"The Valdez Ranchero?" she seemed amazed at his ignorance. "It was where Beverly Hills is now."

The old man nodded and pointed to the background. "Rodeo Drive. Rodeo Drive."

"His father," the daughter explained, "loaned Maria Rita

Valdez one hundred and fifty head of cattle so she could qualify for the Spanish land grant for the ranchero. It was a great event."

The old man nodded solemnly. Chandler tried to see what significance this all had to his problem. The daughter seemed to sense his confusion. "My father thinks writers should know about such things so they are not lost."

"Please tell your father that I'm not that kind of writer. That I only write fiction."

"Yes, but you know about the city. He puts great respect on the written word. And he says what you write about Los Angeles is on the mark."

"I am honored and I will keep that in mind."

The daughter gave a snort to register her doubts. "The other man who came to us said the same things."

"You mean McGrath said he was going to write a history about your father's past?"

"He said he would help us."

"Help you do what?"

"Help us with our problems. We have no bus service no more and now the county will no longer do the road work."

"The city bus line used to run a route up here?"

"Yes, all the time. Five buses a day. Then in February after the bad rain, the bus broke an axle. They tell us they don't run no more buses until the road is fixed. So we call the city. The city say we gotta call the county. It's a county road. But the county say if the bus don't run then they don't gotta fix the road. If the bus run, they fix it. So what we gonna do?"

"Excuse me," Chandler interrupted, "I think I'm missing something here. What was it that Charles McGrath was supposed to be doing on your behalf?"

The old man wanted to know what was going on, so she had to take time to bring him up to date before she could get back to Chandler's question. It was fine with Chandler. His brain seemed to be stuck in neutral and he needed the time to think. He had the upsetting feeling that all of this was supposed to be making sense, but he wasn't making the right connections. He tried to force his brain to the task.

He had trouble conceiving of Corky McGrath as a Good Samaritan. If what the daughter was saying was so, then there had to be another angle that Corky was playing. Maybe an exposé on some of the city fathers? Or a . . . or what? Chandler pinched his eyes to narrow slits and surveyed the bric-a-brac on the small mantel in an attempt to make his head work. He wished now he had laid off the bravery that comes in brown paper sacks. McGrath was trying to get hold of money, supposedly for an investment. How would that tie in . . .

The Spanish chatter was interrupted by the noise of heavy shoes bounding down the stairs in the hall. The three of them looked through the double doors to the hall in time to see the bottom part of two teenage boys hitting the stairs, three at a time, on their way to the front door.

"Michael," the lady of the house called, "Michael, how many times do I got to tell you about them steps?"

"Sorry, Mother," came the reluctant voice from the front door.

"We are sitting down to dinner in a few minutes. You aren't going no place now, young man."

"Aww, Mother."

"Come here. Come in here, let us see you."

With his head down, the thinner of the two boys came into the archway and waited for the rest of his lecture.

"Peppy, you still there?" the woman called.

The other boy called, "Yes'm."

"Come out here so we can see you."

The heavyset boy came in behind his friend. His eyes were down, too, at first, but then he looked up and spotted Chandler.

"*Caramba*," he groaned and poked his friend in the back. Michael looked up and saw Chandler, too, and drew the same startled reaction. Like two minds with a single thought, both boys disappeared and banged their way out the front door with Michael's mother protesting each step of the way.

"I apologize for my son," she said to Chandler once she had given up on getting them back. "I have no idea what's got into him."

Chandler smiled and cleared his throat in an attempt to change the topic. "Could you tell me about what it was that Mr. McGrath said he was doing on your behalf?"

"Well, he came to us—"

"You mean to Mr. Tapia?"

"Yes. Papa is like one of the fathers here in the Ravine. Many people come to him who want to know what it was like in the old days. Or for help with their problems."

"And McGrath just appeared on your doorstep one day?"

"I don't know . . . maybe somebody in the Ravine brought him to Papa."

"When was this?"

She barked the question to her father. He answered and she translated. "In February or March, he thinks."

"Three or four months ago," Chandler thought aloud. "What was it he wanted?"

"He came here saying he wanted to know how the area was settled. What the history was. Who owned what property and things like that. Then later, he started saying it might be possible that the city was going to take over our land. They can't do such things, can they?"

"There is such a thing as 'eminent domain,' I think it's called. The city could declare an area a slum. Or if the land was needed for the public good, they could take over property. It has been done. But they would have to pay you for the land. And it could only be done for an important cause."

"Even if you don't want to move? Can they do such things?"

"It has been done."

At this the old man started bellowing. He seemed to be understanding a good deal more than he was letting on. After his daughter soothed him a bit she said to Chandler, "He is still upset about the taxes the whites put on the rancheros. That is how they were lost. And now he is afraid they will even take this little place."

"Did McGrath tell you of this danger?"

"Yes, he did. He said it might happen, but we wouldn't believe him at first. Only if you don't pay your taxes. Finally he did persuade some of the men it could happen and Mr. McGrath started collecting signatures so we could defend ourselves in the court."

"Signatures? You mean a petition?"

"No, he called it something else. We would have to have an attorney to speak in the courts." Again she had to appeal for help from her father and the answer came back, "Power to the attorney."

"Power of attorney?" Chandler asked.

"Yes, I think that is how it goes."

"You mean McGrath asked the homeowners here to sign power of attorney letters?" He was speaking very slowly, trying to keep his voice level.

"Yes. That is it. You see, that is the only way we can all act together to protect ourselves."

"How many signed the letters?"

"Oh, several I know of . . . once Papa signed."

Chandler slumped in his chair, pushed his glasses up and rubbed his nose. "And McGrath . . . he told you to do this. I suppose he was arranging for the lawyer, too, right?"

"Yes, we don't know no white lawyers and you gotta have a white lawyer to do business in the white man's court. Papa learned that the hard way."

"Was anybody from the Ravine keeping track of McGrath?"

"Keeping track? He would come each day and talk with us. My son wanted to have him followed, but I put a stop to that idea. But now we have not heard or seen him for several days."

"I can imagine."

"Why you asking all the questions, Mr. Chandler?"

He looked into her eyes, wondering how much he should try to say. "I only wish your father's reading tastes had touched a bit on Anglo-Saxon jurisprudence."

"What is that?"

"It's a set of rules this town thinks it runs on. And if you are clever and quick, you can use those rules to steal from the people . . . who aren't so clever and quick."

"Like us, you mean?"

"Oh, I don't know what I mean. Maybe I'm talking out of turn here. Why did your father put so much faith in McGrath?"

"I think it was because he talked such good Spanish."

"I see. That's important, is it? To have a white friend who talks good Spanish?"

"You just try getting anything done in this town with a brown face. In City Hall we are Mexicans. With the bus company we are Mexicans." She studied the backs of her hands, as if they

143

were to blame for her problems. "Only at the draft board are we Americans."

The old man pointed a crooked finger at his own chest and nodded. "Yeah, yeah. *Americano.*"

She put one of her brown hands on the old man's arm. "*Si*, papa. *Americano.*

"What should we do then, do you think?" she asked Chandler.

"Now you are trusting me?"

"What else is there for us to do?"

"I've got problems of my own. Don't look at me. The race belongs to the swift. Get yourself a good lawyer . . ."

But the old man wasn't quite through with his lecture and interrupted Chandler with his last point. He spoke in a slow, carefully enunciated manner that gave Chandler a chance to catch some of his meaning. The daughter refused to translate, but it wasn't necessary. He wanted Chandler to know he was not only American, but there was Castilian *sangre* running in his veins. That he wasn't just your common ordinary field variety *indio.*

Chandler nodded and smiled. Then he laughed out loud. He laughed at himself, really. Laughed at his own naïveté, for what must have been about the one hundredth time. When he left England as a young man he had been under the impression he was leaving the class system behind. Its presence in a myriad of forms in democratic America never ceased to surprise him.

But his laughter was not interpreted that way in this Mexican household where pride was the only commodity held in abundance. Chandler's smile froze on his face when he looked at the offended daughter, whose expression had turned hard, right before his eyes. Her eyes were burning with enough heat to cook her pork chops. He had a very good idea who the kids on the road took their staring lessons from.

"You writers aren't any different from the rest, are you?" she said. "You only pretend to be feeling sorry for troubled people so people will buy your books."

"Look, I've got my own problems. The laughter was about something else—"

144

"Get out. Get out and leave us be. You think we need more grief?"

Chandler stood up and looked at the old man. He was still smiling his proud innocent smile. In a futile gesture to save something from an awkward situation, Chandler reached to shake his hand, but the daughter grabbed him and pushed his arm away from her father.

"And he don't need no more confusion in his life. His sorrow is enough for three lifetimes. Just leave him alone."

Chandler stood with his mouth open, looking at the injured woman and wishing he could start the whole conversation over. He knew nothing about the culture he had just insulted and decided this was not the time to expand his education. He turned on his heel and tried to leave with as much dignity as he could muster. Walking behind him a step, the daughter escorted him to the front door while the confused old man sat practicing his *que's*.

At the porch, Chandler turned. "I don't know what you were expecting of me," he started to say, but she got the door closed on him before he could finish. He headed toward the car; once out of the shade of the porch overhang he found the sun was so bright he had to close his eyes. He fumbled in his breast pocket for his clip-on dark glasses. They helped a little, but he was getting his headache back again. He squinted his way toward the car and was just about there when the boy, Michael, ran up to him out of nowhere. Arnold, who had been moving to open the car door, thought the boy meant him harm and started to intercede. But it quickly became apparent the boy only wanted to talk.

"What did you say to my mother?"

"About what?"

"About . . . you know."

Chandler didn't know, but quickly started to guess. "I didn't tell her anything about last night. What happened to your plump friend?"

"Oh, he had to go home. You want your eight dollars back? We just did it for a gag, you know. We didn't mean anything."

"Eight dollars? Keep it. I think you earned it."

"Oh yeah? Thanks."

"Tell me something. What were you boys looking for over at the studio yesterday?"

The boy's face washed to stonewall blank. It was a cool look, as if suddenly there was nobody home. He had a way to go if he was going to catch up with the intensity of mama. But maybe it was the look of a new generation. More detached. No emotions showing.

"What studio you talkin' 'bout, mister?"

"Ask your plump friend. He was there. Somebody spotted him."

He shrugged. "I dunno nothin' about no studio." His command of English was deteriorating as their talk progressed.

"Okay, Michael. If that's your story you stick with it. But don't be surprised if the police want to know what you were shadowing McGrath around for."

"Police? Forget it, man. I don't talk to no police."

"I'm with you, kid. I feel the—"

"You sic the cops on us, you be sorry, see."

"You want to tell me why you were following McGrath?"

"That's family business." He hitched up his pants and combed his fingers through the long hair above his ears. The motion seemed to suggest he was getting ready for action.

"Look, kid, I'm not your enemy."

"An' I ain't no goat. I look like a goat to you?"

"I'm trying very hard to be your friend."

"Sure. All our friends come up here in cars like this."

"Okay, Pancho, have it your way."

Chandler turned to get into his car and young Michael took the moment to give him a shove. It sent Chandler stumbling onto the floor of the back seat.

"Here, here now, none of this." Arnold, with his white palms showing, made an invisible barrier between the two to stop the physical stuff.

Michael's mother, who must have been watching the scene from behind her lace curtains, hit the porch. Her target was her son, but with her shrill outdoor voice she sprayed the entire area with machine gun Spanish. Michael displayed a decided lack of interest in his mother's tirade, as well as his Sunday pork chop dinner. He took off down the dusty little street and quickly lost himself behind the neighbor's patch of sweet corn.

Arnold reached in and helped his passenger up to a sitting position. "You be all right, sir?"

"Yes, I think so. Just a bit surprised is all."

Arnold brushed at some dust on his cuff. "We don't plan any more house calls up here, do we, sir?"

"No," Chandler laughed. "That one will hold us for awhile, thank you."

That news relieved Arnold. He quickly got behind the wheel of their gigantic catalyst of a car, swung it around, and headed back down the bumpy avenue.

Chandler pressed his left cheek against the backrest and turned to watch the Tapia house recede. Why, he wondered, had he laughed out of place like that? Why hadn't he sensed the situation? Him, the reserved English gentleman, stepping on all that pride. They had it by the bushel. They had a semi-truckload of pride and one gold star in the window, but none of it was going to buy them one minute in this man's world if someone else held the legal right to their dusty little plots.

What would Marlowe have done? The champion of the world's downtrodden. There's no point in pursuing the thought. He only took white men's cases. That's where the readers were. It was a rule: No Mexican clients and no Chinese murderers. Let 'em get their own detectives.

He had forgotten about the headache, but now in the bouncing hot car it started to come back. He reached for his sack and got the last two swigs out of the warm bottle. Nothing.

Still more kids on the road. Would they never stop? They were a prolific bunch, these Mexicans. That's better. Think of them as a group. Not as people with a gold star in the window. That got 'em at a better perspective.

He wondered who the star was for. The boy's father? Or an older brother? He wondered if they really had been the group at the studio. He wondered why the old man was so proud to be an *"Americano."* He wondered a lot of things.

He wondered if Corky McGrath and Clarence were beginning to taint the Jell-O.

17

Arnold got them back onto a paved road before he spoke again. "Where we bound for now, sir?"

"I have a strong suspicion it isn't glory." Chandler sighed and got out McGrath's address book and thumbed the pages absently. Too many names to try reaching them all. There had to be some rhyme or reason to this thing. Some way of finding out who wanted Corky out of the way bad enough to come to the studio and put a bullet in his head from close range. Could it reasonably have been the Mexican boys? There were enough of them at the studio to get the body hoisted into place in the cooler. And maybe they had motive for a revenge slaying if they'd found out Corky was double-crossing the Ravine people. But why, then, did they sit around outside his house that night? And why did they tail a perfect stranger and take him home after he got the bum's rush over at the old movie star's house?

Murder will out and justice must be done, Chandler had written once. It looked so neat and orderly on paper, as if that gave it a life and a truth all its own. He should have added:

assuming someone has the sense and the determination to bring it off. But this wasn't getting shoes for the kids, and Arnold was still waiting for directions.

"Head west on Beverly and I'll tell you where the hunt goes from there."

"Huntin'. Is that what we doin'?"

"Yes. Liquor stores. Sing out if you see a live one."

"This be Sunday, 'member."

"You are absolutely right. Blue laws. And the Chamber of Commerce claims this is a civilized town. Okay, let's press on to 315 Hobart. There is a perfectly good bottle of Four Roses on the kitchen sink there. There's no point in letting it go to waste."

When Chandler reached forward to hang up the intercom he spotted two large beetles climbing up the door panel to his left. He yelled and batted at them with his shoe, then stomped on the floor, trying to kill them before they could crawl under the seat or up his pants leg. Arnold pulled the car over and got out to see what the problem was.

"It's beetles," Chandler cried, still looking about on the floor. "Two big black beetles. We must have picked them up in that damn ravine."

"I don' see nothin'."

"They must have got out when you opened the door. They were monstrous."

While Chandler looked for beetles, Arnold looked at him out of the corner of his eye. "There ain't no beetles here. Can't you see that?"

"But there were. I swear it."

"Mister, you want I take you home?"

"No, I don't 'want you take me home.' Stop talking like that. I keep thinking I'm on an African safari and I forgot my pith helmet."

"Talkin' like what?"

"Never mind, never mind. I got a doozy of a headache."

"Why don' we get somethin' to eat? Ain't you hungry? I'm hungry."

"You're as bad an actor as my wife, you know that? 315 Hobart Avenue."

Chandler rubbed his tired eyes and tried to regroup. He

kept thinking he was missing something that should be obvious. Something a normal person could stumble over. But what was it? And why wasn't his investigation playing like his books? There was supposed to be progression, switches in suspects and story values. The complication of the case was supposed to change with each new revelation. Revelation? What revelation? He was still stuck at square one. Maybe there were more suspects now, but what was he supposed to be doing about it? Whose arm could he twist? How could he put the screws on two teenagers hiding in the corn patch? Or a faded movie star with a walled fortress around her? What was he supposed to do, stand down at her gate and yell tough biting Marlowe-isms up at her?

He came out of his troubled reverie when the car slowed down. "This be the Hobart place you mean?" Arnold asked.

"Yes, this is it. Pull up, will you?"

They rolled to a halt opposite McGrath's and sat watching the neighborhood for a minute. The sprinkler lady was giving the soaking treatment to the other side of her front lawn today. A group of children were playing a sidewalk game. Other than that, the place was quiet and Sunday-afternoon lazy. Chandler got out and strolled slowly across the pavement and toward the side door of the house, trying to whistle as he moved.

But the screen door was now locked and the kitchen window, which before had given him easy access to the key, was pushed down tightly and locked at the top. Chandler cupped his hands against the window screen and peered into the kitchen. The liquor bottles still sat neatly and silently on the sink, just as they had the night before. So near and yet so far. He felt panic start to creep up his back, like a skin rash on a spot you couldn't reach. He knew it was crazy, but he had the overpowering sense that the bottles were mocking him. Why did they sit there so proudly, gleaming so attractively? He threw all caution to the wind and started pounding on the door. Twice, then again. He put his ear hard against the frame, but could hear nothing but the children counting their sidewalk game points, and the lazy whirr of traffic on Third Street. The house itself was absolutely dead.

Who would have taken the trouble to lock up the place like this? Chandler looked around for signs of life, then noticed the garage at the back of the house. Wasn't it standing open yesterday? He walked back and pressed his face against the crack between the two big doors. When his eyes adjusted to the dark, he could make out the shape of McGrath's Model B coupe. Home from the wars, as if nothing unusual had happened.

Chandler frowned and pulled on his ear lobe, like Humphrey Bogart in *The Maltese Falcon*. Had he left a bottle under the seat or hadn't he? It was worth a look-see. He undid the wooden peg that was holding the door latch closed and pulled the garage doors open so he could see what he was doing. He found nothing under the seat. But he was almost positive he had put a bottle under there. No, it must have been in that ambulance they had borrowed. Or was it some other kind of truck? Not an ambulance, but something like it.

He checked the glove compartment and came up empty. Just some old sun glasses with a cracked lens, a *Herald Express* press pass for the windshield, and a fairly new road map for the City of Angels. What the heck, McGrath wouldn't be having any need of a road map where he was, and Chandler could always use an updated copy. He put it in his hip pocket, closed things up, and started back toward the limo on legs that had suddenly turned rubbery.

His brain seemed to be turning itself off in sections. Right now it was night-night time for the motor functions of his extremities. The only way they would operate in a halfway decent manner was to keep a close eye on them. Unfortunately this did nothing good for his sense of balance. He finally solved the dilemma by bobbing his head up and down, first looking at his feet and then the horizon. He needed all of the driveway and a good wide section of the street, but he was finally able to weave his way safely back to the car.

"You better take me home, Arnold. I can't think straight anymore."

In spite of Arnold's helping hand, Chandler stumbled into the back seat and lay with his head on the seat cushion. In a matter of seconds the exhausted knight was dead to the world.

H e was in precisely the same position when he awoke to the pinch of Arnold's meaty hand on his shoulder, shaking him awake. "Boss. Hey, boss, wake up."

"Huh?" He sat up and tried to straighten his glasses, but they wouldn't stay straightened.

"You know anybody drives a black '39 Buick?" Arnold asked softly, almost fearfully. He was halfway in the back door getting his passenger into an upright position and a semi-functioning condition. Nervous, he repeated his question. "You hear? A black '39 Buick?"

"No. Not anyone who comes immediately to mind. Why?"

"Somebody sure be stayin' close to us."

Chandler turned his aching head as best he could to look out the back window. "Why, we aren't moving, are we?"

"Course we ain't movin'. How you 'spect I be back here an' drivin' too?"

"Well how can they be following us if we aren't moving?"

"I means they turn off a piece back."

"Could you recognize anyone in the car?"

"I don' think so. They stay back a ways. I slow down, they slow down. I speed up, they do the same."

"How many in the car?"

"Maybe two. Maybe just a driver. I can't be sure."

"Well, they're gone now. How much farther to my house?"

Arnold smiled. "We's here now. You want I hep you up them steps?"

"You're a good man, Arnold. Whatever they're paying you, it's too much."

"Yes, sir." Arnold chuckled and started their dismount procedures. He apparently had had a good deal of experience with inebriates. Once they were clear of the car he got Chandler's arm up over his shoulder and with something of a rolling stroll walked him up the path, just slow enough and rhythmic enough to let Chandler's legs freely swing forward with his body weight.

Cissy must have been watching for them because she had the front door open before they got to it. Arnold walked him right in and got him leaning against the archway between the living room and the front hall.

"You be needin' me again today, sir?"

"Check with me in an hour." Chandler smiled.

Arnold waited for Cissy to get a hand on his charge, then touched the bill of his cap and exited, closing the door after himself. At the sound of the latch catching, Chandler fell on Cissy's neck in a tired embrace.

"Oh, it's so good to be home. Cissy, speak some English to me will you?"

"What do you want me to say?"

"Anything at all. Tell me about your childhood. I'm so sick of the present tense I could scream. I think I actually would scream, but I'm afraid my head would come loose. Would you be a good girl and get me the aspirin bottle?"

While she was doing that, Chandler aimed himself toward the liquor cabinet in the dining room. His choices of poison were getting slim. He would soon be down to Cissy's decanter of rosé which she usually kept on the end table simply for its color. He took the Jack Daniels bottle with four inches showing and looked for a glass, but Cissy got back before he could unearth one. She had the Bayer bottle in one hand and a good-sized tumbler full of water in the other.

"Not so much water. You want to drown me."

"The aspirin won't work if you are drinking, you know."

"It will if you take enough of 'em."

He shook out five and popped them into his mouth before she could object. He took three gulps of the water, sat down at the table, and pointed to his neck. She came up behind and slowly started working his back muscles with her educated fingers. He was soon groaning in appreciation.

"You know how I frequently have Marlowe get beat up or shot at by his adversaries?" he groaned.

"Yes . . ."

"I'm not going to do that so much anymore."

"I thought you told me your readers expected a little mayhem."

"They're a bunch of sadists. To hell with 'em. Maybe Marlowe is only fiction, but I like him too much to put him through all that agony."

"Yes, dear."

"Besides, he's getting too old."

"He is? I wasn't aware that he was aging."

"Yes, he's old. He's very, very old."

"I take it you haven't had a very good day. Would you like to know what I've been up to?"

There had been just the slightest hint of an edge in Cissy's voice and he was about to find out the cause, whether he liked it or not. He'd try to delay the inevitable a little longer. "Only if it's good."

"I had a call from a voice I thought I recognized. She left a message for you."

Chandler rolled his eyes back in his head, trying to think if Cissy had ever talked to Francine. Something about a bent fender and an unpaid hotel bill seemed to stick in his mind. Then he saw an image of Cissy standing in the outer office of Dabney Oil looking over the secretarial pool for a pair of guilty eyes. The rest was too gory to recall and he forced his eyes back open.

Cissy stopped her rubbing with an extra little pinch that didn't feel appropriate to the occasion. Then she retrieved the message pad from the phone table and with a cavalier toss dropped the pad in front of him. Chandler was afraid of what it might be. He turned his head away and put a shielding hand up to his glasses as if he were adjusting them. But out of the corner of his eye he read the note. He felt it was a subtle sophisticated move. About as subtle and sophisticated as an elephant raiding a jellybean jar.

The note read: "The title of the film you asked me about is *Post-War Los Angeles: The Bridge to the Future.* I remembered it when I saw an ad in the *Times.* It's playing around town."

"I can't read it now," Chandler claimed. "My eyes don't focus so well."

"You want to go see a film tonight? With your little friend?"

"Film? What film? Only if it has a happy ending. You were right about happy endings, my dear. I'm building up a terrific aversion to tragedy. Oh, let me lie me down and bleed a while. Th⌐ ⌐ I'll rise and fight some more."

He tried cutting the unpleasant topic short by heading toward his bedroom. Cissy caught him by the arm and steered him toward the bathroom instead.

"I was wondering what it was that started your drinking again."

"Oh, Cissy, please . . ."

"Good old Cissy, left to clean up the mess."

"My heart is a pure . . . can't you see, I'm defenseless. Would you shoot an unarmed man?"

In silence she backed him up to the toilet and unbuckled his belt for him. He seemed to catch on to the idea and she left him to himself, but left the door open enough so she could still talk to him. She pulled up the phone stool in the hall and sat down.

"You didn't tell me William Faulkner was one of the writers that Warner Brothers had working on *The Big Sleep.*"

"The Duke of Oxford? I didn't know he was still out here slumming. Why isn't he back in Mississippi writing more obtuse Southern novels for those eleven faithful readers of his?"

"Very cute. Do you want to hear this or don't you?"

"Not particularly."

"Well, he called here pleading to talk to you about the book. Are you listening?"

"Aren't you forgetting our more pressing problem?"

"It won't hurt you to give them five minutes of your time."

Cissy heard a suspicious sound that made her look over at the dining room table. The Jack Daniels bottle was missing. Somehow, Chandler had gotten it into the bathroom and was guzzling from it.

"You're going to kill yourself, you realize."

"Good. That means I'll save the state the trouble."

Next she heard the flush of the toilet, which was followed almost immediately by the sound of a bottle smashing on the porcelain bathroom floor.

"Oh, damn," he whimpered in a falsetto.

She went in to find her husband with his trousers and shorts down around his ankles trying to bend over to pick up the pieces of the smashed bottle, perhaps in hopes of putting it back together again.

"Never mind. I'll tend to that," she cried.

"But I hardly got started. All that good liquor . . ." He was starting to fall apart over his great loss.

She finally got him to step out of his pants and to move toward the bedroom without stepping on any major pieces of glass.

"Oh, Cissy, I'm sorry. I'm such a no good . . . Why do you put up with me? I'm such a totally useless human being."

Cissy's excitement and the exertion she was under was getting to be too much; she had to let out two throaty coughs.

"Don't cough," he groaned. "Oh God, don't cough. I can't stand it. Don't you know what that does to me? I don't care a farthing for that girl. I'll never leave you, darling. Never. If only I can prove worthy of your love. . . ."

He had nearly played out his entire repertoire of emotional extremes now. Almost full circle. It was time for a nap, if the beetles would only stay away until he got to sleep.

Through the whines, Cissy got him into the bedroom but barely out of his coat and tie when the phone started ringing.

"I'll bet that's your Warner Brothers people. Can you manage your pajama bottoms by yourself?"

He ardently promised he could. She got the phone on the fourth ring and, after a couple of quick words, was back in the bedroom, extending the phone cord to its maximum, which was the foot of his bed. "Here, it's for you," she whispered.

Chandler had gotten into his pajama bottoms backwards, which was causing him no end of grief. "My strings. What has transpired with my strings?" he whined.

"Never mind that now. I think it's your Warner Brothers call. Can you sound a little more . . . you know?"

"Of course. I'll give 'em my Ronald Colman." He took the phone and cleared his throat. "Hello, this is Ronald Chandler speaking . . . Raymond Chandler speaking."

There was a moment of heavy breathing, then a coarse muffled voice announced, "Too bad for you, Chandler." Whoever it was hung up and Chandler was left looking quizzically at the receiver.

"Bill Faulkner couldn't have heard what I said about him, could he?"

"What's the matter? What was it?"

There was a desperation in her tone now that he didn't like. As if she were nearing her emotional limit.

"Oh, just a wrong number I guess." He shrugged. "Crazy phone company. You can't get any kind of decent service these days . . . I think there's a war on or something."

She got him to lie down and gently started rubbing his shoulders. Usually that did the trick, but the phone call still troubled him. It had frightened him enough to stir some last vestige of reality and he couldn't shake it.

"Too bad for you, Chandler." A nice smooth statement. Not overplayed at all. Just sinister enough to have the ring of truth as a threat. But was that all? What about the words themselves? There was something stagey about it. Maybe too much the Warner Brothers' gangster kind of talk. Maybe he had heard it too often at the movies. That was it. He *had* heard it before, and it wasn't at the movies.

His muscles tightened and he started to sit up, but Cissy

was still there and got him to lie down again. She had started her light girlish chatter, something about a trip they had taken years ago, to the Pacific Northwest. Why was she going on about that now?

But he hardly heard a word she was saying. The vivid sound of the caller was still with him.

It finally rang a bell.

In one of his stories—right now he couldn't remember which one—the suspense tension was beginning to lag a bit, so he had his villain of the piece call up Marlowe and issue an anonymous threat. Everything but the last name was right. It should have been "Too bad for you, Marlowe."

Someone was threatening him with lines from his own stuff.

19

During the years when Chandler was struggling with his writing style, and with his drinking, he had fallen into a convenient habit of napping. But the naps were far from harmless afternoon snoozes. They were an integral part of his creative process. When he faced the writer's brick wall or the block, or whatever they called it then, he would drink himself into a condition that would require rest. Frequently, especially in the very earliest days, this routine would bear precious fruit. When he awoke and faced the glaring empty page again, the Gordian knot would be loosed and the ideas would flow freely.

And there were a few golden times when he awoke to find his pages had been extended miraculously, with words that clicked. Even words that sang, far in excess of what he thought he was capable of doing, but he retained no memory of having written them. The first time it happened he had accused Cissy of having a hand in it. But she had insisted he had done the work himself and then gone back to sleep. It was like writing without the writer's agony. Without paying the price.

He was convinced that somehow the drinking had imbued him with a special boost of creative energy which would not otherwise have been there, and the secret ritual began to take on the mantle of something resembling a spiritual dependency.

Then, as time passed, he found his tricks no longer worked. Nonsense began appearing where the magic had been before. Spilled drinks and torn clothing and strange bruises became his frequent visitors. And the story lines, the damned incessant story lines, kept demanding more and more of his fragile attention.

He and Cissy had run through his meager savings from the oil business and were in the process of doing serious damage to Cissy's small estate when the months of panic set in. The short stories were well received, but it was all too evident the income he could hope to generate from them was simply not enough to keep their household together.

Out of necessity he had taken three major steps. He decided the only way of making a decent living from his writing was to begin writing novels. And, since he had his major difficulties coming up with story lines, he began cannibalizing plots from his earliest short stories. "Curtain" and "Killer in the Rain" were blended together to make *The Big Sleep*. *Farewell, My Lovely* had its roots in "The Man Who Liked Dogs," "Try the Girl," and "Mandarin's Jade."

But the third step was probably the most crucial to his success as a writer. He decided to go on the wagon. If he was going to sustain a story line for a full-length book, he felt he would have to be at his most analytical. So the energetic plots from his earlier days were labored over on a clear-eyed regimen of work, day in and day out. His early training in the classics began exerting its influence in his style as the pages were written and sifted. Rewritten and resifted, again and again, until the quality of the work began to rise above the genre.

But all that was just a nice page in literary history now. Now he had his back to the wall in a different way and was hoping to pull one more chestnut out of the fire by relying on his old afternoon nap routine. He couldn't get over the nagging sense that there was something he wasn't seeing about the whole mess. There had to be something lurking there in his subconscious that could be kicked loose by the booze and a bit of shut-eye. One more trick left in the ol' magic bottle.

When he awoke it was going on five o'clock. He had a sense of having dreamt and quickly closed his eyes and tried to remember what it was about. Perhaps the missing "chestnut" was in the dream. The residue began drifting back his way. He was at the studio again. In the publicity department with its desks and work tables covered with eight-by-ten glossies and press releases and TWXs from New York. Only now there was also a large stainless steel sink in the midst of the disarray. It looked like the sink in the commissary that he had been sick in. Lyle Palmer was standing over the sink in his shirt sleeves, peeling onions. And at his elbow stood Corky McGrath, trying to take the peeling implement away from Palmer. "Let me do that. I can do that. I know how to do that," he kept pestering. But Palmer was wiping at his onion-induced tears and elbowing McGrath away. "You're not ready for the big time, kid. You'd do anything to get ahead, wouldn't you, but you aren't ready for the big time, kid."

Finally McGrath muscled control of the peeler from Palmer and started working on the onions with enthusiasm, dropping large crocodile tears in the process. Only now, as he flaked away, the brown husks of the big onions fell into the bottom of the sink and immediately turned themselves into large black beetles and started scampering up the sides of the stainless steel sink.

Chandler let out a yell and jerked awake again. Then he checked his bed covers for more beetles. They weren't there yet. He heaved a sigh of relief and put his head back down on his pillow. So much for his bright idea of a dream opening up his subconscious.

The bed moved slightly and his eyes refocused. Only then did it dawn on him that Cissy was sitting on the foot of his bed, quietly watching him.

"You have a dream?"

"No. A nightmare."

"You're not seeing the flying ants again, are you?"

"Don't be silly. I haven't had that much to drink."

She sighed and absently rolled up one end of the tie of her

pink housecoat, then let it fall again. Like a little girl, Chandler thought, waiting for her piano lesson. Was it his imagination, or was she moving a bit away from reality? It wasn't the first time he had sensed it. It always seemed to happen when she was extra tired or under some emotional strain. He still held the mental picture of Cissy sitting in her wicker chair in the living room, playing with the hem of her dress, when the Broadway people came to pick up the new radio they couldn't make the payments on, back in '37. What would she be doing if he weren't there at all?

"Your driver is back out front," she said. "Shall I tell him you won't be needing him again today?"

"Wait a minute." He swung his feet onto the floor to see what the world was like if his head was above his body. The screeching mynah birds from the attic had moved outside and were chirping in a waterfall someplace, but otherwise everything seemed to be about as he had left it. He reached for his glasses and got them on his nose. For Cissy's sake he tried to pretend they weren't bent cockeyed.

"Why does Marlowe always seem to know what to do next?" he asked of the bottom drawer of his dresser.

"I don't want you going out anymore today," Cissy whined.

"Where would I go? What would I do?"

"Fine. I'll tell him."

"No, wait. That's a rhetorical question. I'm thinking. There must be something. McGrath worked on a documentary film about Los Angeles. And he was in the process of getting power of attorney rights away from the Mexicans up in Chavez Ravine . . . to do what? He must have found out what the city fathers were planning and . . . was trying to play his own game. . . ."

"You look terrible." Cissy pushed back his hair to look more closely at his eyes. "I want you home, here with me. I never should have let you go out. It's my fault you drink, isn't it?"

He gently put her head on his shoulder and held her. Primarily to stop the words. He whined at her at certain stages when he was drunk and she whined at him when she was tired and in the mood to. But right now he couldn't take the words.

She cried for a minute. As much as her lungs would allow without backing up on her. Then she pushed herself away from him and wiped her face with a bit of tissue from her pocket.

"Where did you get the map?" she asked.

"What map?"

"This map of the city. It was in your coat pocket." She reached over to the dresser and got it for him.

He looked at it in amazement. "My coat pocket?" Maybe the nap thing was magical after all. He unfolded it and spread it on the bed. It was a standard road map of the greater Los Angeles basin. The kind they give away in service stations. But there were some markings on this one. In the vicinity of where Chavez Ravine must be, someone had penciled in a square, or perhaps a three dimensional representation of a building, and then, with a different kind of marker, the square had been crossed out.

The second marker, probably a fountain pen Chandler guessed, had also made extensive markings in the area of the San Fernando Valley. They were lines similar to a branch of a tree, with the main trunk of the tree angling off to the west, through a pass in the Hollywood hills, and ending up near the beach in Santa Monica. At Santa Monica and in two other spots through the hills, squares had also been drawn in.

"What is that supposed to represent?" Cissy asked.

"I haven't the foggiest idea. It looks like a twisted tree."

Chandler turned the map around to look at it from a different angle, but nothing made the markings any clearer. Then, when he was turning it the right way again, Cissy caught his arm.

"What's that by the street listings?"

Chandler angled his glasses on his nose so they magnified more than usual and pulled the corner of the map closer. There were two names he didn't recognize and the words "Saboba Boosters" written in pencil.

"Saboba Boosters," Chandler repeated aloud and reached for McGrath's telephone book, which was on his dresser. He found the listing under S and tapped it like a gold miner on a strike. "I knew I'd seen that somewhere before."

"Seen what? What does it mean?" Cissy whispered.

But Chandler didn't answer. He was already on his way to the phone. He dialed the downtown number from the book and waited with his breath stopped. After three rings, the voice of a young man answered. "Hallo."

"Hello, ah, is this the Saboba Boosters' number?"

"Yes, it is. What can I do for you?"

"I'm not sure," Chandler fumbled. "What kind of a . . . group are you?"

"Look, I'm just on my way out. The regular people aren't here. Can you call back tomorrow after nine?"

"No, wait, wait. This is important. This is Mr. Chandler calling and I need to know about—"

"Oh yes, Mr. Chandler. I didn't know it was you."

"You know me?"

"Certainly, sir," the young man laughed. "I just didn't recognize your voice, is all. What can I do for you? This is Barnie, sir. We just came by to get the horse for the meeting tonight. Otherwise there's nobody here."

"Horse for the meeting? What meeting?"

"Our regular meeting, sir."

"Where is that?"

"Oh, I bet you never got the room change, did you, sir. They had to switch us to the Crystal Room because the military brass is taking over the Catalina Room. They're expecting some news about the surrender in Europe any minute and they got the room reserved for three nights running."

"So we're in the Crystal Room? What hotel is that again?"

The young man laughed again. "The same hotel, sir."

"Yes, I know, but tell me the name again."

"The same old place, sir. The Biltmore, downtown."

"And we're meeting at eight, as usual?"

"Cocktails at seven. We're going to try to start the dinner at quarter to. We got a busy program, as you well know."

"Thank you, Barnie. Now don't forget the horse."

The young man laughed again. "Ah, right, sir. I won't."

The phone call had Chandler so confused it took him three passes to get the receiver hung up right.

"Whoever that was, he seemed to know me," he marveled.

Cissy was right behind him with his slippers. "Maybe you met him while you were . . . tipsy."

He shook his head in confusion. "But I'm supposed to know something about a dinner tonight at the Biltmore Hotel . . . how could I forget about that . . . ?"

164

"What was that about a horse?"

He only shook his head a little more after her question. He wasn't about to tell her that "horse" was a gangland euphemism for cut heroin. But was that possible? A dope party, out in the open in one of the biggest hotels? And he was supposed to know about it? It had to be something else.

"Is my good suit in shape to wear?"

"So. You're going to the movies after all? You're not even asking me, is that it?"

"I'm going to the dinner party. What movie are you talking about?"

Cissy rolled her eyes and retrieved the note she'd shown him earlier. "And don't bother pretending you didn't read it."

He didn't remember if he had, but he read it now. Then it came back to him. Francine must have called the message in and Cissy recognized her voice. Oh dear. Forgetting things because of the drinking had its occasional benefits. But more often it had its drawbacks. Especially when you had to remember things twice.

She shook her head wildly, as if to say she was giving up. "Oh Raymio," she whined and put her tired head on his shoulder. It weighed a ton.

Cissy had been his tower of strength up until now. And his anchor to clear logical reasoning. But the worry and pressure must have gotten to her. In the old oil days, Cissy's extra-sensitive jealousy antennae had put two and two together. Without the aid of a blueprint, she had sensed when the affair had started, and when it had stopped. But now she wasn't so sure. And with each passing day she could sense her ammunition for defense of the homefront was dwindling. Perhaps that explained her mental drifting. Her inability to stick to the real problem at hand.

"Would you lay out my suit, dear?" he asked. "I want to wash my face and shave."

"Please don't go out again. Please. For me."

He wished she wouldn't hang on him that way. It gave him a feeling of drowning in a vat of pink perfume. He disengaged her arm and kissed her finger tips. "Dear, we've only got a few more hours before the commissary kitchen crew starts their Monday morning chores."

Cissy drew in her breath and clenched a knuckle between her teeth, Theda Bara style, as if this was the first she had heard of it. "Oh, yes, of course. You have to, don't you. How silly of me."

While she dutifully laid out his suit, Chandler got his large hip flask out of the dining room buffet and poured what he could of the rosé from the decanter into it, then hid it in the afternoon edition of the paper. Fifteen minutes later, when he was dressed and ready for one more go at the outside world, he kissed his wife good-bye and casually picked up the newspaper on his way out of the house.

20

Arnold was at his post behind the steering wheel and appeared to be sleeping beneath his cap when Chandler got into the back seat. With the movement of the car he roused himself and adjusted the mirror to look at his client.

"Where to now, boss?"

"I think it's time we took in some sea breezes. Let's see what the weather is like in Santa Monica."

"An what about our fren in the Buick?"

"Full speed ahead, Arnold, and damn the Buick."

Arnold only shook his head, Stepin Fetchit style, and turned the big eight-cylinder engine over. "Santa Monica, it is."

Once out of sight of his house, Chandler got out the flask, popped it open, then closed his eyes with a grimace in order to down the first slug of the stuff. It wasn't as sweet as he had expected, but then there wasn't much hope of a kick in it either. He turned the newspaper over to the section listing the local films and looked for an ad that listed short subjects as well as features. Finally he found what he was looking for—the same

167

Wiltern Theatre they had passed earlier in the day was running the Los Angeles promotional film. If they got down to the beach and back in forty-five minutes, he'd have time to see what it was all about. He took another swig from the flask and leaned back, eyes closed, to await its effect. The wine's warmth started to penetrate his midsection as he tried to tell himself he was enjoying it.

Wilshire Boulevard didn't travel as fast as it used to. Not like the old days when the barley fields stretched all the way from Western Avenue to the ocean. Just a few farm patches left now. Where would all the farmers go when the stucco and asphalt sellers were finished with their dirty work? And why was he so sleepy when he'd just finished a nap? If he could only rest his head on the back rest for a minute . . .

"We's here, boss."

"Here? Where's here?"

"We's at the beach in Santa Monica. That be what you lookin' at. Where we go from here?"

"Is there a train going by?"

"No, sir. That be the surf rollin' in. We's got two choices. You wanna go north or you wanna go south? This be as far as we gonna go west."

Chandler rubbed at his bloodshot eyes and got out his trusty road map. "I think we should go north from here, Arnold, if I'm reading this thing correctly."

They rolled slowly up the coast highway, a chain of ugly palms on the left and sandstone bluffs on the right. The dusty sky had washed the color variety out of the bluffs so they looked like tinted monotone scenes from a black and white movie. Was there ever a real green color in the world or had he just imagined it? Someone had told Chandler the strange twilights were all caused by dust in the upper atmosphere. Something about too many bombs going off in the world.

When they came to the first canyon that looked like it ran inland for a distance, Chandler had Arnold pull the car into the empty parking lot on the ocean side of the road. Chandler got out and tested his legs for sobriety. Then he looked back into the canyon as far as he could. Arnold got out, too, and walked over to him.

"What we lookin' for now?"

"According to this map there's supposed to be a big building or something along here." Chandler looked around and scratched at his scalp. "Say, this is still Sunday, isn't it? Why aren't there any beach-goers along this stretch of sand? Don't they still build bonfires and roast marshmallows in the evenings?"

Arnold shrugged. "You askin' the wrong party. Beach sittin's a white man's game."

The lines on the map had ended at the ocean's edge so Chandler decided to carry his query to the limit. After plowing through several yards of loose sand he came to the hard, smooth wet stretch of shoreline the outgoing tide had left behind. Still nothing either north or south, except empty sand and an occasional broken seashell. The walking was easy now so he decided to stroll on farther to the north. Arnold had been holding back by the car but now Chandler waved for him to come along. He pressed his large body into the trek and soon fell in beside Chandler—huffing and puffing.

"We ain't grunion huntin' is we? Tide's almost low enough for it."

"What's a grunion?" Chandler asked.

"Little fishes that come up at some low tides an' plants they eggs in the sand."

"No. I'm looking for the end of a tree trunk."

Arnold looked hard at him. "Well, okay, why not? We ain't done nothin' too usual so far. I guess we don' need to start now. Any pa'tic'ler kind a tree?"

"Yes. The kind that mayors and city councilmen like to keep hidden from the voters."

"What kind a tree might that—" Arnold stopped in midquestion and sniffed at the air. "Do you smell anythin' p'culiar like?"

"I don't smell too well when I'm on the sauce."

They walked on for another two hundred yards, until Arnold stopped. "Sir, I'm beginnin' to think this ain't such a good idea."

"Oh, look at the little white things buried in the sand," Chandler called. "Are they grunion?"

"No, sir. They ain't grunion."

Chandler was fascinated by the loops of little white worm-like objects that stuck out of the smooth wet sand. There seemed to be hundreds of them stretching on ahead. He bent down to examine one. "Why, they're rubbery. What are they, do you know?"

"Yes, sir. They's baby stoppers."

"Baby stoppers? What kind of fish is that?"

"They ain't fish, man. They's used rubbers. You know. For havin' sex with."

Chandler stood up, wiped his hands on his good pants and started backing away from the wet shore line. His foot caught on a bit of slimy kelp and he fell down on his buttocks for a split second before scrambling back up on his feet. In spite of his drinking, he could smell it now, too. He was a slow learner but he had finally gotten the drift. The burgeoning city of Los Angeles was dumping raw sewage from the Valley into Santa Monica Bay.

$\mathcal{A}$t long last, he felt he had something to go on. He had little hope of uncovering the real culprits at this late date, especially since it would probably involve city officials, but at least he would be able to point the police in another direction when they came calling on him. The thing to do in the few hours remaining was to get as much background material together as he could.

When they got to Los Angeles and the Wiltern Theatre, Chandler discovered he had nearly drained the flask. His drinking it must have been a knee-jerk nervous reaction to the situation, because the flat wine wasn't doing anything for him. He had started belching up the taste of sour wine so he popped two Sen-Sen in his mouth, then asked Arnold if he wanted to come into the movie house with him.

At Arnold's request, they sat in the balcony of the crowded theatre. They had just gotten themselves seated when the title of the film short came on the screen: *Post-War Los Angeles: The Bridge to the Future.* Long, low groans could be heard throughout the theatre. The people had come to laugh at the feature and not be educated about the glorious future of Greater Los Angeles. It was a Paramount production all right; Chandler recognized the background music from the studio's canned library. And Corky McGrath's name was seen along with several other contributors during the short list of credits.

And then the film began. First came a short, colorful history of the City of Angels. Starting as a dusty little Indian village called Yang-na, the area changed little until the great Spanish migration and the establishment of the large rancheros. But even this was merely a preamble to the real story, which was the filmmaker's way of saying that nothing of import happened in the area until the railroad and the Protestants arrived.

The gist of the narration was that Los Angeles had met the test of greatness by producing war materials at a record pace, contributing in no small measure to the impending Allied victories, and now it was the City's destiny to take its rightful place beside such illustrious eastern cities as New York, Chicago, and Philadelphia. Interspersed with this palaver were pictures of Eastern big league baseball games in action and packed Eastern stadiums watching football teams running up and down the field. Apparently the true test of a city's greatness was to be measured by participation in athletic events. Or maybe by the size of the crowds at such events. The film left the viewer confused at this point.

Next came the promise of a city on wheels. Because of the great geographical size of the area, it was necessary to create a transportation system that would accommodate the growing needs of industry and the population in general. A special type of super road was already being planned that would allow cars to travel all the way from Los Angeles to Pasadena without the hindrance of a stop sign or red light for the entire distance. And this was just the beginning. The old would have to give way to the new as Los Angeles, the Citadel on the rim of the great Pacific Basin, fulfilled its destiny of a brilliant future.

Beauty shot of City Hall, camera tilted. Shots of smiling faces. Asian, Mexican, and white. Music up to a crescendo and "The End."

The whole effect of the big finish the filmmakers had worked so hard to achieve was ruined when only a handful of people out of the large crowd of theatregoers applauded halfheartedly. A moment later when Betty Grable's title card hit the screen the entire thing was forgotten.

Except in the mind of a confused bespectacled spectator in the balcony. As he and Arnold made their way toward the exit, Chandler began to have second thoughts about his land-swindle theory. About the most sinister secret McGrath could have known would be something about a new sewer bond for the fast growing city.

Back on the street, Arnold asked, "You likes to go to the movies just to see the shorts?"

Chandler smiled, then asked, "What did you think of the film about Los Angeles?"

Arnold shrugged his massive shoulders. "What is there to think?"

"Don't you buy this business about a grand and glorious future for our city?"

"We had us a big talker back in Looziana, too. When the King Fish talk 'bout buildin' stuff it gen'ly mean slum clear'nce. An' guess who be livin' in the slums he be clearin'?"

"Ah, yes. I see your point."

"Course maybe they build 'nuf roads, we all get jobs drivin' white folks about."

"Do I detect a note of bitterness in your voice, Arnold?"

"What do you think?"

Chandler jerked his head upright and stared at his driver. The Negro had crossed the invisible line. He had gone from being the good natured helpful servant to something else Chandler wasn't ready for. Arnold had gotten uppity.

Arnold walked ahead to open the limo's back door, but Chandler's movements had suddenly turned quite jerky. Sitting in the hot theatre, then walking down the balcony stairs had done something strange to his legs. He had gotten the shakes only once before and had ended up in the hospital that time. After taking a couple of spastic steps sideways, he finally had to reach out for help. Arnold came over and gently guided him into the safety of the back seat.

Chandler felt about for the flask and fumbled for the last few drops. There wasn't enough to soothe an ant. But he was damned well determined he was not going to ask Arnold to look for a booze source among his Negro friends.

He put his arms around himself and squeezed. That seemed to help, because the shaking started to fade.

"What time is it, Arnold?"

Arnold looked at the dash clock. "It be jes about eight o'clock, sir."

"Take me to the Biltmore, downtown, please."

Arnold looked him over, as much to say, you ain't in condition to go into no hotel, but ended up obediently nodding.

"And you'd better give me the hand gun, now." When Arnold hesitated, Chandler snapped, "Come on. I paid for it."

Arnold reluctantly got out the old automatic and handed it to Chandler.

Chandler snatched the gun and plopped it on the seat beside him. "Let's get going. I'm late."

They drove in silence down Wilshire for several blocks. Then without warning, Arnold started to speed up. He switched lanes several times, dodging in and out between cars and finally darted through a stoplight well after it had turned red. Chandler at first thought he would ignore these shenanigans, but then they swerved off south onto a side street. By the time Chandler had gotten his shaky hands on the communication tube, they were approaching Olympic Boulevard.

"What the devil do you think you're doing, Arnold?" he bellowed.

Arnold swung east on Olympic and checked both his mirrors before answering. "I think we ditched 'em, Mr. Chandler."

"Ditched who? What the hell are you talking about?"

"The Buick, what's been following us."

Chandler got his obstreperous body turned about so he could look out the back window. The sickly pink western sky had turned to blazing magenta now, and it forced Chandler to think of the time he got sick on maraschino cherries in his cocktails. The glare was coming from everywhere. The street, the office buildings lining the street, the hoods and grillwork of the cars bobbing along behind them. The world wasn't real anymore. The sky was too high and the air was too thin. And the nerve endings in his body were too close to the surface.

Freedom. That was the problem, he decided. There was too much freedom in the atmosphere here to keep an English schoolboy in his place. He rolled up the window to minimize the risk of his body floating out of the car and dissolving in the cloudless haze like so much cotton candy. Then he wrapped himself in his arms again to gather a bit of warmth.

Chandler looked at the seat next to him. Was there somebody there, or was it a figment of his strained imagination? Then the image made a move on his own. Just a slow headshake to signify his disgust.

"Look, I'm doing the best I can," Chandler whined. "Where have you been? I need you. What am I supposed to do with these big people at the Biltmore? What's the answer?"

But his detective only shook his head with a great sadness, as if he alone understood nobility. As if he were the perpetually crucified redeemer of all men's sins.

"Is that all you can do?" Chandler demanded. "Is that all you're going to tell me?"

Marlowe relented. He pointed a thumb at the back window and formed the word "Buick" with his lips.

Buick. Yes, that was it. Chandler obediently craned his neck around to look behind him. He was supposed to be looking for Buicks. But he couldn't for the life of him remember why.

He turned back to Marlowe for more help. But just then the car passed a grove of dark trees and the image in the glass clarified. It was only his own reflection staring back at him, bleary-eyed.

22

Arnold let him off on the Pershing Square side of the hotel leaving Chandler to climb the long marble staircase on his own. He was half expecting to see Barbara Norman at the head of the stairwell, waiting for her spotlight. It was her kind of lobby. About halfway up he decided he'd have to grab onto the brass railing if he ever hoped to make it to the main landing of the large hotel.

A solicitous bellhop saw him in trouble and came over and gave him a hand navigating the last few steps. Once they had made it, Chandler continued to hold the bellhop in his grasp and waited for his thoughts to clear. When they didn't, he chuckled.

"Young fellow, I'm here for a dinner, but I don't remember the room. Boosters . . . Something Boosters. What room are they?"

The bellhop helped him move forward and pointed to a room down a secondary corridor. He thanked him, but the bellhop held out his hand, expecting something more substantial. Chandler patted it, like a kindly old aunt would do.

The main lobby was filled with military brass and others in

expensive suits hovering around several big illustrations of air-planes that were manufactured in Southern California. Some of them had been drawn without propellers. Chandler decided the local plane builders were hosting a victory party for the services. The next layer of Southern California civilization making its big move.

Down the corridor he heard the sounds of clinking glasses and the general conviviality that went with an open bar, and he stumble-trotted forward. Salvation was at hand. The hall and the room ahead were crowded with middle-aged to elderly men who all seemed to know one another. The boisterous camara-derie and backslapping going on told him they were on their second or third drink and he had some catching up to do. He shouldered his way through the blue and grey three-piece suits until at the door an arm reached out and stopped him.

"Don't forget your badge, brother. Can't let you in without your badge now, can we," a bucktoothed sergeant-at-arms told him.

Chandler looked back in the direction the man was pointing to and saw a large bulletin board on a tripod. At the top of the board was a wooden plaque that said SABOBA BOOSTERS, the let-ters burnt into the wood like ranch brands. Still attached to the board were eight or ten large round buttons with the names of the members who apparently were absent. He was about to grab just any one of them in order to get into the dining room, but lo and behold, one was made out with his own name on it: R. CHANDLER. Granted, someone had done a poor job of forming his first initial but this was no time for quibbling or questions. Didn't the kid on the phone say he was expected? Why should he look a gift horse in the mouth? Acting as casual as he could, he hung the pin on his breast pocket the way he had seen the others do and made a second charge on the gauntlet. The toothy man at the door gave him a wink this time and waved him on.

He made straight for the crowd standing about the portable bar and was shouldering his way forward when one of the men he had been pushing against turned around.

"Why, Mr. Chandler, what are you doing here?"

It was Lyle Palmer from the studio. He smiled and stuck

177

out a hand in greeting. Then he noticed the badge and did a couple of double takes back and forth between Chandler's face and the badge, but he didn't say anything about it.

"I might ask the same of you, mightn't I," Chandler said. "Is it possible to get a decent drink in this place?"

"Of course," Palmer smiled. "I'm up next here, I believe. What'll you have?

Chandler eyed the bartender's selections like a kid in a candy store. "How about an old-fashioned double. And a second one for my friend at that table with the wooden leg."

Palmer laughed and gave his order. When Chandler finally got his drinks, he sipped a bit from both of them so he wouldn't spill anything valuable. He and Palmer moved over to an empty table nearby and sat down together.

"Seriously," Palmer semi-whispered, "what are you doing here, Mr. Chandler?"

Chandler couldn't think of anything to say yet, but he could feel his blood flowing again. He tapped his badge as if that were to supply enough explanation, then asked, "Now it's your turn. You a member here?"

"Member?" Palmer laughed. "Hardly. I'm just doing a bit of escorting for my old firm. In the public relations business you can never have too many contacts. I used to work for the *Times*, or didn't you know . . . ?" Palmer couldn't keep his eyes off the badge on Chandler's coat. "You know I had no idea you were part of that family. I thought I knew them all. . . ."

"Escorting?" Chandler interrupted. "Who are you escorting, if I may be so bold?"

Palmer looked about the room. "You see the portly chap over there in the corner? The one with the ruddy cheeks and the cigar? He's the business manager for the Cleveland Rams." Chandler spotted the man in question. A plump man with a huge double chin that caused him to speak with his head held at a haughty angle. He wondered how the man got his head low enough to do his book work, but Palmer was going on. "That's a professional football team. You know, American-style football?"

"What are you squiring him around for?"

Palmer looked a bit ill at ease, Chandler thought. He coughed and brushed at some invisible crumbs on the tablecloth. "Oh, you never can tell. They might be thinking about making a move to the West Coast. It wouldn't hurt us to know him, would it?"

Chandler played thoughtfully with the ice in his first drink. His hands would soon be steady enough for him to lift the glass and drink it like a man, one-handed. Just having the glasses there in front of him was already doing wonders for him. He tried raising the glass, using both hands, and got two hot gulps down. They hit him like a blockbuster from a B-29, and he fought to keep the conversation going.

"American football, you say? I'm afraid I'm not much of a fan. Why would the Cleveland Rams want to play out here? Aren't all their fans back in Cleveland?"

Palmer laughed again, brushed back his unruly blond hair and changed the subject. "This your first dinner here, Raymond?"

"Yes, it is."

"Do you know much about the group?"

Chandler scanned the room, trying to think of something to say that would shield his own ignorance, yet draw out Palmer.

"Say, isn't that what's-his-name Butterworth over there? I remember him from my oil days. He's a big refinery man, isn't he?"

Palmer followed his look. "Yes, it is him."

"What's he doing here?" Chandler asked.

Palmer laughed. "You don't get in this place unless you're a mover and a shaker. You see those two chaps he's talking to?"

"Yeah, what about 'em?"

"The guy on his left is General Motors. The other guy is named Firestone. Nice little group, that."

"No kidding? What are they hatching?"

" 'Hatching' is right. They're forming their own little city transit company for L.A. and they're here for the blessing of the city fathers."

"Wait a minute, wait a minute." Chandler frowned and tried to clear his head. "That's cars and tires and petrol. And transit? That's like streetcars and trains, right?"

Palmer smiled. "That's right, it is."

"What's oil and cars and tires doing buying streetcars?"

Palmer smiled and nodded again. "That's what a lot of

people are wondering. Sort of like having the foxes in charge of the chicken coop, isn't it? Some people think they want the streetcar lines so they can put them out of business."

Chandler didn't follow the logic of it all, but his eyelids narrowed and he nodded, using a bluff technique he had mastered during many story conferences with ninety-day-wonder producers.

But his mind was working faster now and his peripheral vision seemed to be improving as well. For the first time he was able to have a good look at the room. It was not a large place, but quite elegant with a high ceiling and plenty of delicate gold leaf wrapping itself ornately against the patterned walls. It reminded Chandler of the Palace at Versailles. Well, why not? After apartment towers out of the Arabian Nights and balloon worms on the beach and raspberry parfait sunsets, what could be more fitting to top off an evening than a touch of Louis the Fourteenth? What's one more non sequitur after such a day?

The room had bowed to one necessary modernization. The middle of one wall had been opened up to accommodate a raised platform with curtains. It would normally be used as a small bandstand, but tonight it held only an upright piano and some other unusual trappings. One item especially—a rather elaborate sawhorse with ribbons and buttons, with what appeared to be the head of a child's hobby horse attached to the front of it. Was this the "horse" the young man on the phone had been talking about? And next to the sawhorse was another tripod, this one holding a poster showing a series of capital letters: F,V,N,E,M? F,V,N,E,X?, and so on. The board was displayed quite prominently center stage with a baby spotlight on it, and Chandler became convinced that it was somehow at the heart of this group. It had to be a part of the ritual or the key to "Saboba." If he could unlock the meaning of that board, he had a feeling he would know what this was all about.

Palmer was getting restless and just about to join his new friend from Cleveland, when Chandler held him by his sleeve and pointed at the bandstand.

"What's the story with the funny letters up there?"

"Ah, something dark and mysterious, my friend."

"Saboba? What's Saboba supposed to mean, anyway?"

Palmer studied him, then smiled, and sat back down. "You really don't know, do you? I didn't think you did. Listen, Ray," he put a consoling hand on his shoulder. "Let me give you some real sound advice. As soon as you finish up your drinks here, you get up and leave."

"What's Saboba?"

"It's just a ranch most of these men have visited at one time or another."

"Who owns it?"

Palmer looked at the badge on Chandler's suit coat and smiled. "Never mind who owns it. I don't know how you got here, but believe me, these people can play rough. They don't tolerate practical jokes very well."

"You mean they're all gangsters?"

"No, no. They're . . . just businessmen. But one phone call from the right people, Ray, and you'd never work at Paramount again."

"Is that what happened to McGrath? One call and—" He tried to snap his fingers, but they refused to go off.

"Say, what is this with you and McGrath?" Palmer wanted to know. "He's never worked much to begin with. What are you always bringing him up for?"

"Never mind. Forget I said it. How about Councilman Bodecker? He about anyplace?"

Palmer had run out of patience. "Look, I've got to introduce my Cleveland porker over there to a couple more people. Do yourself a big favor, Mr. Chandler, and be among the missing very soon. Okay?"

Palmer left to attend to his P.R. duties while Chandler nursed his first drink down to the lemon twist, getting increasingly angered in the process. Who was Palmer to tell him when to come and when to go? He didn't even have the decency to give him straight answers to his questions. Raymond Chandler wasn't about to be bullied or scared off by the likes of him. Palmer probably couldn't write a decent dramatic scene if his life depended on it. That was the real test of a man.

Chandler drained his first glass and decided the second one needed some company. He drank enough of the second so he could carry it without fear of spilling and headed back toward the bar. But before he could reach it, some yokel in Western attire stood up on the platform and started banging on a large steel triangle. The noise level was deafening and couldn't help but stop all activity.

"We're runnin' late, gentlemen," he bellowed. "Too much gabbin' goin' on. Get to your places so's we can start this here shindig."

This brought on much laughing and general agreement from the audience and men started moving toward their places and sitting. Chandler found himself alone at the bar and asked for his refill. The barman said the bar was closed, but Chandler raised his voice and demanded his rights. He'd gotten a late start, he said, and he damn well was entitled to at least one more drink. The barman, in order to keep him quiet, decided to give him what he wanted.

An enthusiastic piano player started beating out an up-tempo tune and, under the cowboy's musical direction, the entire room was soon swaying and singing, with each man's arms interlocked with his neighbor's.

*"Sea, sea, sea, oh why are you angry with me?*
*Ever since I left Dover,*
*I thought the boat would go over . . ."*

Chandler wandered in and out among the swaying bodies, looking for a safe harbor for his cargo. Once he saw Palmer's face, turned an ashen white and scowling in his direction. Why wasn't the man singing with the rest of the cowboy-sailors? He finally found one empty seat, which placed him near the center of the room with his back to the bandstand podium. He sat and tried to get into the spirit of the song, but they were into the second verse by now and the tempo had picked up yet again which made the swaying back and forth more of a jerking back and forth. Just when he was about to lose his balance, and whatever he had on his stomach, the song mercifully concluded. The members erupted in joyous laughter, as if something wonderful had just transpired.

The next thing he knew the happy round faces around the table were looking at him and holding out friendly pink hands for him to shake. There was Murdock from the Valley, he was in real estate. There was Geiger, with a mortuary, Overholt the lawyer and Luer the meatpacker. And then there was Wilson with city planning. Bingo! A bell went off in Chandler's brain. The names and faces that followed were a total blank, for he was too busy formulating questions to put to Wilson in city planning.

"Now tell me again," somebody was saying to him, "which Chandler are you, again?"

"I'm Raymond, the writer."

"Oh, really. How interesting. I didn't know . . ."

"Say, would you mind terribly, changing places with me?" Raymond the writer asked. "I'd like to chat with Wilson next to you there, don't you know."

He had affected his British mannerisms in order to get what he wanted. He had found from experience it worked wonders among a certain type of American. True to form, the man next to Wilson hopped up and was more than happy to oblige by changing places with him. It also happened to place Chandler right next to the triangle they used for their dinner bell.

"Level with me, my good man," he started in on Wilson, "what does the city have planned for Chavez Ravine?"

"Well, Mr. Chandler, I imagine you know more about that than I would," Wilson demurred.

"I would? No, I wouldn't. Really I wouldn't. Tell me about it."

Wilson eyed him and laughed for the benefit of the other men. Then, when someone else started a second conversation at the table, he tapped Chandler's sleeve and spoke in a soft voice. "I'm sure you understand, this isn't the time or the place to be bringing that up."

Chandler had lost the ability to speak softly. In full voice he growled, "What's wrong with this time and place? It's a simple enough question. What the hell are you people doing with Chavez Ravine?"

While Mr. Wilson was still nervously wetting his lips in place of an answer, the cowboy at the podium rang the triangle again— much to the dismay of Chandler's eardrums—and announced that it was time to introduce tonight's honored guest. Lyle Palmer started escorting the fat man from Cleveland up toward the stage as the cowboy began listing the man's accomplishments: a thirty-second degree Mason, co-founder of the Boys' Club of Greater Ohio, et cetera, and current acting general manager of the great Cleveland Rams, "a football organization which is second to none in the world today."

The clapping started building with "Rams" and without waiting to hear the man's name mentioned, the audience arose as one man and gave Cleveland a hearty round of applause. All, that is, except the party crasher, who took the opportunity to even out liquid levels in his drinks and consider his next move.

Cleveland, meanwhile, was invited to be initiated into the Saboba Riding Club and Chowder Society, if he was up to it. He proudly said he was and was given an Indian spear and told to sit on the sawhorse. He grunted to get one chubby leg over the sawhorse and eased downward. Once in place he was challenged by the cowboy to decipher the peculiar series of letters on the board in front of him. Cleveland good-naturedly sat on his mount, spear in hand, and scowled down his nose at the puzzling board. He finally admitted he could not say what the message meant. This, the audience was anticipating and they all joined in with an exaggerated, "Ooooh, toooo baaaad," followed by more laughter.

"Boys," Chandler muttered to himself. "That's what they bloody well are. They aren't grown men at all. They're a bunch of bully boys."

Wilson and the man on the other side of Chandler scowled at him. Someone else shushed at him. He smiled back. The cowboy, using an Indian spear of his own as a pointer, was deciphering the message and the room full of boys joined in:

*"HaFe Ve aN-E haM? HaFe Ve aN-E eXs?*
*YeS Ve haFe haM. YeS Ve haFe eXs.*
*Ve haFe haM aNd eXs."*

While the room full of revelers applauded themselves, Chandler finished his second drink and fumed at himself. So this was the big secret he was waiting for. How dare they!

In a defensive move, Mr. Wilson was trying to draw some-

184

one else at the table into conversation about something earth shattering, like the price of the new double breasted suits at Bullocks, so Chandler got the man's attention back by leaning against him.

"Okay, don't tell me what you are going to do about Chavez Ravine. I'll tell you what you're gonna do. Shall I?"

"I'd rather you didn't," Wilson whispered and pushed his tormentor back into an upright position.

Chandler was feeling the heavy effects of the new drinks, and his speech was sliding rapidly. "You're gonna tell everybody the city's gotta have a sewer treatment plant, ain'tcha?"

"Of course we are. That's already on the ballot for the next election. Everybody knows that. We've had unprecedented growth. . . ."

Wilson was now growling a bit, with his whispered answers. And there was another slight disturbance going on over by the entry way now as well, but Chandler was oblivious to such minor distractions.

"An' you jokers are gonna tell everybody the sewer treatment plant's gonna be built in Chavez Ravine, ain'tcha? Only it ain't gonna be built out there. You're just sayin' that now to get those poor damn Mexicans outa the way."

"Shut up, man. Are you crazy?" Wilson barked at him.

Then came one of the precious moments when time seems to stand still. Or maybe it was that everything seemed to happen at once. Hidden wall panels leading to the kitchen opened up and a horde of waiters of Latino extraction appeared with plates of tossed green salad and rapidly began serving the tables. The cowboy, who had been trying to administer the next step in the initiation, by having the Cleveland man balance a plate of eggs with his free hand, had to stop because the commotion at the front table was beginning to be distracting. He resorted to another clang on his large triangle. "Simmer down there, podners."

Chandler grabbed at his ears. "Will you knock off with that damn clattering, 'podner,' before I wrap that thing around your head."

Cleveland laughed, uneasily. "Is this all part of the initiation, gentlemen?" He started to lose an egg and had to drop his spear in order to keep his plate upright. The spear clanged against the triangle and sent it tipping into Mr. Wilson's lap.

Meanwhile, from the opposite direction, the bucktoothed sergeant-at-arms was bearing down on the center of activity, an angry-looking elderly man at his side. "There he is, Mr. Chandler. That's him."

"So," the old man with him pontificated. "So."

"Who? There's who?" Raymond Chandler asked, assuming the bucktoothed one was addressing him.

"My name badge, if you please, young man," The old man demanded with his hand extended. He had a white mane of hair, steel-rimmed glasses, and a demeanor that was used to being kowtowed to.

"We certainly don't have programs like this in Cleveland."

"Come on. Off with it. That's my name badge."

Raymond Chandler clutched his breast. "What do you mean, your name badge. I'm Raymond Chandler."

"That's not an 'R', that's an 'H', you idiot. 'H' for Harry." The old man beat at his own breast.

Wilson rang the triangle by accident, getting it back on the stage. "Honestly, Mr. Chandler, we thought he was a relative. Honestly."

The buck teeth sneered at Raymond, "I suppose you're going to say you don't know who he is."

Raymond eyed the old man up and down. "I have a pretty fair idea who he is. He fell out of a Sinclair Lewis book I shook once."

"Sal-eeds?" a little Mexican in a white jacket asked. "Everybody at dis table got sal-eeds?"

"Aaaright, this has gone fer enough," the bucktoothed one drawled and reached across to get the name tag off the interloper. Wilson helped by holding Raymond's arm and at the same time stage whispering to the white-haired old man: "He started talking about the Ravine. He's on to it, I'm sure."

"Well, who the devil is he?" the old man squeaked. "Who knows him? Speak up."

Silence fell on the scene like a fart in a one-room country school. Raymond saw Palmer in the distance, moving toward the exit as if he had a nosebleed. The old man got his name tag back and patted it into place on his suit coat. Finally, Raymond, in a delayed flash of revelation, pointed a finger in Harry's direction and cried: "*Los Angeles Times*. Harry Chandler, right?"

"Get rid of this clown," Harry Chandler said to his friend with the buck teeth.

Several of the men started to move in on Raymond now, but he elbowed them away and got a chair between himself and the lot of them.

"Of course. It's all hanging together now. The *Los Angeles Times*. Just like the good ol' days when you boys stole the Owens Valley water for Los Angeles. Up to your ol' tricks, aren't you? You're gonna Eminent Domain the Mexicans out of the Ravine by telling the voters you need the land for the sewer thing. But then you're gonna do your ol' switcheroo. You're gonna build the sewer thing someplace else and give the Ravine land to the fat guy on the horse up there for his sheep or goats or whatever they are to play in."

The "fat guy" on the horse went from pink to red. "Now just a minute, here. Just a darn minute. This isn't funny anymore. Not one penny of city funds will go into building the stadium."

The Cleveland Porker tried to dismount, but his oxford caught on the hind flank of his steed. Unfortunately he had already committed his center of gravity to a spot two feet to the left. In a desperate move to right himself he swung his arm holding the egg plate into an underhand loop like a softball pitcher. This move got most of the eggs onto the floor ahead of him and had the beneficial effect of greasing his fall. He landed flat on his left side, did a rolling half gainer, ending up in a sitting position at the edge of the bandstand apron. A few people laughed, but most only aahed in hushed sympathy.

"And McGrath was on to you, wasn't he," Raymond said without missing a beat, continuing his lecture to old Harry. "He was gonna print a story to blow your nice little plan out of the water."

"My suit. Look at my suit."

"McGrath who?" Harry Chandler demanded.

"Don't give me 'McGrath who,'" Raymond scoffed. "Charles 'Corky' McGrath, whom you and your cronies had to eliminate. You even got the Hearst paper to go along with you. You murdered him in cold blood."

"Murder?" Cleveland stopped wiping egg yolk long enough to repeat. "My God, Harry, what have you gotten me into?"

"Now simmer down, Ralph," Harry consoled his Cleveland friend. "Do I look like a murderer to you?"

"I don't know. I don't know what you look like."

"You look like a man who's been dead for two years to me," Raymond offered. "Here, get Humpty Dumpty here a towel or something."

Raymond reached for the towel that was over the arm of a petrified Mexican waiter standing too close. Unfortunately, when the towel came off the waiter's arm a bowl of Roquefort dressing also came off the tray he was carrying and landed on the right kneecap of Ralph from Cleveland.

"My God, this is my one and only suit. Is everybody in this town insane?"

"Will somebody get this fruitcake out of this room?" Harry Chandler squeaked in his piercing falsetto voice.

The Boosters began moving en masse toward the retreating writer. Raymond fumbled in his pocket for the gun and finally came up with it just before they were to lay hands on him.

"Look out, he's got a gun."

"My God, he's a Nazi."

Chandler would like to have fired a warning shot into the air, but he had forgotten how to cock the mechanism. Getting his Wild West mannerisms mixed up, he waved the Luger over his head in a circle, lariat style, until the barrel caught on the pesky triangle with a resounding clang. The triangle tipped toward Cleveland, who angrily pushed it onto the floor. Next the buck-toothed man tried to pull an end run to get behind Raymond, but slipped on egg dropping, landing hard on his backside.

The cowboy master of ceremonies strapped on his guitar and started strumming a few bars. "What say we all do a few campfire songs before things get out a' hand?"

"Campfire? My God," Cleveland cried, looking for a dry spot to wipe his hands on. "This entire state belongs in a camp."

Old man Chandler helped up his fallen lieutenant and barked at him, "Get the police in here, right away."

"No, no. Oh no, you don't," Raymond cried, waving his gun

again and backing away from the group. "If anybody is going to the police, it'll be me."

He held them all at bay until he reached near enough to the door to make a break for it. But just before he did, he had the nagging sense of having seen this entire scene played out in a Mack Sennett comedy sometime after the first World War. Without bothering to jump up and click his heels in the air he headed for the main lobby.

Instead of finding the muffled and reserved atmosphere of his first entry, the lobby was now alive with shouting, singing military brass overflowing from a party of their own. Chandler made for the exit stairwell, but was nearly knocked down by a full bird colonel in hot pursuit of a young blonde. The colonel caught her by her skirt and brought her to a halt like a team of horses. Her skirt ended up around her waist and she protested, slightly.

"It's okay, honey," the colonel was explaining. "The Germans surrendered. It's okay. It's just celebrating."

Chandler's first impulse was to berate the colonel for conduct unbecoming. But then he noticed the soft white flesh just above the girl's stocking line and he stood transfixed at the banister railing, watching the girl. There was plenty of time for him to get away or call the police or whatever he had in mind, but his brain wasn't working with any semblance of logic. The Germans' surrender didn't seem nearly as important as the view at hand.

"There he is," Harry Chandler called out for the benefit of the lynch mob he had gathered about him, and pointed an Indian spear across the lobby in Raymond's direction.

Raymond felt a hand on his arm and before he knew it, he was being pulled down the marble steps. Palmer was there, telling him to hurry. Then other hands were upon him. A black man in a uniform and maybe a Mexican waiter with three salad plates balanced up the length of his left arm. Marlowe had finally showed up to lend a hand, too. And he had brought along Corky McGrath, just for laughs. Chandler lost sight of the girl with her skirt raised and other thoughts started taking center stage. He felt himself being carried out, but he still struggled against it.

"Wait, no wait. I can't leave yet. I haven't finished my drink."

23

The leg shaking routine had started again. Twice earlier he had been able to incorporate the shake into snatches of dreams that came and went, but this time it was too persistent to ignore.

"It's Monday morning, Ray."

He rolled over quickly and looked at his tormentor in her pink wraparound. "Are the police here?"

"No, they aren't here." She smiled.

At least he thought she smiled. All he could really see was her general outline in front of the infernal, ever present Southern California sunlight, bouncing off the white house next door and streaking through the window of his bedroom.

"What time is it?"

"A little after seven-thirty. I think you should get dressed and go in to work just as if nothing has happened. I've been thinking it over and I think that's our best course of action."

He brushed at his cowlick and tried to think. "The kitchen crew must have been there a good two hours by now. I wonder how long it's going to take them to put two and two together. The longer it is before the doorbell or that phone rings, the happier I'm gonna be."

"Are you steady enough to handle this?" She held out his morning "tonic."

He extended a hand to see for himself. She automatically watched it for tremors, then put the glass into it.

"How'd you manage to get raw egg on your good suit last night?" she asked.

"Raw egg? I don't know. It must have been some kid's idea of a joke. We sat upstairs at the movie. It must have happened then."

"We? I thought you said you were going alone."

"Did I say we?"

"It certainly sounded like 'we' to me."

He scratched the back of the hand that always acted up from his drinking, then sat up. "Give me a little time and I'll think of something."

"Mmm."

"Is there an interesting story in how I got home last night?"

"Oh, Ray, it wasn't all that late. Don't you remember? Your friends from the studio brought you."

"Friends from the studio?"

"At least he said he was. The one that talked. Your Mr. Palmer, and someone else, along with your chauffeur."

"It took three of them?"

"No. I think the little fellow just came along for laughs. You are drawing an audience. Next time I'll phone old Mrs. Pierce and her sister from next door. We can sell tickets."

"But no Mexicans?"

"No, the Mexicans sat this one out." She got to her feet slowly. "Is the drinking over now, Ray?"

"I think so. I think it's run the full course now."

He reached for his glasses, started to put them on, but he wasn't quite ready to see the day in focus. He tossed them on the bed and covered his face in his hands. "Oh, Cissy, what am I gonna do? I've done everything I can think of. I'm fumbling and floundering around like an idiot. I'm just a writer. That's the only damn thing I have any talent for. I can't even face the real world sober anymore. What am I gonna do if they arrest . . ."

He started to lose it, so he stopped the talking. She put his head against her breasts and patted his back, as if she were trying to raise a burp out of a baby.

" . . . and you. What's going to happen to you? I've failed you again, haven't I."

"Oh, Raymio, no. You haven't failed me. Don't even think it. I'm sorry for the things I said yesterday. I'm just an old worrisome busybody when I get tired. You know that."

They were still clinging to each other, like *Life* magazine photos of displaced persons from the war, when the telephone rang. It sounded like the only noise in the world. So grating on the nerves. So impersonal.

After the third ring Cissy went into the hall, cleared her voice to calm it, then picked up the receiver.

Chandler put on his glasses and got up to look at the mirror of the dresser where Cissy had put another news clipping. He forced his mind to the task of reading it. It was a report from a psychiatrist in Syracuse who had come up with a surefire treatment for alcoholics. It seems that by getting them pets to cuddle and look after, alcoholics lost interest in drinking. . . . Wonderful. Someday, Chandler told himself, he'd have to send them a picture of Taki, his old drinking companion.

Then Cissy was standing in the doorway. And she was smiling.

"What is it?" he asked.

"It's Howard Hawks. He wants to talk to you about their script for *The Big Sleep*."

Chandler was so happy to hear who it wasn't, he almost ran to the phone.

"Hello, Hawks. This is Raymond Chandler."

"Chandler. My God man, but you're a hard man to reach. I suppose your good wife told you why we have been trying to reach you."

"Yes, it's something about the story line I believe." He moved with the phone through the hall to his workplace in the dining room. It felt so good, he felt like putting in two or three good working days without once moving out of the chair.

"What seems to be your problem?" he called, cheerily.

"It's this murder of the Sternwood chauffeur . . . his name is Owen Tailor. Are you with me?"

"Yes, what about it?"

"Well, who killed him?"

"What do you want to know for?"

"What the hell does that mean, 'what do I want to know for?' "

"Just what I said. Is it all that important?"

"Well, of course it is. We're making a murder mystery here. The people who go to these films want all the loose ends tied up nicely with a bow. You can't have a murder that isn't solved."

"As I recall I have six people killed in the book. The five others you can figure out, right?"

"Yes, I think that's right." Hawks didn't sound too sure.

"Well, there you go. Five out of six isn't all that bad."

Hawks was beginning to sputter. "This is the damnedest conversation I ever had in my life. What kind of writer are you, anyway?"

"Look, you've had the property for a year and a half now and it's taken you this long to figure out you don't know who killed the Sternwood chauffeur. Doesn't that tell you something?"

"And what is that supposed to tell me?"

"It tells you your audience is not going to be too worried about it either. Remember, they're seeing it all for the first time."

"Look, Chandler, this plot is screwy enough the way it is now. We got a girl who's got a dope problem, only we aren't allowed to mention dope because of the motion picture code. We got a guy who runs a pornographic book store only we can't talk about that either. And now you tell us not to worry about wrapping up a murder. We got the craziest mixed up plot going I ever—"

"Yes, but all the scenes work, don't they?" Chandler interrupted.

"Well, yes they do. I hope."

"You're damn right they do. Because I wrote 'em to work. You followed the book nice and tight, didn't you?"

"Yeah, fairly tightly," Hawks admitted. "Except we cut out all that first-person social commentary jazz."

"How come?"

"Because I don't go in for knocking the town I work in. What have you got against Los Angeles, anyway?"

"Oh, not a thing. It's a lovely little burg with all the personality of a Dixie cup. I think the moral high point of the place was when the Spaniards used to buy and sell the squatter Indians like so much chattel, and the place has been going downhill ever since."

"Oh really, now. Well, I say we have a pretty darn nice little community here, for my money."

"What an appropriate expression. A haven, made safe of, by, and for the millionaires."

"Look, Chandler, I make entertainment films. That's my business. You wanna go into the soapbox business, that's your business. If you want a little friendly advice, I'd knock off that kind of Commie b.s. It's not gonna go over in this town."

"Everybody is so anxious to give me such good advice."

"Mister, you're crazy."

"That's fine. Now let's see if you can call me dishonest."

Hawks sputtered again on that. "I wonder if you'd be talking to me like that if we'd hired you to write the script for us."

Chandler laughed. "Probably not."

"Look, I don't want to start World War Three over this. I just want to know who killed the Sternwoods' damn chauffeur. You have him drive off the end of the Santa Monica pier with the dash throttle pulled out and a bump on the back of the head. Now how'd he get out there?"

"Look, every case has its loose ends. The police will tell you that. Things that never get answered. Why not leave it at that?"

"That's reality you're talking about. When you do fiction you can't afford such luxuries."

"Why not? Shouldn't fiction try to reflect reality?"

Hawks groaned. "Now don't get artsy-craftsy on me. Are you trying to tell me this chauffeur thing actually happened?"

"It could. The police files are filled with unsolved cases just

194

like this. Things that should have been investigated more thoroughly but weren't for political reasons, or because somebody's kinky son-in-law might get exposed. . . ."

"Look, what is this Sternwood thing? Is it fact or fiction?"

"It's Los Angeles."

Oh, it felt so good. To be back in his element, talking about story values. Arguing with directors. And he even did it sober. The fire in the belly was still burning. If God would only let him get back to his own little world of make-believe he would never, never, never ever leave it again, as long as he lived. Dorothy was right: There's no place like home.

He didn't have the heart to tell Hawks he didn't know who killed the Sternwood chauffeur. It had been one of those slippery little details he had planned to work out later, but with the thousand and one other things needed to finish a mystery pressing at the time, the matter had slipped his mind. What did they expect for seven thousand dollars? For that kind of money they only get the book rights. The blueprint on how the book came about was extra.

Cissy got him his breakfast and laid out a tweed sport coat and the only clean pair of slacks he had left. He liked to dress a little on the scruffy side for his work at the studio, partly as a psychological thing—the poor struggling writer, et cetera. Today that effect would not be difficult to achieve.

He was surprised at how calm he felt. Perhaps it was because he knew it was all over. He'd done everything he could and nothing had worked. He was resigned to his fate, whatever that might be.

It came time to open the front door. A new driver got out of the limousine at the curb and held the back door open for him. Chandler kissed his wife good-bye and started down the steps.

24

Clarence wasn't at the main gate when he got to the studio. It probably meant nothing, but it made Chandler's heart beat a bit harder just the same. He was looking for signs of normalcy and, with his imagination, any variations in the routine of the place could be read in a million different ways. His new driver let him off next to the writers' building. He decided to stroll in whistling a popular little melody, but all he got for his efforts was wind whooshing by dry lips. Simone sat plugged into her switchboard as if she had spent the weekend there. He started on by her with just a wave, but she stood up and called, "Mr. Chandler, stop!"

This was it, he told himself. This was how it would begin. He cowered against the opposite wall, like Peter Lorre playing a child molester.

"Oh, I'm sorry," Simone laughed, "I didn't mean to startle you. I just wondered if you had a radio in your car."

"Radio in my car? Why?"

"It's just come over the air. There's a German general going to sign the surrender papers. The war in Europe is really over now. Isn't that wonderful?"

For the first time, Chandler noticed the girl had tears in her eyes. And he thought her French accent might be a little thicker than usual.

"Yes. Yes, that is joyous news, isn't it? By the way, where is everybody?"

"Oh, things are so topsy-turvy. I think most of your friends are over at the commissar—"

"Commissary. Why? Anything unusual going on over there?"

"It's the peace reports. The technicians have set up a loud-speaker with the radio. Isn't this a glorious day?"

"Yes, it certainly is. No . . . no messages for me, though?"

"Mr. Houseman called. He said he'd call back."

"Thanks, Simone."

He hurried up the steps and to his office and closed the door quietly behind him. He thought that would make him feel better, but it didn't. The austere decor only made him think of interrogation rooms and prisons.

The coffee spill had been cleaned up by the night crew. That's one thing you'd have to say about the place. They do keep the cages clean.

If Simone didn't know about the bodies by now, it must have been because the studio had arranged with the police to keep it quiet. But the Houseman call worried him. Did the police talk to Houseman, and then did he get to wondering about Chandler's strange actions on Saturday and put two and two together? It was best not to get too carried away with such thoughts, he decided.

Let's see now, he had left the Ladd vehicle around here someplace. Oh yes, there it was in his center drawer, right where he had stuffed it a century ago. He decided to at least make it look like he was working. He sat down and started thumbing through it.

A war veteran comes home and finds his wife has been unfaithful. Then she gets herself murdered and it looks like the husband did it . . . just like somebody else he knew. Why hadn't the similarity struck him before? Surely it must have and he'd forgotten. Let's see now, what does Alan Ladd do? Maybe the same would work for him . . . no, no, he'd been down that road with Houseman. The clues don't come out of the woodwork like they do in fiction, when you do the steering. Mustn't start confusing fact and fiction.

But maybe that was his problem. Too much murder and mayhem in his life because of his work with fiction. First the short stories and novels, then the big *Double Indemnity* script with Wilder. Then more murders on celluloid. It was coming out his ears. But the bodies had been real. He hadn't imagined all that. Not the morgue stiff named Clarence. What a stupid stunt. What a stupid, stupid stunt to try to pull. McGrath had talked him into it. McGrath and the booze. If only he could get out of this he would never, never . . .

The phone on his desk exploded in his ear like a stick of dynamite. He grabbed at it before it could do more damage.

"Hello, Chandler here."

"Yes, Mr. Chandler. This is Miss Hernandez. I'm Mr. Wilder's secretary. Mr. Wilder would like you to come over to his office in the new building right away."

"Oh, he would, would he? And what would I want for to be seeing Mr. Wilder about, *por favor*?"

"He didn't tell me what it was about. But . . . you don't want to see him?"

"I can only think of one reason why I would want to see Mr. Wilder—unfortunately, I left my gun at home."

There was a trace of a stifled laugh on the line. "He said you were quite a jokester. I should tell him then, that you won't be coming?"

"I have a script to whip in shape, thanks to him. And I'm awaiting a call from my producer. Tell him that."

"Yes, sir. I'll tell him."

Two minutes later, Bill Dozier, himself, was on the line. "What's this I hear about you not wanting to go over to Billy's office?"

"My days of running after Billy Wilder are over. If he wants to see me, I think he knows where I am. Half of the blood on the floor here is still his."

"Don't think of it as blood. Think of it as afterbirth. And the two of you made a beautiful baby. Remember that."

"What a bilious thought. Tell me, which one of us did the impregnating? On second thought, don't tell me."

"Raymond, it's the end of the war. Why not end your own personal war as well? So you don't like the guy's personal style. It's no reason to carry on this giant and, if I might say so, rather unreasonable grudge."

"Unreasonable? I think that's a rather poor choice for an adjective, Bill."

"Look, the guy got his appointment for the Ministry of Culture thing. He's off to Germany within the week and he'll be out of your hair. Is it going to kill you to go over and see what he wants? Maybe he's going to apologize."

"I take it that's an order, then."

"It's a strong request. And if I don't see you by our ten o'clock meeting time, I'll send in the marines."

He would rather be spending the time looking in the mirror and practicing his surprised and innocent looks. Billy Wilder was a man of many unusual and convoluted attitudes, but apologizing with no attendant reward in sight was quite beyond his capabilities. He could apologize if it meant he was going to end up with a producable story line as a result. He could apologize if it meant some star-struck damsel would then let him have his way with her. But Chandler could not conceive of another set of reasons.

When he got to Wilder's office, Miss Hernandez was on the phone—to Allied Headquarters in Europe, she explained during a break in the conversation—and would be right with him. She seemed nice. She was gracious, without any of the I-told-you-so smirks most of the girls would have delivered for Chandler's benefit. And she looked about as much like a Hernandez as the Queen Mother. When she hung up the phone, she got quickly to her feet.

"He said we should go right in when you got here." She smiled and led the way into Wilder's new office. The place was a graphic reminder of the dramatic rise Wilder had experienced in the studio's pecking order since the release of *Double Indemnity*.

It was a practical room, but the furniture was upgraded and personalized, a far cry from the institutional trappings of the writers' building. Wilder was beginning to fancy himself an art connoisseur and two Impressionist works were displayed on the wall behind his desk.

"Hello, old bean." Wilder waved a greeting. "Be with you in a second." Then, to Miss Hernandez, "What was that call about? Could you follow what they wanted?"

"Yes, there is a town in Germany named Oberammergau—"

"Yeah, yeah, what about it?"

"And every ten years they put on the Passion Play."

"Yeah, yeah, I remember."

"And they are seeking permission to put it on again, now—"

"So what's the problem? I can't see any problem with that."

"It's about one of their actors. An Anton Lang—"

"Yeah, yeah."

"They want him to play the part of Christ. But they have to get special permission from the Culture group you are with. It seems Mr. Lang was a storm trooper in the war—"

Wilder cracked one quick laugh. "A storm trooper Nazi playing Jesus. Is Christopher Isherwood writing their stuff? Okay, okay, let's see . . . take a telegram to the head honcho over there. Ready?"

Miss Hernandez, used to his rapid delivery, got her steno book ready and nodded.

Billy leaned back and scanned the ceiling. "Okay Storm Trooper Anton Lang for part of Christ, stop. Only this time we use real nails, stop."

"Oh, Mr. Wilder," she said, frowning, "what are they supposed to make of that?"

"With my name on it, they'll know what to do with it. And be sure Western Union sends me a copy, too."

With his cat-that-ate-the-canary smile, he turned his attention to Chandler, who had seated himself in a far corner of the room. "Well, Raymond, just like old times, eh?"

"What can I do for you?"

Wilder winked at his secretary. "Honey, why don't you bring

us some coffee? You still take it black, Raymond? She can fix it just the way you like. She's very good at it."

After the elaborate business about coffee orders, the girl left and Wilder started his familiar pacing in small energetic circles behind his desk.

"You know, Raymond, old bean, I've been worried about why it is that we don't hit it off better together. I've asked myself what could be causing all this friction and how do I get it stopped. My reputation is not the greatest in the world, I'll admit. But I can't see having people going around, knocking me behind my back. It's bad for me. It's bad for the studio. Bad for the business. Why do you suppose we have this problem? You got any ideas?"

Wilder slowly pushed a hand across the sparse hair on the top of his head and scowled, as if he were in a story conference. Then, without waiting for an answer to his question, he supplied his own. "You suppose it's because we have such different outlooks on life?"

"By different, you mean—"

"Well, look at you, now. A mystery writer with an analytical mind on you. You got your education in one of those high-toned private English schools. You got sort of set ideas about the world. Like right and wrong and how things are supposed to go and how people are supposed to talk."

"Of course. Doesn't everybody?"

Wilder sat down at his desk and tapped his little cane lightly on his blotter. "I think maybe that's why the English do such a good job with the mystery story. You know, the idea there's something wrong with the world and they're gonna set it right. You're very big on decorum, aren'tcha?"

"But you aren't, is that it?"

Wilder smiled and spun the cane like a baton. "No, I guess I'm not. Me, I went to school at the movies, with Herr Lubitsch as my schoolmaster. I look at life without making a lot of judgments, you understand. I see what's really there and then I have a little fun with it."

"Is all this talk designed to make me love you, Willie?"

"Oh, I'm not expecting miracles . . . Ah, here we are."

Miss Hernandez returned with a tray and put it on Wilder's

201

desk. One cup of coffee she placed in front of her boss, who thanked her kindly. Next, she presented something to Chandler. But it wasn't coffee in the cup and saucer. It was a bowl of diced red Jell-O, just like the Jell-O from the commissary.

She quickly finished her duties with a straight face and left. Wilder checked the ceiling again, waxing philosophical about his poor upbringing and his show business struggles during the twenties. For his part, Chandler was able to keep his body quiet. After a few seconds of not knowing what to do, he returned the strange offering to the tray on the desk and sat down again.

"What's the matter, old bean?" Wilder cooed. "Too much sugar?"

"I take it you wanted to see me about something."

"Perhaps not enough sugar?"

"I always felt the ancient Greeks did sarcasm best," Chandler lectured. "Returning the severed heads of their enemies' messengers in the form of gifts."

"Oh, really? Well, you see there what a classical education will do for you? I hadn't heard about that one. Around here we have to make do with whatever we find in the icebox. The war and all, you understand."

Chandler tried to smile back at his nemesis, but found his face wasn't working. "Are we going to sit here and stare at one another until V-J day, or is there a point to this object lesson?"

"Now see, there you go again. Does there have to be a point? Why don't we simply enjoy this little moment we have together? We have been having so few lately, Raymio."

He had been stymied, not knowing what line to take, up until then. But with the flagrant misuse of his wife's pet name for him, Chandler's course of action became clear. Displaying a surprising burst of energy, he got up and seized the coffee tray. "Why you son-of-a-bitch, you—" Using an overhand delivery any cricket player would have been proud of, he took dead aim at Wilder's head and sent the tray and its contents splashing against the top of the window drapes, a good four feet from where Wilder was laughing.

"Hey easy, man. You almost hit my Monet."

"You bloody bastard, you—"

Chandler spotted a large pair of scissors lying in their scabbard on Wilder's desk. He grabbed them just before Wilder could and flung the scabbard into a corner. The scissors remained in his shaking hand, like a paring knife.

"If I'm going to hang, it might as well be for something I'm going to enjoy . . ."

"Easy. The joke's over. Enough, already."

But the result of the joke wasn't over. Chandler started counterclockwise around the desk with venom in his eyes. Wilder, much the younger of the two and quick with his mouth and arms, was surprisingly slow afoot and found himself stumbling backwards, trying to keep the desk between himself and his imminent demise, all the while doing an Errol Flynn imitation with his cane. Chandler was growling like a British lion, while Wilder was squawking like a chicken in the hands of a schochet rabbi.

"My God, man, that's enough. Don't hurt me, please. I'm a great director. Charlie, get in here. Charlie, the game's over. Get your ass in here."

Wilder was trying to shout for help, but he wasn't getting enough volume out of his fear-constricted throat. Finally, on the third chase around the desk, a door to an adjacent office opened and Charles "Corky" McGrath walked in.

Chandler's anger had closed down his peripheral vision, and it took him another half turn around the desk before he realized they had a visitor.

"You, you . . ." he sputtered and finally collapsed into Wilder's desk chair as it dawned on him the dead was walking.

"Hello, Mr. Chandler," Corky smiled. "It's really me."

Wilder collapsed, too, onto his knees in front of the desk. He was near tears as he shouted, finally in full voice, at McGrath, "You goddamn idiot, didn't you hear me call you? He damn near killed me. Get the scissors. Get the scissors."

"Mr. Wilder," McGrath protested, "you told me not to come in till you hollered, 'And the dead shall rise up and smite thee.' You never said that."

"Of course I didn't," Wilder gasped. "This wild man never . . . gave me the chance."

"How . . . how did you . . ." Chandler was trying to say, "I saw you dead with . . ." He pointed at his own temple.

"Great makeup," McGrath smiled. I'm sorry, Mr. C., but I . . ." He shrugged like a goofy kid. "Mr. Wilder saw you coming out of the commissary after we put Clarence in the fridge and he came nosing around. He talked me into it. I couldn't pass it up. Don't be mad. I'm gonna be his associate producer. Screen credit and everything. I couldn't pass it up, you see."

"Oh, no, of course not." Chandler deadpanned. "I often wondered what qualifications our producers brought to their work. Now I know it comes from sitting on dead bodies in iceboxes."

"It's the same joke, only I did it on you instead of Billy. And I'm getting screen credit on his next picture. Don't you see?" That fact seemed to justify everything in McGrath's mind.

"How'd you know I'd open that refrigerator door?"

"We rigged my jacket so it stuck out of the corner of the door. Mr. Wilder said you were so neat, you wouldn't be able to pass it up. Trying to tuck it in, I mean. He set it all up like he was directing a scene. He called Wally Westmore down to do the makeup. He even locked the front door of the commissary so you'd come in the back way and have a better viewing angle of the cooler doors." McGrath rubbed his back pockets. "I almost froze my buns off waiting for you. I thought you'd never open that door." He laughed and sallied nervously about the room like a bad actor. "We kept thinking you were going to catch on. I thought for sure all that theatrical gelatin blood that got smeared on your shirt from my 'wounds' would tip you off. But I guess you don't know that much about the technical side of movie making, do you?"

Chandler didn't answer at first. He was too busy breathing and staring. Then, "But Clarence . . . what about the other body . . ."

"Oh, he's long gone, on his way back to Iowa, none the worse for the wear. Curtis and I took care of that, with a bit of help at the gate from Mr. Wilder, here." McGrath smiled.

"The scissors . . ." Wilder whispered again, but nobody moved to get them out of Chandler's hand.

"We had no idea it would go on so long," McGrath was

saying. "We thought when I sent Miss Norman's chauffeur over to my place for my script, you'd start figuring things out. When you showed up at her place I thought the jig was up. Didn't you see my car in her garage?"

"You . . . knew about that?"

"Sure. I was upstairs when you fell on the steps. We got you outside, but we didn't know what to do with you. Then I spotted the Mexican kids that had been following me around and I paid them to take you home. You owe me five bucks."

"And the Chavez thing?" Chandler asked. "The sewer bond and the land switch thing with the Saboba people . . ."

"Yeah, I think you figured out the same thing I'd figured out. The big boys downtown are planning to pull a switcheroo for that land to build their stadium. When I couldn't get my story about it published, I figured I might as well make a few bucks on the deal. I've been trying to buy up some of the land around the Ravine." He laughed again. "But after your demonstration at the Biltmore, I don't think they'll have the nerve to try to pull off that little stunt."

"My demonstration? How'd you know about that?" Chandler asked.

McGrath giggled. "Who do you think it was who brought you home with Palmer? You were the cheapest weekend entertainment in town. I even walked you to the door. Billy . . . Mr. Wilder said you drunks got memories like a sieve."

Chandler tried to smile, to show he could appreciate a joke like anyone else. But he knew it wasn't coming off that way. His silly look only enhanced the glory of the moment. He turned to Wilder.

"What kind of car do you drive? As if I didn't know."

Wilder still wasn't showing any of his sly wit. "A Buick."

"It figures. You would have a garter belt fetish," Chandler grunted. "You know that girl tried to kill herself? You bastard."

"Yes. Things got a little out of hand," Wilder said softly.

Chandler snorted, trying to display disgust with the man, then tossed the scissors on the desk. Wilder ducked, but recovered quickly when he realized they weren't headed for his head. Then he grabbed the scissors and got to his feet. His cocky demeanor was suddenly back, intact.

"Let this be a lesson to you, old bean. Never try to kid a kidder."

That wasn't quite the homily Chandler would have chosen for the matter. He had something about lying down with swine in mind. But he wasn't about to dignify the affair further with his presence. He rose, tugged at his British tweed sport coat to straighten it, and left the room as if the group had never been properly introduced.

McGrath made one more attempt at an apology, but Chandler shut the door on him in mid-sentence.

In the hall he closed his eyes and took in a deep jerky breath. He needed some time alone to lick his wounds. To rationalize himself back into existence. Who was Wilder to lecture him? To scoff at his sense of decorum? The world today was full of foolhardy heroes just like himself and Marlowe, who risked their lives to put the crazy, sick world back in order. The villains were dying off because of people like him and the thousands out there still in the trenches. Not because of anything Wilder had done— him and his "having fun" attitude.

That's what he should have said to him. Why didn't he think of it earlier? But no matter what he told himself, it came out the same way. As usual, the snake, had all the lines.

Outside on the studio streets he could hear the familiar voice of Ginny Simms, probably from her morning radio broadcast being piped over a loudspeaker. She was singing about bluebirds and white cliffs of Dover, working in some new lyrics to fit the happy occasion.

When he rounded the corner to the commissary, Chandler saw a large group of studio workers gathered around a loudspeaker that had been placed on the steps. Most of them were unashamedly trying to sing along with the radio. Three couples were enthusiastically dancing to the slow ballad in the dusty street. Still others just stood by, watching or wiping away bittersweet tears.

Chandler was in no mood for celebrating. He turned away from the revelers and trudged toward the writers' building.

"Raymond, just the man I wanted to see."

It was Houseman, waiting for him on the steps. He extended both his arms in greeting.

"Quite a day of jubilation, isn't it? If the reports are to be trusted. There'll always be an England, and all that."

Chandler could only smile and shake Houseman's hand lamely.

"I know there will not be a great deal of work done today," Houseman continued, "but I wanted to keep in touch, all the same. Did you manage to have a good day of rest?"

Chandler looked at him as though he were insane. "Day of rest . . . ? Ah, very good. A day of rest."

"Now I don't mean to press you, Raymond, but I have Alan Ladd over in my office right now, and he's a bit out of sorts about the script. You know we're scheduled to start shooting this Thursday and he's a bit beside himself."

"Tell him that makes two of us."

"But we are making progress, are we not?" Houseman gave a hopeful nod, expecting his writer would follow suit.

"Tell him I've decided to make Adolf Hitler the murderer. It seems he's been hiding out in his wife's linen closet until one day when she decided to change the bed sheets and she got the surprise of her life—"

"Yes, very funny, Raymond. Actually, Alan's not so concerned with the matter of who did the killing, as he is with . . . Well, without a completed script in his hands, the man doesn't know what he's supposed to wear. . . ."

It was a small thing. Perhaps even a reasonable thing, from a performer's point of view. But Mr. Ladd's burning problem seemed to bring about a profound change in Chandler. Perhaps it was the accumulation of things. The straw that broke the camel's back.

He looked about at his surroundings as if seeing it all for the first time. The little flower bed next to the writers' building, where some idiot had planted a desert century plant next to a fern. And both plants were flourishing. The hazy blue morning sky without the decency of a cloud in sight. And the stucco, everywhere. In the permanent buildings—as if anything were permanent—as well as the sets. Stucco. In Southern California, oh, can you get stucco.

A giggle escaped his lips. A sound he thought himself incapable of making while sober. He turned on his heels and started for the De Mille gate without another word.

Poor John called, but finally had to trot after him and touch his arm to get him to stop.

"Raymond, where are you going?"

"I'm going home, John."

"But what about the script? And our ten o'clock meeting?"

"Tell Dozier I'm going home to write my little heart out. Oh, I'll finish the script, all right, because that's the kind of person I am. I feel a responsibility to you and a sense of obligation to the studio. Old school tie and all that. Honor. Honor and good taste. You do remember those words, don't you, John? I'll finish the damn script. It may well be I'll be dead drunk when I do it, because this business seems to make more sense to me that way. But rest assured I'll finish your script. In the meantime, tell Mr. Ladd he is to wear a blue dahlia rapped around his dingus in the opening shot. Good-bye, John. Don't think it hasn't been an education."

Houseman, totally befuddled, could only watch his retreating writer and friend, and wonder how on earth such a small matter as an actor's wardrobe could bring on such a firestorm.

Chandler found his chauffeur and headed west, toward the safety and sanctity of his little rented house.

By rights he should have been dancing in the streets with the others. Who had more to celebrate? The war in Europe was over. He was not about to be charged with a murder he didn't commit. Even the onus of being dismissed by the studio had been lifted.

But there was within his makeup the ability to turn even this one happy ending that the fates had granted him into a tragedy. He saw the entire affair as one devastating blow to his person, for never, never again, as long as he lived, would he be able to hold his own at the writers' table at Paramount.

# WRAP-UP

In 1946, Raymond and Cissy Chandler moved away from Los Angeles and Hollywood. The reason given was Cissy's health. That was the same year that moviegoers were rushing out to see Billy Wilder's new film, *The Lost Weekend,* the story of a troubled alcoholic writer and his two-day struggle with himself and his drinking problems.

In 1948, Wilder made *A Foreign Affair,* the story of an American square bent on preserving the morals and customs of the past while all the time being upstaged and out-talked by a worldly German.

In 1950, Wilder made *Sunset Boulevard,* the story of a struggling young writer and a washed-up silent movie star and their doomed attempt to reignite her career.

In 1951, he made *Ace in the Hole,* the story of an opportunistic newspaper reporter trying to get a story scoop at the expense of the downtrodden of the world.

In 1957, he made *Witness for the Prosecution,* a murder mystery with a surprise twist, revealed at the end, just as the injured party takes a knife after the guilty party.

In 1960, he made *The Apartment,* the story of a junior executive making points with his superiors by lending his home out for clandestine love affairs.

And on April 10, 1962, baseball's "Brooklyn" Dodgers played their first game in their new home, Chavez Ravine.